A *Fall* FROM *Grace*

CLAVERING CHRONICLES 1

JENNIE GOUTET

Dedicated to the very best of sisters, Stephanie—
who always buys my books, even though they are not in her genre of choice

CHAPTER 1

HERTFORDSHIRE, 1817

SIR LUCIUS CLAVERING, sixth Baronet of Mardley, had just loosened his cravat and settled into the deepest armchair his hunting box boasted when he heard the loud echo of the knocker on the front door and the footsteps of Briggs proceeding to answer it.

He wasn't expecting visitors and couldn't imagine why anyone should arrive at this hour to trouble him, but he'd instructed Briggs not to disturb him, and so, with a satisfied smile, he closed his ears to the noises outside the library and reached for his warmed brandy. A log in the fireplace cracked and the well-cleaned chimney pulled the smoke upward. For the past hour or so, welcome aromas of roast game and simmering French sauces had wafted through the small stone house—the inviting scents of refuge. He had endured a wearisome round of Christmas obligations at the estate, brought on by his widowed mother who still lived there, and the incessant demands of youthful, entitled siblings that came with such a reunion. A quiet meal in his own company would be just the thing to restore his peace.

A soft knock at the library door put a chink in his hopes. Lucius sighed audibly and wondered what could be important enough to disturb him. "Enter."

"A young...*ahem*, lady, sir," Briggs said. "It appears she has lost her way in the snow and is seeking shelter."

"Unaccompanied, I presume?" Lucius inquired with the lift of an eyebrow. This was hardly the first time. The number of *accidents* occurring outside his London property requiring him to come to the rescue of comely young maidens was impossible to credit, and Lucius was impatient with such a tiresome ploy. It appeared he was now not even safe in Hertfordshire.

"Naturally," Briggs replied, eyes twinkling. He was as wise to the ruse as his master.

"Show her in then," Lucius said on a sigh.

The girl ushered into his library minutes later was a prime example of one such maiden. She certainly was a taking thing, with a sweet apple-shaped face and doe-like eyes, framed by a perfect halo of golden curls that were tucked into a chignon in the back. This he was able to appreciate, as she had removed her bonnet.

"I am dreadfully sorry to disturb you, my lord," she said, in a voice little more than a whisper.

"I am not 'my lord'," he responded with as much patience as he could muster. "Merely 'sir'. Let me know how I may assist you."

"You are very good." The young lady surveyed the room with wide eyes, and upon spotting a gory painting of a hunting scene covering the entire back wall, shuddered and turned her back on it, the root of which gesture appeared to be more from artifice than delicacy.

Lucius waited, his irritation tinged with ready amusement. "But how came you to be here, Miss—?"

"Miss Woodsley. The stagecoach set me down on the knoll, and I mistook the location. I believed it to be the road leading to the Craigsons'."

"The stagecoach already? It must be the first time ever it has arrived early." When she didn't respond, he inquired, "And who are these Craigsons?"

The girl bit her plump lower lip and looked fully into his eyes. She was quite pretty and, with a jolt, Lucius realized there was also something familiar about her. London Society? A local family? He could not place her.

"The Craigsons are a large family from Hertfordshire," she said. "I was invited by their daughter, Constance, to visit."

Lucius frowned. "I thought I knew every family in the neighborhood. Unless they have rented the Burnham Estate?" He looked at her. "In what village are they located?"

"They reside at Coddicot, my lord—sir."

"Coddicot! Good heavens, child. You are quite a distance from there. The stagecoach splits south of here at Welwyn, and you are now east of where you want to be in Woolmer Green."

Any potential humor he might have felt over her studied innocence vanished at the fix he now found himself in. He would be honor-bound to escort her to the home of these Craigsons' without delay. And in this weather, too! It spoke a rapid end to his peace. "How came you to travel alone with no one to see to your safety?"

Miss Woodsley cast her eyes upward before answering. "The head mistress at Paisley Seminary said a maid could not be spared to accompany me, sir, and that I would do very well on the stagecoach."

"Indeed. What an odd notion for a head mistress to have, as one who should be concerned for your well-being. A delicately nurtured— and young—female such as yourself left to make her own way? I cannot comprehend it." *I cannot credit it either.*

Miss Woodsley ducked her head and studied the melting snow on the sides of her boots. Lucius felt the burden of her presence. How he'd needed this evening of solitude and calm, and how little he relished taking the carriage out in such weather.

He paused. His sister was likely still at St. Albans and therefore of no use, but perhaps Lady Harrowden would take her in. It would be deuced awkward to see his old neighbor again after having neglected her for the past two years, but surely she would see he was in a fix?

Lucius shook his head. He couldn't disturb her this late. He'd have to go to Coddicot.

"Have you eaten?" Lucius asked at last. "I can ask Cook to bring you something sustaining while we sort out what's to be done."

"You are too kind, sir." His unwelcome guest lifted her gaze slowly to meet his, her lashes flipping upwards at last. "Although I am anxious to be off, something sustaining would be most welcome."

This is it. The seduction begins. Surely they would be halfway through their meal when the doorbell rang, and the outraged father, uncle—whoever it was—who had been led to his hunting box by divine intervention would burst into the dining hall and gasp at the thought of his innocent daughter or niece dining alone with such a *reputed rake* as Sir Lucius Clavering, declaring they must marry *at once* to spare her pristine reputation.

Miss Woodsley, he was sure, would not wait until the vows had been exchanged before she showed herself to be a managing, cunning sort of female. As soon as the contract was signed, she would begin the slow interference of his comfortable existence until all his friends shook their heads in pity. Lucius ground his teeth at the image.

"Briggs will show you into the dining room, where I will ask the maid to attend to you," he replied with icy politeness. "She will ensure that propriety is maintained." And although he could not be certain, he thought he saw a flash of disappointment in Miss Woodsley's eyes. His first assessment of her had been correct.

✲ 2 ✲

THE NEXT-TO-LAST PASSENGER TO quit the stagecoach—a buxom woman who'd claimed to be a sick nurse for the gentry—exited the tilting vehicle in a swirl of snowflakes that did not appear to worry the driver if his shouts at each stop were any indication, and therefore Selena Lockhart decided they would not worry her. The fat flakes would seem harmless, friendly little things were they not accompanied by a biting cold.

The departing passenger graced Selena with a generous whack on the shoulder from the basket she'd slung over her solid back, a blow that would surely leave its mark. Although she had been garrulous and smelled of garlic and spirits, Selena missed her presence the minute the door to the stagecoach closed and they rejoined the road. When two of them had shared the warmth of the enclosed carriage, Selena had been able to dismiss her bleak thoughts about the future. Alone, she shivered.

At first, the cold caused little tremors as she adjusted to the invasion of frigid air, and she tried in vain to wrap her cloak even more tightly about her. Then, her teeth began to chatter. Audibly. *Well, Selena. You insisted on this course of action and now must see it through.*

5

Besides, anything must be better than the disagreeable attentions of Robert Bromley, who was entering his dotage and still imagined she must be grateful for his offer.

After another half-hour of fruitless meditation, the stagecoach jerked to a sudden stop and tilted on its axis. Selena lurched forward, banging her head on the opposite seat with a force that brought tears to her eyes. With her luck, that would leave another mark, and one more visible. There was a bustle and shout as the driver, along with the lone passenger seated on top of the stagecoach—who had tried to coax his way inside without success since he had not paid the additional fare —climbed down to inspect the damage. Selena lifted the heavy leather curtain and watched the activity from her window.

"Right stuck we are," the driver said with a scowl. He batted the snow off his hat and shoved it back on his head.

"'Tis no surprise with thee tooling the coach in that neck-or-nothing way." The passenger shook his head in disgust.

The driver stuck his chin forward. "What'd you say?"

Selena bit her lip. The two had been exchanging sharp words since the roof passenger was taken up several hours earlier, and the bickering added to her sense of isolation. A thought occurred to her, borne out of desperation. Perhaps she was close enough to her destination to walk since the next stop was hers. Their voices kept rising in pitch, and before the men broke into an outright brawl, Selena picked up her portmanteau and pushed open the door. If courage could not spring up on its own, she must conjure it.

"Miss, no need for you to be leaving the carriage." The driver paused in his altercation, treating her to the dismissive tone he had used with her since he recognized her low station. "We'll be on our way again in two shakes."

"Whot's this you're jawing on about?" The passenger balled his hands and placed them squarely on his hips. "This carriage ain't going nowhere. We'll need a job horse to pull us out—and several men asides."

The driver puffed up his chest like a prize cock about to fight. "'Tain't you the driver of this vehicle."

"Excuse me," Selena interrupted. She would not be deterred by the driver's high-handed manner. What did he know of her station anyway? "Do either of you know where we are?"

Serving her with an impatient glance, the driver gave a curt answer. "Just entered Woolmer Green." Turning back to the passenger, he added, "And this is a broad stretch of flat road—"

Woolmer Green meant nothing to her. "How close are we to Harrowden Estate?"

"Harrowden?" With deliberate disdain, the driver pulled his gaze from the passenger and rubbed his chin. "It's nigh four miles from here, I reckon."

Selena's determination began to waver and she huddled in her cloak, taking refuge from the flurry of snowflakes. "Then it will not be possible to walk from here." She looked at the coachman. "What are your plans, sir? Do you truly think we shall become unstuck?" She pleaded him silently with her eyes. *No blustering. I need the truth.*

The driver opened his mouth to give a quick answer but paused when the passenger raised his eyebrows. At last, he spoke as if the words were forced out of him. "P'raps he's got the right of it. The wheel's hit a frozen rut and the axle's broke. It's only three miles to the last posting inn."

He then surveyed her cloaked figure with interest. "We'll jest unhitch these horses, and you can ride with me."

The flash of revulsion that hit her was involuntary and instantaneous. "No, I don't think I shall join you," Selena said in a strong voice that surprised even her.

The portmanteau, which she had been cradling in her arms, she took securely by the handle. "I will seek shelter at the house over yonder, whose windows are lit. I am quite sure they will take pity on my plight and lend their assistance. You are to bring my trunk to the next stop as planned, and I'll have Lady Harrowden send someone to pick it up at the posting inn there tomorrow."

Selena spoke with a confidence she was far from feeling. "In any case, should brigands come to loot the carriage while you are away, goodness knows I have nothing of value to steal." She did not wait for their reaction but turned and began to walk.

A few feet into the tree-lined path, and she could no longer hear their argument, which had sprung back to life in her wake. The silence was a relief. All too well did she know what a vulnerable position she was in, traveling alone with only two men of unknown morals to accompany her. The quicker they forgot about her the better. No, it was more prudent to head toward the manor she saw in the distance. It was of a decent size, which meant servants and respectability; and mentioning she was to visit Lady Harrowden would give her the protection she needed.

The silence became less friendly as she trudged on in the snow, and the house seemed farther than she had first judged. There was a movement in the trees to her right, which set her heart pounding, and her arms ached from the weight of her portmanteau and the books she had stored in it. Her feet burned from cold, and bits of snow slipped into the top of her boots as she sank into the white powder with each step.

Selena arrived at last and rapped the knocker on the front door, which echoed inside. She attempted to swallow the lump in her throat, as she waited in the cold silence, and she cast her gaze about the two-storied stone manor decked with eight windows on each floor. The hoot of an owl came from the trees to her right, and she jumped at the eerie, lonely sound.

Three years should have been sufficient to prepare her for this, but the stretch of time didn't seem to be enough. One year to recover from the shock of her father having gambled away his entire fortune and plunged himself headlong into drink, for Matthew Downing to rescind his offer of marriage, and for the fickle attention of former friends in the *ton* to dwindle to nothing. One year to dash all hopes that a new life could be created at her mother's small property in Bedford where enough of the gentry were connected to the pulse of London's Society and its delicious gossip. One year to sink further into poverty as her father succumbed in his weakened state to the influenza and the collectors came to take what little there was left.

It was hard enough to leave home, the responsible daughter and the eldest of four, but she had persuaded her mother it was the only thing to do after refusing to enter into a loveless marriage, and indeed it was. They had no means to give her sisters a London Season where their sweetness of temper and charming countenances might cause some gentlemen to contemplate an unequal match. At least with Selena gone it would be one less mouth to feed for her mother. And Lady Harrowden was offering a respectable salary. If ever Selena had needed a sign from Providence that she was on the right path, the timing of this position was it—or so she had thought until now.

The door opened, but the man behind it did not have the look of a servant. His clothes were too fine, and he had a handsome chin and noble brow with a prominent crease in the middle of it. There was a look of haughty superiority on his face, and if she wasn't mistaken —irony.

"Yes, miss? How may I be of assistance?"

"Good evening, sir. I was bound for Harrowden, but the stagecoach has broken down. I saw the lights in this house from the road and had hoped to find assistance here."

"I did not expect to host a henhouse when I had the shutters opened today," was his cryptic reply. "Harrowden? At least you're in the right town."

What an odd greeting. It was nothing Selena could answer, so she waited for him to continue.

"And what is your business with Lady Harrowden?" His cynical gaze swept over Selena, and she was made to feel as shabby as she surely looked. Not only was her cloak several seasons old, but it had lost its luster in patches. "A companion, I presume?"

Selena fumed for a moment. If only this man had known her before her disgrace, he would never dare to speak to her in such an impertinent manner. She couldn't give him the set-down she longed to—not when she was dependent upon him for help.

Why should his reaction surprise her, though? It was the way of Society. "You have surmised correctly, sir."

Selena waited, still on the doorstep with the cold at her back, but he did not bid her enter. Perhaps she had made a grave error in coming here on her own, but she had nowhere to turn now. The stagecoach driver was long gone, and all she would have was an empty coach or a four-mile trek to Harrowden, where she was sure to get lost or freeze to death before ever she reached it.

Behind the gentleman, a movement caught her eye and revealed itself in the form of a young woman, smartly dressed in a cream gown and Evening Primrose yellow spencer. She looked young to be this man's wife, but no other explanation offered itself.

Selena relaxed at once and gave her a brilliant smile. "Good evening, ma'am. I am relieved to see the mistress of the house is at home. I had begun to fear I had fallen on a bachelor establishment."

The look the woman sent her husband confused Selena, because it was not one of self-assurance. Was she newly married then and not comfortable in her position? Selena narrowed her eyes. Perhaps this house was run by a despot whose own wife cowered before him, which would be very like this gentleman if his initial greeting were any indication. But she could not give up this chance to appeal to another woman. Her whole safety depended on it.

"I assure you, I shall not trouble you for long," Selena said, ignoring the gentleman. "If word can be sent to Harrowden, I am quite certain they will send someone immediately to fetch me."

"This is rich," the gentleman murmured, as he looked at his wife. He took a step back and folded his arms, a mocking smile on his face. Without sparing him a glance, Selena turned the full force of her pleading gaze on the one who could help her.

"I...I..." the woman hemmed.

"Go on," the gentleman urged his wife, waiting for her to speak. He almost seemed to take pleasure in her discomfiture. Had Selena stumbled on a madhouse?

With a timid glance at her husband, the young woman said, "I am sure a supper might be prepared for you in the kitchen—is that not so?"

A voice came from beyond the hosts. "Sir, the supper has been brought up and is waiting for you in the dining room."

His gaze fixed on Selena, the gentleman called over his shoulder. "Set another plate."

So he was intending to let her in. Good. She could no longer feel her toes, and even her warm cloak was beginning to be ineffective against the biting cold. He opened the door wider, and she took a step in.

"Thank you, sir." She turned to his wife and graced her with a small curtsy. "And you, ma'am."

"Miss Woodsley is not, in fact, my wife," the gentleman said, as he led the way to the dining room.

He did not look back as he said it, and Selena was left to decipher its meaning. The implication came upon her at once, and she felt a flush mount to her cheeks. She had not stumbled into a madhouse—no! She had stumbled into a house of vice. No wonder that poor girl looked so uncomfortable. Would he expect something of Selena? Was she to be another one of his conquests? Even the snow was preferable to that.

She followed behind numbly. At long last her courage deserted her, and Selena felt tears prick at the back of her eyelids.

Her host stopped before a dark wooden door and opened it, ushering the young lady in before him. When Selena came to the door, he glanced at her face and stayed her with a light pressure on her shoulder. She trembled from cold and fear, unable to meet his gaze, but he stepped closer until she was forced to look up. He seemed to be studying her, searching for something in her eyes, and Selena's heart beat strangely.

"I will not hurt you," he said, his voice low, as if soothing a wounded animal. Without releasing her from his gaze, he called out to his servant.

"Can we drive to Harrowden in this weather? Find out from Finn. We are going to escort this young woman there this evening."

"Right away, Sir Lucius." The servant hurried off to do his bidding.

"Thank you," Selena whispered and, released from his nearness, stepped in front of him into the dining room where a servant was pouring the drinks. Any thought that Miss Woodsley might be as terrified as she was vanished as the young woman sent a calculating glance at the gentleman entering the room behind Selena.

Turning with a seductive smile that was at odds with her wispy, childlike voice, Miss Woodsley leaned forward. "Sir Lucius, you were beginning to tell me how we might make our way to Coddicot. It is so good of you to offer."

He sat and leaned back as the servant dished soup into his bowl. "We shall have to hope the weather will hold so that we may indeed set out tomorrow. In the meantime, I believe fate has sent us an answer in the form of Miss—" He turned to Selena and raised his brows in question.

"Miss Lockhart," she supplied.

"In the form of Miss Lockhart. As we are to bring Miss Lockhart to Harrowden, we shall request that Lady Harrowden put you up for the night to keep your reputation safe. In the morning, I shall come to relieve them of your unexpected presence and bring you to Coddicot where I might restore you to your friends—who must be beside themselves with worry."

His eyes twinkled with private amusement, and now Selena was truly confused. Was this woman not his mistress? Perhaps he was not the rake Selena had assumed him to be.

She hadn't noticed the servant filling her bowl with steaming soup, but now she felt its warmth on her face. "I am much obliged to you, sir," Selena replied, glancing at Miss Woodsley. Upon closer inspection, she could not be more than eighteen. How came she to be here?

Miss Woodsley wound the napkin around her fingers in a nervous gesture, and when she spoke, she had lost some of her self-assurance. "Sir Lucius, I admire your noble impulse to protect my reputation, but...Lady Harrowden will not be expecting me. I cannot impose upon her household in such a way."

She paused to take a convulsive breath, and Selena thought she might be suffering from fear, until Miss Woodsley blurted out, "Surely we can contrive to protect my reputation whilst I stay here, and then set out at an early hour in the morning with none the wiser?"

Selena's eyes widened. It had seemed at first glance that Sir Lucius was the hunter and Miss Woodsley the hunted, but now...

"You mistake me," Sir Lucius replied, picking up his spoon. "I am not concerned with your reputation."

Selena wasn't the only one who received a jolt from his harsh words. Across from her, Miss Woodsley looked as if she had been slapped.

"I am, at present," Sir Lucius continued, "only concerned with my own." No sooner had he spoken the words than the rap of another visitor echoed through the house.

Sir Lucius picked up his wine glass and held it in his hands. A smile hovered on the corner of his mouth. "Ah. Now the fun begins."

3

IT WAS JUST as he had predicted. In minutes, following on the heels of Lucius's servant, a dashing young man rushed into the room, his brow thunderous. He tossed his cape back, revealing a thin blade. He would have looked comical in his dramatic entrance were it not for his stern expression. With one hand, he removed his hat, and with the other, raised a shaking finger toward Lucius.

"You—you, sir, shall answer for the seduction of my sister. How little it surprises me that her innocence has led her right into a trap set by a known rake. Her reputation will not survive after you've been closeted together in this way. I will see that justice is done, even if it has to come from my own hand."

The bold nature of this statement was somewhat lost when he reached into the pocket of his waistcoat in search of a handkerchief and wiped his nose, which had begun to run. Lucius shot an amused glance at Briggs, then at Miss Lockhart, who was staring at the sight before her as one transfixed by an oddity.

When the gentleman had tucked the handkerchief back into his waistcoat, he allowed himself to look around the room. It was then that he peered more closely at the small group gathered around the table. He stopped short at the sight of Miss Lockhart.

Lucius stood. "Allow me to introduce myself. I am Sir Lucius Clavering, Baronet of Mardley. Although, it appears you already know me by reputation—" Lucius narrowed his lids at the word, for although he had once dabbled with fair Cyprians like all men of his age, they had long ceased to hold any interest for him. If his reputation was less than pristine still, he knew it had more to do with his according only the barest civility to young ladies without coming up to scratch with offers of marriage. Rake was an epithet used purely out of spite.

"I do not have the pleasure of knowing you at all," Lucius continued, "and I cannot say I am the poorer for it. You will recognize your sister, Miss Woodsley, of course. And this"—with a nod to the most recently arrived guest—" is Miss Lockhart."

The young buck's eyes widened as he fixed his gaze on Miss Lockhart, and he visibly faltered. "I don't know what kind of deep game you're playing at, sir—"

"Why, none at all," Lucius replied smoothly, forcing down his irritation. Who did this greenhorn think he was? "If you thought I had designs on your sister—a girl upon whom I had not laid eyes before she forced my hospitality this evening—let me assure you it is no such thing. And Miss Lockhart's presence safeguards her reputation quite nicely."

Mr. Woodsley fingered the sword hilt, as if he still hoped it might come to a challenge. *Fool.* The young man would not come off the victor.

"But what kind of propriety does *that* woman lend?" Mr. Woodsley asked, as he glanced at Miss Lockhart's outdated attire with an expression of aversion. "How came she to be in a bachelor's establishment without accompaniment?"

Miss Lockhart astonished Lucius by leaping to her feet and taking her own defense. "My situation is none of your concern, sir. But if we are looking to point out irregularities, I might ask the same of your sister."

"Wh..why, I don't see how that is any of your concern—"

"Precisely," Miss Lockhart responded, her eyes flashing dangerously.

"Spiked your own guns," Lucius murmured, as he gestured for the hovering footman to bring the second course. The evening that had so threatened to cut up his peace was beginning to look quite promising. He wasn't even bored.

However, it was time to put this farce to an end. "I can see how concerned you were for your sister's welfare and how lucky to discover her whereabouts. You must be reassured to find her reputation intact. Your arrival is timely. I was about to escort your sister, along with Miss Lockhart, to Harrowden, where Miss Lockhart will be residing with the countess."

"Lady Harrowden?" the man exclaimed, sending a startled glance at his sister.

"How relieving that I shall not need to inconvenience Lady Harrowden by foisting an unexpected guest upon her, as I had planned to do until I could restore your sister to her friends on the morrow. Briggs, will you see that our guests have everything they need to continue their journey?"

Miss Woodsley's silverware clattered on the plate as she stood, her face livid. Without sparing Lucius a glance, she swept past her brother, who had been rendered momentarily speechless, and made her way to the door.

"Well, sir...I am, of course, much obliged to you. I see I quite misread the situation, and if I've caused you any inconvenience, why, I apologize for it." Mr. Woodsley attempted a placating smile. "I wouldn't want this to bring us any discomfort should we meet again in London—"

"Joseph, let us go." Miss Woodsley cut his effusions short, much to Lucius's relief. Before the door closed fully, her exasperation led her to betray herself. "You're late."

Her brother's muffled reply came through the shut door. "Don't imagine I am always to appear at the snap of your finger, even if you do discharge my debts. Save that for your suitors." Their footsteps and voices trailed away as Briggs escorted them out.

Miss Lockhart locked eyes with Lucius, who gave a shake of his head and the hint of a smile. She took her seat again. "I had convinced myself I'd landed in Bedlam upon arriving here, and I am still not entirely sure that is untrue. However, I see it is not all of your own making." Her expression was severe, but he thought he detected a flash of something in her eyes—if not humor, then relenting.

He wiped his mouth with the thick cloth napkin. "Some women are...determined."

Miss Lockhart lifted her chin and drew in a sharp breath. "Let me be perfectly clear. *I* am not one of them."

Lucius nodded, oddly chastened for having jumped to the wrong conclusion. He looked at her more closely and was struck by her mouth that was tinged the natural hue of raspberries, and her eyebrows that arched perfectly over gray eyes that had already expressed many emotions in their short time together. Miss Lockhart had arrived, dressed in a red cloak from several seasons ago, and the gown she wore underneath was almost shabby. For all that, as soon as she spoke, her quality became apparent. He would have to remember not to be hasty in his judgments.

Briggs opened the door. "Sir, your carriage is ready when you wish for it. The snow has nearly ceased."

"Very good." Lucius turned to Miss Lockhart, feeling more kindly disposed toward her now that the worst of his concerns had been dealt with. "We are not in a hurry. May I offer you some pudding? You were nearly blue with cold and will need to be warmed before we venture out again."

～

SELENA FELT MUCH MORE cheerful after having eaten, and now that she was thawed from the chill, knew a great temptation to stretch out on the sofa that was placed temptingly before the fire and go to sleep. This could not be, of course, and she forced herself to remain alert. Harrowden Estate would be her home now. *Please God, let it be a welcoming one.*

Before long, Sir Lucius was ready to set out, and she reluctantly put her cloak back on, knowing the cold would feel cruel after the all-too-brief reprieve. The cloak had not thoroughly dried before the fire, but the baronet surprised her with his thoughtfulness. She not only had a hot brick at her feet, but Sir Lucius tucked blankets securely around her in his phaeton.

At least now she knew his name. Sir Lucius Clavering. Selena warned herself against thinking kindly of him. It would only be a matter of time before he reminded her of her station and the chasm that separated them. It was better that she accepted his brief gesture of condescension for what it was.

Apart from the horses' hoofbeats and the carriage wheels rolling over the snowy path, all was quiet as Sir Lucius drove, his groom perched behind them. Selena was overcome by fatigue from the combination of warmth under the blankets and the frigid air outside— that and the comforting sensation of having someone else in charge for the first time since she'd left the safety of her mother's house. Despite her resolution to remain alert, the sensation of protection settled about her like a warm cloud. She yawned.

"You are under no compulsion to tell me, of course, but how came you to be companion to the countess? Where do you come from?" Sir Lucius looked down at her, and his superior height, coupled with his handsome and imposing demeanor, weakened her defenses. It had been some years since she'd encountered a man she felt to be a paragon —that is, if she overlooked his initial arrogance—and it was harder to bear when she knew she stood no chance at winning his good opinion.

"Forgive me," Selena said as she tried to swallow another yawn, her eyes watering from fatigue and cold. "I was lately living in a village near Bedford where my mother has a small property. Lady Harrowden is my father's second cousin, so it is not a very close relationship but enough to claim a connection and be of service to her."

"Have you never had a London Season then? Why hide yourself away in a role where you are likely to be little more than a drudge? You cannot be more than twenty."

"I am three and twenty," she replied after a brief hesitation. Wasn't the answer obvious to him? "When my father died, his estate passed over to my cousin, who..." Selena stopped short as a series of memories flashed before her "...who did not require any advisement on the running of his estate," she finished. Selena pressed her lips together. "So we soon found ourselves new lodgings. It only made sense that I would not remain a charge upon my mother, and she remembered this connection, the end result being that I am here."

"*Hm.*" Sir Lucius frowned and when at last he did speak it was only to say, "Don't let her frighten you. Lady Harrowden is known for her sharp tongue."

Selena pulled the blanket more securely around her shoulders. "Well, I should not think she can *eat* me."

This brought forth a smile from her transitory benefactor, and they did not speak many more words before they pulled up in front of the Harrowden residence. It was not extremely large as far as estates went, but it was three times the size of Sir Lucius's house. The carriage wheels were muted in the snow as they drove along the path that led to the front stairs, and Selena's tremors of cold turned to those of trepidation. If she could not find her place here, she did not know where else she might go.

~

LUCIUS HOPPED down from the carriage and handed the reins to Finn so he could help Miss Lockhart alight. With the blankets discarded in the carriage, the slender woman shivered at his side, and he knew a strange impulse to put his arm around her and shield her from the worst of the wind. He settled for offering his arm as they climbed the steps. The door opened shortly after the sound of the knocker ceased to echo.

"Good evening, Mullings," Lucius said. "I believe Lady Harrowden is expecting Miss Lockhart this evening. Her stagecoach had a run-in near my hunting box. It is most likely still there with her trunk attached to it if the drivers have not been able to pull the coach out of the rut. We came by the back roads."

The butler stepped aside to let them in. "Indeed, sir. One of the footmen had already gone to fetch her at the posting inn and has come back. The inn had no knowledge of why the stagecoach was delayed. If you will wait here inside where it's warm, I will make Lady Harrowden aware of the young lady's presence."

When the butler disappeared inside a door along the corridor, Miss Lockhart glanced around at her surroundings, and Lucius had a chance to study her more closely. Despite the fact that her eyes were too close together to label her a beauty, her slender nose and sweet mouth lent her quite a pretty appearance, and when she tilted her chin inquisitively, it revealed a willowy neck and a neat chignon just visible when she turned to the profile.

Miss Lockhart had not complained about the cold, although the tips of her nose and ears were red. She didn't spare him another glance, and with her attention off him, Lucius wondered just what she made of her new circumstances. Neither spoke and, when minutes later the door opened, it was Lucius's sister, Maria—not the butler—who exited the room to fetch Miss Lockhart. Lucius bit back an oath.

"Lucius!" Maria Holbeck advanced into the room and held out both her hands. He kissed them dutifully, attempting to hide the scowl that threatened to form. Any last hopes of having a New Year untroubled by further family obligations were quashed by this unexpected encounter. Maria had told him she and her husband would be remaining with their family at St Albans.

Maria turned to Miss Lockhart with a calculating look. "Lady Harrowden told me she was expecting you, and we were both wondering what could have happened to the coach. What a charming...coincidence that you fell into the hands of my brother. I will bring you to Lady Harrowden."

Maria had gestured Miss Lockhart forward, but she turned back and gave Lucius a penetrating glance. "I know you had hoped to be left quite alone, but I believe fate has aligned itself against you. Since you are here, you may save me the trip to your house and say that you are happy to attend the Twelfth Night ball for which I will be sending out invitations."

Lucius turned to follow Miss Lockhart, keeping his voice even. "I have no plans to attend any balls. It's why I came to my hunting box."

"Life is often not what we planned," Maria replied austerely.

How true that was for Miss Lockhart. Lucius was sure it was not by her own choice that she left her family to come serve as companion to a cantankerous old woman. However, Lucius should hope he had more control over his destiny than that. At least, that's what he spent most of his energy trying to secure. To be left in peace and comfort—that was all he asked. And if that was true for him at age thirty, Lucius didn't imagine it changing as he aged.

He should go now—he had no desire to see Lady Harrowden. But there was something that compelled him to remain for Miss Lockhart's sake. He was curious to know what would come of her.

Miss Lockhart stopped in her tracks with his sister at her side and turned to look at Lucius, her head held high. She opened her mouth to speak.

In the end, Lucius did not discover what Miss Lockhart was going to say, nor was he given a choice whether or not to remain. "Lucius, you may as well come in too," Maria said, as she advanced toward the drawing room. "Lady Harrowden has not seen your face for two years, and she will want a glimpse of you."

Lucius entered the room in time to see Lady Harrowden's brows snap together as Miss Lockhart came to stand before her. He was struck by the change in the widow's face. While she had always been a rather severe old woman in all the time he had known her, her severity seemed to have been replaced by bitterness.

"What do you mean by coming to me in this ramshackle manner?" she demanded of Miss Lockhart. "And in the company of a known rake no less—Sir Lucius, you know very well it is true, no matter if I have known you since you were in short coats." Turning back to Miss Lockhart, Lady Harrowden added, "I sent my footman to get you, and he returned empty-handed."

Although Miss Lockhart's expression remained veiled, Lucius saw her rising color. *This is not a woman who will take to her new position easily. She will likely not last the week.*

"My lady, you can hardly expect me to be blamed for the stage-coach breaking down—" Miss Lockart was cut off.

"Do not try your impertinence with me, young lady, or your employment here will be short-lived."

Lucius began to be uncomfortable. He could in no way defend Miss

Lockhart—what right had he? But something had happened to Lady Harrowden to cause her to be so uncivil.

Miss Lockart's color rose further, and Lucius knew by instinct that it took every ounce of her self-control not to respond in kind. Miss Lockhart was gently bred, but with her straitened means, she might not find a position in more favorable circumstances.

Miss Lockhart met the widow's gaze and remained silent. There was nothing challenging in her expression, but neither did she back down. The silence stretched.

"Lady Harrowden, I am happy to see that your companion has been safely restored to you by my brother. She will be a great help to you, I daresay."

"A very odd thing to have an unmarried man and single woman arrive together—"

Maria continued in a commanding voice, as if the countess had not raised an objection. "It is a fortunate thing the weather detained me here long enough to keep you company until her arrival. Well..." Maria clasped her hands together in front of her. "I must be off now that the snow has abated. I promise to come more often, and I do so hope you will grace our Twelfth Night ball with your presence."

"If the weather is anything like today, you may be assured I will not," Lady Harrowden snapped. She seemed to recollect herself, however, and softening, added, "However if it is warm enough, I will come. I know the importance of showing support for local celebrations."

"Well, I shall hope for good weather then," Maria said, "and I must bid you good night. As it is, Charles will be beside himself with worry —especially since his dinner was held up." She laughed at her own pleasantry.

"Come again before the ball, Maria," Lady Harrowden said, adding in her most acidic tone, "Sir Lucius, I suppose I shall see you here again in another two years."

Lady Harrowden had every right to hold a grudge against him, and Lucius acknowledged her snide comment with an inclination of his head, but he did not apologize. He was not going to give the countess his head for washing.

He turned to face Miss Lockhart. He didn't like the idea of leaving her here, and he bestowed a final glance upon her before turning to follow his sister. Her cryptic smile held a hint of mischief that made him stop in his tracks to see if she would divulge the reason behind it.

"Sir Lucius, I am much obliged to you for rescuing me from, what I imagine was near certain death. I was chilled through, and I'm grateful for your chivalrous nature in taking me in so promptly—and with such an air of hospitality."

Although her tone was perfectly pleasant, the sardonic edge to her words did not escape him.

"I am happy to be of service, Miss Lockhart," Sir Lucius replied gravely, though the corner of his mouth twitched. There was a bite to her, this one. He bowed before the countess. "My lady."

Alone with his sister in the hallway, the footman standing at the front door, Lucius muttered under his breath. "How is it possible you are here already? You made no mention of this when we were together over Christmas. I left St Albans precisely for some time apart from the family."

"You must blame our grandfather then for purchasing a hunting box not twelve miles from the family estate."

"And then our father for arranging your marriage to Holbeck, who lives no more than three," Lucius grumbled. "You said you would remain with Mother through January."

Maria smiled patronisingly. "How often our dearest wishes are not accorded. But Mother changed her mind and said she'd rather not plan a Twelfth Night party so I am throwing a ball here." His sister smoothed the fur on her muff. "The number of unattached ladies far outweighs the number of single gentlemen, and I know I can count on you to do your duty."

Lucius curled his lip. "You cannot be so naïve as to think *that* will tempt me."

"Oh no. Merely to warn you," Maria replied. "I know you too well to think that such a thing will be tempting. However, you may as well come, you know. You have an entire week to yourself and may grumble in your library to your heart's content. Soon you will long for company, and this is just the event to provide it."

"I hardly think so. Why are you at Harrowden on such a day? Surely Holbeck does not permit you to traipse about in this sort of weather. And I shouldn't think you and the countess had much in common."

"No, but someone has to visit her if you won't," Maria said tartly, with a significant look that sparked a twinge of guilt in Lucius—an irritating sensation considering there was no limit to what his own family would ask of him. But it was true he hadn't kept his promise to the dying earl to look in on Lady Harrowden and see she was well taken care of. Well, technically speaking, Lucius had done so once, but he could not fool himself into believing that one visit was true to the spirit of his promise.

"I came early in the afternoon," Maria continued, "and I was meant to stay just for the time it took to have tea together. But it soon began to snow, and I thought it safer to stay put while the snow lasted. Thankfully, it stopped, and it is now safe to return home. I much prefer my own bed."

"A sentiment with which I highly concur." Lucius had given a signal to Mullings and before long their two carriages were brought around to the front.

Before they made their way to the front door, Lucius said in a voice only his sister could hear, "Miss Lockhart does not have the easiest of circumstances before her. Lady Harrowden will not set herself out to be pleasant to a mere companion. She is more likely to treat her like a drudge. In fact, she seems decidedly more bitter since I last saw her."

"Lady Harrowden is lonely. And that is why she has engaged a companion. Miss Lockhart will only be fulfilling her role. And I'm sure it's a situation that will suit both very nicely. Miss Lockhart will earn her living, which is something she clearly needs, and Lady Harrowden will have someone to amuse her and run her errands."

"*Hmph.*" The conversation irritated Lucius for reasons he could not understand, and he was ready to end it. "Do you need me to accompany you?" he asked, hoping fervently the answer was no.

His wish was granted. "It is two miles in the opposite direction, and I have both my groom and a footman. I shall be perfectly comfortable."

Lucius nodded. "Good night, then."

Maria exited into the frigid air, her breath coming out in a cloud. "Mind you come to my ball. I am counting on you."

Lucius grunted and waved one hand.

4

AFTER SIR LUCIUS and his sister left, and the door was closed behind them, Selena found herself alone with Lady Harrowden. The cold draft sweeping under her skirt made her shiver, and the chimney to the right of the countess gave off more smoke than warmth.

Lady Harrowden studied her in silence for a moment before saying, "Well, here you are at last. We will see how this arrangement suits, I suppose. Ring the bell there, and the maid will see you to your room."

Those were dampening words. Her brief correspondence with Lady Harrowden, cold and perfunctory in nature, should have warned her not to expect much consideration from the countess. She had nevertheless romanticized the adventure, since it was the means of escaping a disagreeable marriage prospect and a stifling home environment. To have imagined her new life as an improvement in circumstances was a mistake, and the reality came as a rude shock.

"What time tomorrow would you like me to be at your disposal, my lady?"

"The maid will apprise you of my habits. I am not an early riser, so you will have the mornings to yourself. I will expect you to tend to me starting from eleven o'clock." Lady Harrowden's papery skin shrouded her with frailty, and the deep pockets under her eyes gave her a disconsolate air. But there was an edge to her words when she dismissed Selena. "That will be all."

Lady Harrowden turned her gaze to the flickering logs in the chimney, signaling an end to their conversation. Selena rang the bell and waited quietly until the maid entered the room. Only then did Lady Harrowden stir from what looked to be a sober contemplation.

"Show Miss Lockhart to her room. Tomorrow morning, I will expect Mrs. Randall to give her a tour of the house, so she knows where to find everything. Miss Lockhart knows when she is to come to me."

Selena gave Lady Harrowden a curtsy and turned to follow the maid. The corridor was drafty, but surprisingly not much colder than the drawing room. Her own room, however, although small, was nicer than she expected and warmed by a small fire. Her apprehension over her new position, that had increased with the day's events, now abated somewhat. She would have time to walk in the mornings or read, and she had a warm fire. The role was likely to be tedious, but there were these small pleasures, at least.

"You have no trunk, miss?" The maid looked around in confusion. They must not have communicated belowstairs what had happened.

"No, the stagecoach broke down, and I only hope they will find my trunk and bring it to me without delay. I have one change of clothes in my portmanteau, and that will have to do until I have the rest." Selena tried to speak with more confidence than she felt. "And what is your name?"

"Hazel, miss." The maid dipped a curtsy. "There is hot water, and I will bring you more in the morning. Will you take your breakfast in your room?"

Selena shook her head. "I am an early riser. I will go for a walk before breakfast if the weather permits it, but I will come to the breakfast room to take my meal."

The maid dipped another curtsy and left. Selena was alone. She looked around her room. There was a large, single four-poster bed and enough space to move comfortably between the bed and the wardrobe. The corner of the room to the right of the fire held a writing desk, and she could hardly believe her luck. If only she could reconcile herself to Lady Harrowden's dragon-like personality she might be easy.

Selena unpacked her portmanteau. It was only then she realized the maid should have thought to help her remove her dress, and Selena should have thought to ask. She had grown self-reliant in their straitened means at home. However, by the time the idea of requesting help had occurred to Selena, she was hesitant to call the maid back. Did she merit any of the attentions paid to a guest? Selena was a gentleman's daughter, after all. She really did not know what to think.

In the end, Selena did not ring the bell but reached behind her back and undid the laces the best she could. Then she pulled her shift over her head, replacing it with a fresh one, and climbed into the bed, wiggling her bare legs rapidly until the cold sheets started to feel warmer. She stilled, drowsily staring at the fire, which gave off warmth and a cheerful glow. In this instant, Selena could almost imagine finding contentment in her life here. For the first time in two days, it was with pleasure rather than worry that she drifted off to sleep.

The next morning, Selena woke when the maid brought in the hot water and went over to turn the burning logs. This time she was not going to miss out on getting help.

"Good morning, Hazel," she said. "Would you mind helping me into my dress?"

"Right away, miss. I'm not trained as a lady's maid, though." Hazel dropped the poker and came to the side of the bed where Selena stood. The maid began to tug the strings hanging from her stays.

"Never mind about the training," Selena replied briskly. "I am here as a companion, and I will not be overly particular."

When Selena was properly dressed, she asked Hazel whether Mrs. Randall might be spared to take her to visit the house once she had eaten. The mounds of snow outside did not recommend her to a walk, and she thought it best to set out at once to familiarize herself with the house.

"I believe Mrs. Randall is aware of it, miss. I will just see when she is available and will send word to the breakfast room." Hazel dipped a curtsy before leaving, and Selena turned to the dressing mirror and tied her hair in a simple knot she knew would have to do. Her position did not require elegant hair, which was a bit of a shame, because with curling papers, she knew her hair was one of her best assets.

Selena examined herself in the small glass, trying to assess how she felt—trying to judge how she looked, and perhaps what impression she might have made on the masculine, sardonic Sir Lucius, who had a surprising tender side tucked away. She frowned at the last thought that had crept in. *Ridiculous girl.*

Once downstairs, a footman directed Selena to the breakfast room, where she ate in silence. Afterwards, she entered the corridor and turned to where she thought there might be stairs leading to the kitchen. Perhaps the housekeeper could be found there. Selena passed an open door in the corridor when the sound of a gentleman's voice reached her from inside the room.

"Miss—Miss! Might I help you with something?"

Selena retraced her steps until she was once again looking through the door of a library where a young man stood, dressed in the first stare of fashion. The stylish clothing leaned toward extravagance, and although his face was handsome enough, his lips had a petulant air to them. He raised his eyebrows as he took in her appearance, and heat crept up Selena's cheeks. She had traded yesterday's gown with the muddy hem for her only change from the portmanteau, which was a dull brown cotton print dress that had begun to fade. Even her best gown would not have done for this meeting.

"Good morning, sir," she said, hiding her dismay. "I am Miss Lockhart, and I am Lady Harrowden's companion. I was not aware she had other guests."

Selena paused, thinking that perhaps it was no business of hers to know whether or not there would be guests. She wished she'd had a manual of how to be a lady's companion—what she was entitled to and what she certainly must or must not do.

"I am not a guest," he replied, his smile ready as he took a step toward her. The smile changed his appearance and made him more attractive. She began to think her first assessment that he was of a querulous nature was incorrect.

"Perhaps that is why you were not aware of it," the gentleman went on, "but allow me to introduce myself." He bowed. "I am Lord

Harrowden, nephew to Lady Harrowden, and the current earl since my uncle died two years ago."

Selena was considerably surprised. There had been no mention of anyone in residence other than Lady Harrowden, and it had not occurred to her to wonder who had inherited the title.

"Excuse me, my lord. I was not aware Lady Harrowden had anyone else living with her. Do you reside here permanently, if...if such a thing is not too bold to ask?"

"I have been residing in London and had left my steward in care of this estate, permitting my aunt to continue to live here as long as she wished. But I arrived a week ago to take up residence. I have recently become absorbed in the affairs of the estate and must spend time here to better understand how it is run." Lord Harrowden puzzled his brows. "I had not been made aware that my aunt had engaged a companion."

Selena received this news with bafflement. Why would Lady Harrowden not tell her nephew something as significant as that? "Perhaps your wife knew of it, my lord," she volunteered.

"Perhaps she would have, were I married," Lord Harrowden responded with a self-deprecating smile. "However, I have not yet found a lady to fill the position."

Selena darted a glance into the corridor then back at him, as she considered how best she should answer. This was likely to be an uncomfortable situation and something she had not been prepared for —to live in such close quarters with an unmarried man. She wondered that Lady Harrowden had not thought to mention it. But then she remembered that Lady Harrowden had sent for her before her nephew had taken up residence.

"Well, I am on my way to find Mrs. Randall so that she may give me a tour of the house. I bid you good day." Selena curtsied and turned, hoping to make her escape, but the earl precipitated her movement toward the door.

"Please, allow me," he said. "I would be delighted to show you my house and grounds, and I have nothing so important it cannot wait."

Selena could not refuse without sounding churlish, but she did not wish to have more time alone with a strange gentlemen than she could avoid.

"I...um." She sought inspiration for how to refuse, but none came to her. "Very well," she said at last. "However, the maid has warned Mrs. Randall of my wish to speak with her, and I should hate to think she was waiting for me. Allow me to inform her of my intentions, and perhaps she might later show me the areas that are more within her domain."

"I think you need not trouble yourself about Mrs. Randall. Once she hears that I have taken you for the tour, she will find it perfectly natural, as I am the master of the house."

Selena now found herself in a bind. She was somewhat under this gentleman's power, being employed in his house, but her aversion to anything that hinted at lack of propriety made her pause, as did a new fear that had just struck her: she did not want Mrs. Randall to think she was acting above her station.

"Do come," Lord Harrowden urged, as he reached for his gloves that were resting on the side table next to the door. "I may not have something of more importance to do now, but it does not mean I have the entire day at my disposal."

His tone was friendly enough, but there was a tenor to his words that Selena did not like. She stepped aside and let him lead forward, her heart sinking as she followed.

LUCIUS AWOKE TOO EARLY for his liking. Dim rays of sunlight peeked through the curtains in his room, and the fire had not been stoked. He couldn't remember the last time he had awoken before his servant had arrived. Lucius went over to stoke the fire himself when he realized he could see his breath in the dim light.

He couldn't get last evening's events out of his mind. His encounter with Lady Harrowden for the first time in nearly two years served to remind him just how short he'd fallen of his promise made to her husband to look in on the countess after the earl died. Partly from compassion for Miss Lockhart—for she had not seemed at all comfortable when he left her—and partly from a sense of guilt, he'd suffered a temptation to go visit.

However, Lucius wasn't accustomed to listening to his own conscience, and he decided to dress himself and have breakfast instead. The feeling would surely pass soon enough. He had just finished a leisurely breakfast and was perusing *The London Gazette* while drinking his second cup of coffee when he heard the dull echo of the knocker at the entrance. *Who is it this time?* May a man not have a reprieve in his own house?

Briggs entered a moment later. "Sir, there are two men who wish to deliver a trunk belonging to the young lady who came here last night— Miss Lockhart."

Lucius looked up in surprise. "Well, I hope you told them to take it to the Harrowden estate since that is where it belongs."

"I attempted to do so, sir," Briggs replied, "but they said the road is blocked, and they have no choice but to leave the trunk here."

Lucius was betrayed into a hasty retort. "If they set the thing outside my door, that is precisely where it will stay."

His butler made to leave the room when Lucius thought the better of it. This was Miss Lockhart's trunk, and she should not suffer for the men's lack of diligence or his loss of temper. "Stay a minute, Briggs. I will see to the trunk."

At the door was what looked to be the stagecoach driver with his cape and tall hat perched on his head. He was accompanied by a second man who Lucius recognized as a hostler from The Songbird, a nearby inn.

"What brings you here?" he asked them. "Did Miss Lockhart not give you instructions for her trunk?" The article in question, a brown stiff leather box with a rounded lid and thin straps held in place by metal studs, sat between the men on the ground. It looked too small to carry all the effects of a woman setting up permanent residence in a new place.

"There's a tree that fell last night from the high wind, sir—along the road. We can't bring the coach to be fixed until the tree is removed, but the trunk must go either way. We thought p'rhaps the miss might still be here."

"This is my hunting box, and she is a lady," Lucius replied with a degree of exasperation. "Of course she is not here."

The men did not seem to know what to make of that and looked from the trunk back to their poor conveyance. Lucius paused for a moment. Perhaps this was fate's way of telling him he needed to do his duty to the countess and see how she was faring—and this time to stop and converse with her. He owned to some curiosity over whether Miss Lockhart was in better frame today than she was last night. She had been subdued before the countess, though she'd taken pains to hide it.

She had certainly let him know precisely what she thought of his welcome. The memory made Lucius smile.

"Very well," he said. "You may leave it here. I will see that Miss Lockhart gets it."

The men wasted no time in setting the trunk outside his front door and turning to climb into their gig as if they feared he would call them back. Lucius watched them turn the carriage and go the way they came, which must have been the unencumbered portion of road leading to The Songbird. He turned his face to where the stagecoach must lie, but the sight of it was hidden by the trees. They had not had any more snowfall, and it wouldn't be difficult to bring the trunk this morning. He would access Harrowden through the private road he'd used last night.

Lucius stood looking at the modest trunk for a moment. He might as well take it over now. Then he would be done with the errand and could get back to his solitude.

"Finn, hitch up the phaeton. I have a call to make."

His groom had come around to the front of the estate when Lucius was speaking with the men, and he now hurried off to do his master's bidding. Lucius went up to put on more layers as the air was even colder today without the falling snow.

He drove in silence, appreciating the road that wound through the bit of woods, then across the meadow. He could still see his tracks in the snow from the night before. It was nearly silent apart from the horses' hooves and the creak of the phaeton as the wheels went over the frozen ruts. The brisk air that bit at him through his cloak was invigorating.

Lucius wondered when he had lost that sense of enchantment that came from the outdoors—from friendship, family, and the little pleasures life afforded. It seemed that ever since he had inherited the title eight years ago, his life had become more about all the things he must do, and therefore there was always this vague undercurrent of wishing to escape. He rode by an evergreen with red berries set cheerfully against the white snowy backdrop, and as he passed it, the large branch overhead spilled a mound of snow on one of the horse's backs, causing both horses to speed up as the wind powdered Lucius's face with the flakes. A quiet chuckle escaped him as he wiped the snow off his face with his free hand.

He was just coming up the road leading to Harrowden Estate, when he spotted two figures walking along the path that led from its gardens. The couple was quite far from the house, which was odd. With the frigid air, it was not a day for pleasure walking.

It was the red coat belonging to Miss Lockhart that next caught his attention. What gentleman could have been so improvident as to suggest a walk when it was this cold? As he drew near, he saw it was indeed Miss Lockhart, accompanied by the new earl, whom Lucius knew only by face and name. Harrowden was younger than he by a good six years, and therefore they had no friends in common.

Lucius pulled up to the pair and found Miss Lockhart nearly blue with cold. "Good morning, Harrowden. Miss Lockhart," he said, catching her gaze. "Your trunk was delivered to my doorstep, and I came to bring it to you."

"You are very kind, sir."

Miss Lockhart's smile was frozen, and Lucius wondered if it was simply the cold, or if there was something more sinister behind it, like fear. *Why is she here?* He responded to an instinct that told him Miss Lockhart needed help, even if it was just to get her quickly to warmth.

"Harrowden, I am sure you will not mind if I take Miss Lockhart up in the carriage so that she may see to her trunk."

A look of annoyance passed over Harrowden's features, but he gave a short bow. "Yes, of course. You must certainly do so. Miss Lockhart, we can finish our tour at another time as we have not yet visited the orchards."

Miss Lockhart returned a stiff curtsy, then moved to the side of the carriage. Lucius wondered what the earl had hoped to achieve by this walk? He intended to find out as soon as they drove away. Harrowden stood by while Miss Lockhart assessed the carriage then reached up her hand to grasp the side of it.

"Perhaps you could assist Miss Lockhart," Lucius suggested, carefully hiding away his irritation. It would do no good to provoke someone he did not know, and who did not act in the usual way of a gentleman.

"Of course," Lord Harrowden replied, equally as polite. He offered Miss Lockhart a gloved hand and, with some difficulty that was likely due to cold, she stepped into the carriage.

When Miss Lockhart was settled next to Lucius, he tucked her securely under the blankets that his groom had thought to provide, stopping long enough to fold them around on the other side of her. She appeared to be even colder than she had been last night. He clicked the reins.

"What brings you so far from the estate?" He felt Miss Lockhart shiver next to him, and she replied through chattering teeth.

"Lord Harrowden insisted upon showing me the grounds. He kept leading me farther away from the estate, although I told him I was not properly dressed for the cold. He did not seem to hear me, and I dared not refuse him since he is, in some sense of the word, my employer."

"My dear Miss Lockhart, Lord Harrowden is not your employer, and therefore you need not do anything he suggests unless it accords with your own wishes. *Lady* Harrowden is your employer. Your salary will come out of her trust."

Miss Lockhart turned to him in surprise, and Lucius was caught by the brilliance of her clear, gray eyes, set as they were against her rosy cheeks and the white that surrounded them. His stomach lurched in an unfamiliar way. Turning forward again, Lucius could only be glad she was sitting comfortably beside him, as it would have taken a good half-hour to walk back to the estate—and the earl had not even begun to lead her back in the direction of the house.

"I am unfamiliar with my role," Miss Lockhart admitted, her gaze directed toward the house they were fast approaching. "I do not know what I owe Lady Harrowden—how much I must cater to her wishes and to what degree I might remain my own master. How much of what others request of me must I do?" She spoke in a musing way, as if there were no ready answer.

"Who is your father?" Lucius asked, the question leaving his lips before he had thought it through. It was unlike him to ask such a personal question. His entire aim was generally to keep a distance, as he had enough family and friends to occupy him without adding more. Nevertheless, he persisted. "You were not born to this role."

"I suppose not, but it is my role now." Miss Lockhart stared ahead. "My father was John Lockhart of Kingsbury in Warwickshire—a gentleman but not a nobleman."

"And your mother?" Lucius glanced again at her profile and saw her tighten her jaw. Although the unusual manner in which they met cut through some of the superficiality of the *ton*, he was pressing her for details he usually preferred to leave alone.

"My mother is caring for my three younger sisters, who live in Bedford where she grew up. She met my father in the usual way during the London Season. The ending to their match was not in her favor, so I am doing what I can to assist her. We are an ordinary family with an ordinary tale, I suppose."

"I don't believe there is such a thing as an ordinary family," Lucius said, pulling gently on the reins. "I suppose your circumstances must at times be hard to bear. I imagine it was not easy for you to leave your family and come to Harrowden?"

By now they had arrived at the estate, and Miss Lockhart did not respond right away. Lucius waited before jumping down from the carriage, curious as to her answer. *He* certainly would not mind a little distance from his family, but she likely pulled strength from her mother and sisters and regretted the necessity of having to leave them.

"Oh, there is no point in thinking of what might have been, is there? Rather only looking forward. After all, the future is all that is left to us." Miss Lockhart looked pained, and he saw that he had pushed her too far.

Lucius hesitated, wondering if he should utter some form of an apology for having intruded, but in the end said nothing as the under-groom came forward. He handed him the reins and halted the footman moving toward the carriage to assist Miss Lockhart.

"I will help her down. You—take Miss Lockhart's trunk and have it sent to her room." Lucius walked around the carriage and held out his hand to help Miss Lockhart alight. She did not move at once, and he wondered if it had been his intrusive questions that made her shrink back from him.

She surprised him then with a smile, her frank eyes turned on him from on high, as though she were placed on a pedestal. "It is the most ridiculous notion, but I have almost started to thaw under these blankets and have no wish to leave them, even if the house is warmer."

"I believe you simply wish to punish me by making me suffer the cold while I await your pleasure," Lucius replied, the corner of his mouth lifting. "Come. You will be much the better for a cup of hot tea and a seat before the fire. I will accompany you in. I would like to see Lady Harrowden again."

There was a gleam of humor in Miss Lockhart's eyes as she held his gaze, and in a quick gesture, she threw off the blankets and scampered down. He held her arm close as he hurried her inside.

"Goodness, what time is it?" she asked, her teeth now chattering again, as they climbed the stone steps and rushed through the door that opened for them from the inside. "I am to appear before Lady Harrowden by eleven o'clock."

"It is past eleven. I will explain the reason for your tardiness," he said. "I hope the connection between our families will compel her to listen. Besides, you are not to blame."

"That is very kind of you, sir. Although I am sure she would listen to you, I believe I must present myself to her first. She will not have left her bedchambers."

Lucius raised his head as the butler came toward them. "Perhaps you are right. Mullings, if you will be so good as to show me into the drawing room, I will wait for Lady Harrowden to receive me. I have sent a footman to bring Miss Lockhart's trunk that arrived at my doorstep today."

The butler bowed, and Lucius turned to Miss Lockhart. "You have your trunk now. This should give you something to change into."

"You are right. My boots are soaked through. But I must hurry."

True to her word, Miss Lockhart wasted no time in rushing off, as Lucius was shown into the Harrowden drawing room, to which he hadn't set foot in two years, barring last night. The fire in the room gave off ineffectual heat, and the only sound within was the ticking of the clock on the shelf, the soft crackle of burning logs, and distant footsteps in another room. It took only five minutes in such stillness before Lucius began to wonder what had prompted him to come on what could only be described as a fool's errand.

6

SELENA HURRIED into her bedroom where the trunk was waiting for her, and she untied the straps. She would not change her dress; there was little enough to choose from. However, she could find something dry for her feet.

Selena changed her boots, pulling at the laces with clumsy fingers that burned as they thawed in the warm room. What she should have been thinking through was what to say to Lady Harrowden. The clock on the mantel showed half-past eleven, and Selena redoubled her efforts. This was not a good beginning to her employment.

She knocked softly at Lady Harrowden's door. When there was no response, she knocked again and heard a sharp—*Enter!*

The curtains were thrown open, and the room was flooded with light. Lady Harrowden was still in bed, and the empty cup of chocolate sat on the small table to her side. The countess's grey hair had retained hints of red, and it was currently fanned over her shoulder against the pillow. Her face was pinched with irritation as she waited for Selena to speak.

"My lady, I beg you will forgive my tardiness. Lord Harrowden wished to show me the grounds and did not heed my warning that it would make me late in presenting myself to you. Fortunately, Sir Lucius was coming to deliver my trunk—"

Lady Harrowden's eyes widened, stopping Selena short. "Why did Sir Lucius have your trunk?" she demanded.

Selena paused, abashed. This did not look good, and the awkwardness had not occurred to her until now. "The...the stagecoach driver brought it to his house, and he came upon me walking with the earl and brought me to you straight away in his carriage."

"So, Lord Harrowden has sought your acquaintance, has he?" The countess studied Selena's face keenly. "And how do you find my nephew? He is pleasing to look at, I am told, and his title only adds to his attraction."

How could Selena answer such a question? Lord Harrowden's title was of absolutely no interest to her. And since she was not a suitable candidate for him, there was no point in considering such a thing. However, truth be told, he awakened Selena's instinct of self-preservation. He seemed bent on reminding her she was under his power, even if only by the subtlest of hints. Discovering him at the estate, lent a sense of peril to Selena's situation that was more than she had bargained for.

She chose her words carefully. "I can see why members of the *ton* have their eye on Lord Harrowden, as he is certainly charming. As for me, I wished only to show him the respect that was due as lord of the manor and for that reason agreed to accompany him. Even as it grew late, I did not dare oppose him by returning to the house against his will."

"So he forced you to walk with him?" Lady Harrowden's tone was a mixture of curiosity and annoyance.

"Not...exactly." *How could she answer this?* Selena tried again. "I had hoped to view the estate with Mrs. Randall, as you suggested. But when Lord Harrowden insisted, I could not refuse him. Fortunately, Sir Lucius came upon us, as I mentioned, and I must say his arrival was providential, for not only was I late in coming to you, but I was half-frozen."

"And where is Sir Lucius now? Did he scurry back to his hunting box—or wherever it is he is currently residing?"

"As a matter of fact, he did not, my lady. He said he wished to speak with you, and is waiting in the drawing room if you can spare the time."

Lady Harrowden sniffed and looked to the window. "So he seeks an audience with me, does he? At last."

Selena was beginning to accustom herself to Lady Harrowden's rapid questions, not all of which required an answer. The countess threw off her covers and stood in a movement that was brisk for someone her age. Selena rushed over to help.

"I am not such an invalid as that," Lady Harrowden snapped. "Ring the bell and get Morgan here. She will know just what to do with my hair."

Selena did as she was bid, and while they were waiting for her maid to arrive, Selena ventured, "My lady, perhaps you will be so good as to tell me what you expect of me. I should like to be a useful companion to you, but I have no experience."

Lady Harrowden sat in front of the vanity and met Selena's gaze in the mirror. "You will discover easily enough what I require, as I will make my wishes clear at all times. However"—The countess tightened her mouth— "I expect you to be on time. I expect you to avoid scandal."

Selena swallowed convulsively. Was the countess referring to her family's disgrace or was she anticipating some future scandal?

Lady Harrowden continued. "I expect you will not disclose to my nephew anything personal about me. I do not want him to know when I go to sleep or when I rise. I do not wish him to know what I talk about or what I like and don't like. In fact, it will suit me very well to remain a complete mystery to him. Oh, I have no doubt he set out to please. He is amusing himself with your company, as there is not another young lady on hand more worthy of notice."

The words cut, although Selena should have steeled herself against them by now. She had received enough insults, veiled and outright in the past.

Lady Harrowden turned to face Selena. "I am equally certain Lord Harrowden wishes to get into your good graces with the object of discovering things about me he would not otherwise learn. I will be extremely displeased if I find out you have obliged him."

Selena resolved never to displease Lady Harrowden. She could not afford to. Shoving down the sting that came with the reminder of her low station, Selena focused rather on the implications of Lady Harrowden's speech. "So you are not on terms with your nephew?"

"My nephew is what they call a rake," Lady Harrowden said with an impatient wave. "He is what *I* call a scoundrel."

"A rake...like Sir Lucius is a rake?" Selena asked. Perhaps she was treading on thin ice to remind Lady Harrowden of her own words, but she had called Sir Lucius that very thing last night. And Sir Lucius and Lord Harrowden were not at all cut from the same cloth, from what Selena could tell. Lord Harrowden ignored her wishes, reminding Selena of her vulnerability. On the contrary, and despite the inauspicious start, Sir Lucius seemed to adhere to a gentleman's code, and beyond that, she had to own—he appeared to greater advantage with each encounter.

"I am irritated with Lucius," was all the countess would vouchsafe, as if that answered the question. She did not quite meet Selena's gaze.

Mrs. Morgan, the countess's maid, entered the room, and Selena stepped aside to allow her to assist Lady Harrowden to dress.

"Morgan, is Sir Lucius still waiting for me?" Lady Harrowden asked her maid.

"I do not know, my lady. I was not aware he was here." Mrs. Morgan continued to tug at the countess's stays.

Lady Harrowden studied Selena in the mirror, then dropped her gaze to Selena's attire, her expression showing increasing displeasure. "The Twelfth Night ball will be a good opportunity to see how you carry yourself. I will give you an advance on your salary, so that you might buy material for a dress." She narrowed her eyes at Selena's Egyptian brown dress, which was both worn and several years out of date. "I assure you. You will need it."

"Thank you. That is kind of you." Selena's gaze flitted away, and she bit her tongue rather than assure her employer she did not need instruction on how to carry herself in Society. She had been trained for it and had at one time received stacks of invitations. But the advance was indeed necessary, as she was in dire want of a new wardrobe, and she would not risk irritating the countess.

Selena drew a breath and looked directly at Lady Harrowden, deciding she would set one thing straight, at least. "Despite my father's...disgrace, I know how to comport myself. You shall have no need to be ashamed of me."

Lady Harrowden harrumphed. "Go down and, if by some miracle Sir Lucius is still here, tell him I will arrive in due time."

Selena left the countess and went directly to the drawing room, thinking it would be nothing short of astonishing if Sir Lucius were still there, since he did not seem to be a man who allowed himself to be easily inconvenienced.

However, when she entered the drawing room, Sir Lucius stood before the fire, and he turned at the sound of her footsteps. Selena experienced a curious rush of comfort to see him standing there. She realized with a start that she had come to associate Sir Lucius with protection, which was a very odd thing indeed since he also appeared to be selfish and bent on having his way.

Nevertheless, he had opened his door to her—well, eventually— when she was lost, and he'd tucked robes around her against the cold and had brought her safely to her destination. Then he'd returned the next day, carrying her trunk with all her worldly possessions, had whisked her out of the power of a gentleman she could not like, and tucked the robes around her once again. A shield of warmth against the brutal cold.

She would have to guard her heart.

The thought shook her into awareness and provided an effective remedy against an overly romantic turn of mind. It was ridiculous to think Sir Lucius would look twice at her, and she would not open herself up again to ridicule by handing her heart over to someone of the *ton*.

"What is it?" Sir Lucius asked. His eyes had softened as he looked at her, threatening her carefully built fortress. Goodness—she must've been staring at him.

Selena cleared her throat and stepped forward. "Lady Harrowden said she will be down and will see you." She permitted a tiny smile.

"She made me understand that she is not pleased with you at the moment. Although I am not sure what you could have done to earn her displeasure."

"I can answer that." Sir Lucius turned to look at the fire, as if it were more comfortable to confess to the flames than to her. "My grandfather bought the hunting box close to Harrowden, because he was friends with the late Lord Harrowden. I've been coming here to hunt since I was young, and the Harrowdens have watched me grow. When Lord Harrowden was on his deathbed six years after my own father died, he gave me a charge to look after his wife. They had no son of their own, and although he did not say the words, I do not believe he thought his nephew would have Lady Harrowden's best interests at heart. He laid a charge upon me to look after her."

Sir Lucius turned to Selena, his mouth set in a firm line and his countenance forbidding. "I did not do it. I have been to see her but once since her husband died two years ago."

Selena studied his face. Did he truly regret having neglected his duty? Or was he just like everyone else she'd met in Society—fickle?

"Why did you not keep your word?"

Sir Lucius walked from the mantel to her side, his voice gruff when he responded. "Selfishness, I believe."

Such honesty compelled Selena to meet his gaze. She was oddly relieved. "And this is your repentance?"

"I can at least try." Sir Lucius looked up as the doorknob turned, and Selena, realizing how closely they were standing, took a step back.

7

IT WAS ONLY when Miss Lockhart stepped away from him that Lucius became aware of how near they had been. This would not do, even if she did invite a man's confidence with her poise and gentle manner. He hoped her gentleness would not lead her into other situations, such as following Harrowden around on another pleasure walk in the bitter cold.

It was Harrowden who had entered the room. Upon seeing them together, he widened his eyes and with a thin veneer of cordiality, said, "Sir Lucius—still here?"

Before the earl could address Miss Lockhart, she excused herself. "Lady Harrowden requested I speak with the housekeeper. I must do so." Without another word, she turned and glided toward the door, quickly as if to escape.

When the door shut behind her, Lord Harrowden walked over to the fire where Lucius was standing and positioned himself with his back to it, facing the room. "Your arrival was timely this morning, Sir Lucius. Miss Lockhart was able to avoid having to traipse back on foot, and I'm sure she was beholden to you. But I assure you, it was not necessary. We had not long to go before turning back, and she will have to grow more stout if she's going to serve as companion to my aunt."

Harrowden's arrogance goaded Lucius beyond what he could bear, and his resolve not to pick a quarrel vanished. "What were you thinking, bringing a woman out in such weather with no more than a thin cloak to keep her warm? She was nearly blue with cold by the time I came upon her."

Harrowden paused for a long moment before curving his lips into a tight smile. "Perhaps you have the right of it, though I stand by my assertion that she will need to be made of sterner stuff. I was willing to show off Harrowden's grounds, and as she will be here for some time, I thought she should see everything. I daresay she is warm enough by now."

Lucius looked toward the door, wondering what was keeping the countess. "Surely." He leaned against the mantel.

Harrowden wandered over to the escritoire and rifled through the letters there. "I imagine a man like you has much to attend to. What keeps you here?" He darted a glance from the papers to Lucius before hiding his gaze again.

"I had promised your aunt I would visit, and I have not yet done so. I merely wish to rectify my mistake."

Harrowden laughed. "Why? I cannot imagine what you and my aunt have to discuss."

"Surely nothing that would interest you." Lucius lifted a brow. He would let Harrowden suffer from curiosity. For one thing, it did not concern him. For another, Lucius had an instinct that he would do better not to entrust anything to the man.

Harrowden glanced at the door, which remained shut. After another minute, he folded his arms and fixed his gaze on the floor. "Well, I suppose I shall not keep you then." He waited, and when Lucius didn't respond, added, "I am sure my aunt will be down momentarily."

"Undoubtedly," Lucius said. He was thankful when Harrowden left the room. Robertson's brother had been at school with him, hadn't he? He would write his friend today to find out what he could about the young earl. Lucius thought there was something unsettling…something false about him.

When Miss Lockhart reentered the room some time later, she paused on the threshold as if to ascertain whether Lord Harrowden was still there. Her cheeks were tinged pink from having climbed stairs, or perhaps some other emotion had played upon her. Lucius would like to know what it was. It had not been lost upon him that Miss Lockhart was an attractive woman, but in the soft winter light that streamed into the drawing room through the windows, it struck him that she was more than in the ordinary way.

"Lady Harrowden will be down shortly," Miss Lockhart said. "And Mrs. Randall has promised to have the tea sent. I'm sorry—I fear you have been kept waiting long."

"Why do *you* apologize? It was not you who did so, I believe," Lucius said. Most people had enough faults of their own without apologizing for someone else's.

"I suppose not, if you put it like that." Miss Lockhart advanced into the room and when she came to where he stood, smiled up at him shyly. "It is the way of things. Or at least my way…" Her voice trailed away.

"To what?" he prodded when she didn't continue. "To apologize for things that are not your fault?"

She pursed her lips. "Perhaps. I believe women often feel the need to do so. To soothe and placate, although"—Miss Lockhart grimaced—"why we should is anyone's guess."

"Yes, why should you?" Lucius shrugged and laid his arm along the mantel. "It is a concept entirely foreign to me."

Miss Lockhart laughed. "Oh, very well, sir," she said, her eyes sparkling. "I shall take a lesson from you. I will not apologize for an inconvenience I did not cause."

"Very proper," Lucius replied, gravely. The door opened, and at last the countess entered.

"Good morning, my lady," he said with a bow. "May I escort you to a chair?"

"I do not require being escorted in my own home," Lady Harrowden said acidly. He ignored her words and came to her side, and she put her hand in the crook of his arm without further remonstrance and allowed him to bring her to the armchair closest to the fire.

Once seated, she turned to Miss Lockhart. "You may leave us now. I have some things I wish to say to Sir Lucius."

Miss Lockhart gave a nod and turned to Lucius to take leave of him. "I thank you again for all you have done for me, sir." She curtsied and turned to leave.

Lucius refused to let his gaze follow her out the door, knowing he would be under the eagle eye of Lady Harrowden. However, his thoughts dwelled on Miss Lockhart, and he felt they had not had enough time to talk. He had the strangest compulsion to return and see her again. Of course he would not trouble himself to do so without good reason. It was unthinkable to act so out of character as to visit Harrowden with *her* as the object. He was not the marrying kind and did not wish to give her a false impression.

That said, he would be sorry not to see her again. *She'd smelled of apples when she came back in the room.* She must have snuck one from the kitchen. The idea made him want to laugh.

His smile died away quickly, though, when he saw that Lady Harrowden was studying his face and had missed nothing. It appeared the direction of his thoughts had not been as discreet as he would have liked.

"You are not dangling after impoverished females at your age, are you?" she inquired in a sharp tone.

He must quickly rid her of that idea. "No, my lady. My heart is safely intact."

"Good." Lady Harrowden twitched her shawl more securely around her shoulder. "It is enough that my nephew has begun to take an interest in Miss Lockhart. If I had wished to send for eligible marital candidates instead of a companion, I would have looked higher."

"And yet she is a gentleman's daughter—and a relation," Lucius could not resist replying.

"Only of the most distant." Lady Harrowden pulled at the handkerchief that was clutched in her hands. "But I did not sit with you to talk about that. I see you have finally decided to visit me after all this time. What brought you, if not Miss Lockhart?"

He would not flatter her. She would not appreciate it, and it was against his nature. "Her trunk brought me," he said, lifting a boot to warm it by the fire. "My sense of having been remiss is what kept me here, I suppose."

"You *have* been remiss." Lady Harrowden narrowed her eyes peevishly. "You gave your word. Harrowden told me so before he died."

Lucius didn't like being chided, but he deserved the rebuke. She was right. His word should mean something, and he had not considered her worthy enough to honor it. Keeping a rein on his temper, which only sprang from embarrassment, he said, "I offer you my sincere apologies, my lady. I shall make myself more available."

Lady Harrowden frowned and pulled herself up. "I do not desire your pity."

"I do not offer you my pity." Lucius studied her ageing face and softened. "Our families have a long history together, and I am here to set things right. How may I be of service to you?"

Lady Harrowden assessed him for a moment and at last put her hands on the armrest of her chair. "How well can you read legal documents and entails? You followed the coursework of a barrister, I believe."

Lucius had studied law, but he had not liked it. He only wanted enough knowledge to serve him in his estate. "I understand only the basics. Why? Is there a problem with yours?" He left his position by the fire and came to sit by Lady Harrowden.

"That is better," she said. "I cannot bear when people hover over me."

"You should have said something. I would have sat," Lucius responded in a mild tone.

"As if you've ever done anything other than precisely what you wished to do," the countess retorted. Lucius wisely kept silent, and when she saw he would not rise to the bait, continued. "I believe my nephew—as if he did not have enough with the entire estate—I believe he is trying to encroach upon my jointure."

It would seem like such a petty thing to do—to take money from a widow when Harrowden had so much. Lucius thought over the possibilities. Surely Harrowden would have no reason to do so. And most wills were ironclad. He would not have had much room to cheat the countess.

Lucius leaned on the armrest and rubbed his chin as he studied her. "What makes you think he is doing such a thing?"

"He encourages me to remove to the dower house at every turn, although he has not yet found himself a wife. He says it need only to be painted, but he has been saying that for well over a year, and I do not believe a painter has set foot inside that house."

She clutched her hands together in an impatient gesture. "The notion was preposterous while Richard was staying in London. Who would care for the estate? But now that he has returned, and it appears his stay will be prolonged—or perhaps indefinite, although there is no Lady Harrowden at present—I am quickly learning that I will not be able to live under the same roof with such a popinjay. I believe I shall have to make the move." She added in a voice laden with irony, "He was quick to assure me that he would help."

Lucius crossed one leg over the other. "That seems more proof of his generosity than his villainy."

"Perhaps, were it not for the fact that my accounts seem more meagre than they should be, and I'm wondering if my nephew thought to run *his* estate on *my* portion. After all, the estate's solicitor oversees both accounts. I would like you to find an accountant who has had no interaction with my nephew. When you find him, bring him to me without Richard's knowledge, and I will have him look over the figures of my income to see how it's being used."

"Does your nephew have access to your funds?" Lucius asked. "I will do as you wish, of course, but it seems odd that he could have the means of reducing your income without your consent or knowledge."

"Richard has the handling of my bills and accounts," Lady Harrowden said, with an annoyed huff. "Both the steward and solicitor have said it is the most natural arrangement. Yet I am constantly receiving word that my portion cannot permit such and such expense. I was not led to believe my husband had left me in such straitened means. I can only think those two are under his power."

She leaned forward in her chair. "In addition to the accountant, I would like you to find me a solicitor, who is not employed by the estate. I need someone who can assist me in protecting my interests. May I rely on you?"

"I can do that for you," Lucius replied, vaguely conscious that his willingness had something to do with seeing Miss Lockhart more regularly. "I cannot go to London until after Twelfth Night, which will probably be necessary if I am to locate a solicitor who can be trusted. I would offer mine if he were not already overworked. But I will endeavor to find a local accountant before then in the meantime, and I have one in mind who might do the trick."

Lucius took his leave of Lady Harrowden and walked toward the front door. It was currently empty of footmen. He would have to wait to have his carriage brought around or go out to the stables himself. He turned as Miss Lockhart stepped into the corridor from the morning room.

When he saw her, a smile touched his lips, and he bowed. "I will take my leave of you, Miss Lockhart."

She curtsied, her eyes somber, despite an answering smile. "I have already thanked you, perhaps one time too many, but I feel I must do so again. Your arrival was timely."

Lucius paused, struck by her features and dignified mien. The more time he spent in her presence, the harder it was to imagine her in this role. She was better suited to be countess—if the earl were not so undesirable.

"It is my pleasure," he replied, reining in his thoughts, which were beginning to unravel. "And if you should be in need of assistance, please do not hesitate to send word. I am not far. My sister, Maria, has twisted my arm, and I suspect we will be meeting again at the Twelfth Night ball. That is, if Lady Harrowden is well enough to go."

"We shall see," Miss Lockhart said. "At any event, wherever she is, that is where I will be." The words were spoken lightly, as if in jest, but they held a forlorn sound to them.

Lucius looked toward the footman, who had entered the corridor and was now standing at the front entrance. He turned his back on the servant and leaned toward her, saying in a quiet voice, "Miss Lockhart, may I suggest you keep your door secured at night?" He did not trust

Harrowden and was not certain enough of his being a gentleman for Miss Lockhart to be safe in the same house as him.

She blanched at his suggestion, and after a pause, nodded. "I will do so."

Miss Lockhart looked as if she wanted to speak again but closed her lips and gave another parting nod before turning to enter the drawing room. Lucius glanced around the corridor at the austere furnishings of the front entrance, the high ceiling offering no warmth, and wished, most irrationally, that he might whisk Miss Lockhart away from it.

~

THE NEXT MORNING, Selena entered the breakfast room and her heart sank when she saw Lord Harrowden sitting at the table. She had hoped he would not be an early riser. His eyes widened in interest as he looked up from his plate and perceived her. Although the smile he gave her molded his handsome features into amiability, she knew not to trust it. He seemed like a boy suffering from boredom, in search of some amusement that would pall soon enough.

"Good morning, Miss Lockhart. You appear fatigued." Lord Harrowden greeted her with a self-satisfied smile. "I hope my aunt is not too difficult."

Selena paused before serving herself a roll and sitting at the table. She would have to shove aside her feelings of unease and make conversation. "Lady Harrowden and I spent a very pleasant day together yesterday."

She poured a cup of coffee and buttered her roll. The faster she finished her breakfast, the faster she could escape Lord Harrowden.

"I imagine it will wear on you with time. You are young, and waiting hand and foot on an old lady cannot be pleasing to you. Surely you must aspire to more." He leaned back in his chair, settling in for a long conversation, it seemed, when she wanted nothing more than to break away from his presence.

Selena swallowed her bread. "I am quite satisfied with my role," she said. "I do not ask for much to be content." She thought for a minute, then added for his benefit, "Respect, a roof over my head, and simple diversion is enough for me."

"Have you had a Season?" the earl asked. "I do not recall having seen you in London, but then I imagine you wouldn't move in all the best circles. Almack's would be out of the question."

Selena gave a fleeting smile. Her family had had regular vouchers for Almack's before her father's catastrophic finale to his gambling career became public. However, she would not lower herself to puff off her own consequence, particularly as she now had none. "I imagine so. I have been to London, but it is big. And, as you said, we were not likely to move in the same circles."

"If you did go, then apparently no offers were made." Lord Harrowden looked up from studying his fingernails, his sharp eyes scrutinizing her.

"I am not hanging out for a husband," Selena replied. "My wish is to provide for myself and my family. I have no need of marriage." She certainly wouldn't lay her heart and longings bare for him to mock.

As if he could read her mind, Lord Harrowden sent her a coaxing smile. "Surely you have affectionate yearnings in your heart," he insisted. "I cannot imagine that you truly desire a life as a spinster."

Selena repressed a shudder from his words, which took on a sinister tone when coupled with his leering grin. She remembered that he was not her employer and took courage from that. "I consider your question impertinent, my lord."

He raised his eyebrows and his lazy smile appeared once again. "You are out of reason cross. I am only looking out for your own interests."

Selena finished the last bite of her bread. She coughed when she drank the coffee quickly, and the hot liquid scalded her throat. It was probably the fastest breakfast she had ever eaten, and it would not sit well. She set her napkin on the table and rose to her feet.

"I bid you good day, my lord. I have an appointment with the housekeeper to make myself acquainted with the estate."

"Why don't I show you?" Lord Harrowden said. "I promise we will not leave the warmth of this house, and I can give you the history behind each of the rooms—old stories that the housekeeper will not be aware of."

Oh no you won't. I will not fall for that again. "You are very kind, and I appreciate your offer, but I will have to decline. It is important for me to be on terms with the housekeeper, and I will not put off our interview for a second time. Good day." Selena made her escape.

Mrs. Randall had been inclined toward coldness when Selena went to make her excuses the day before. Now, as she saw Selena coming off the stairs and into the kitchen just when she promised she would come, the housekeeper's smile held more warmth.

"I shall just restore the china back to its cupboard, and I'll be free to take you around the house." Mrs. Randall put away the tea cup she had been inspecting and finished with the rest of the china that had been spread out for inventory.

There were twenty-seven rooms, and since they were laid out in an orderly fashion, Selena didn't think it would be difficult to remember where to find everything. She took note of where Lord Harrowden's bedroom was and was relieved to see that hers was on the other wing much closer to Lady Harrowden's. If she called out, the countess would surely hear her.

Mrs. Randall did know quite a bit about the estate's history as it turned out, so Lord Harrowden's trump card had been a bluff. As they were winding up their tour, the housekeeper said, "I heard young Sir Lucius was here. It will do Lady Harrowden good to see him again. The families were close before the earl died."

"Perhaps he will come more often, now that he and Lady Harrowden have...rekindled family relations," Selena said, unsure if 'rekindling' most aptly fit the acerbic scolds the countess applied to Sir Lucius. She hoped he would come more often, however.

"He is a good man. If you won't think me forward for offering my own opinion?" Mrs. Randall looked to Selena for confirmation, who shook her head. As a matter of fact, she was very interested in hearing Mrs. Randall's opinion on Sir Lucius. And apparently Selena, a mere companion, was not above being taken into the housekeeper's confidence. She was glad, as she would need some friends here.

"My husband was a groundskeeper for the former baronet, and I have watched Sir Lucius grow. Whenever he is present, you are sure things will be done as they should. It's a small wonder his family relies on him the way they do, what with his mother coaxing him to accompany her to the watering holes in search of a cure—although she does not seem to suffer from any clear ailment—and Miss Philippa and Master George always getting into one scrape or another. It's a shame..." Mrs. Randall smiled and closed her lips. "But what am I going on about? There is no need for me to ramble," she said.

"Please go on," Selena said. "I am interested."

"It's just..." Mrs. Randall paused, "When the former Lord Harrowden was alive, and Sir John as well—Sir Lucius's grandfather—the two friends spent a great deal of time together, and the two families were often in each others' company. Things were peaceful in Woolmer Green."

She sighed and shrugged before continuing. "I suppose when Lord Harrowden's nephew became earl..." There was a long pause, before she said, "But I should not speak about my employer that way." Mrs. Randall gestured forward, and Selena accompanied her toward the stairwell leading to the floor below.

She could only infer from Mrs. Randall's comment with all she'd left unspoken—and her own gut feeling—that with the new earl, things were not as peaceful.

8

THREE DAYS after Selena's arrival, she entered Lady Harrowden's bedroom and found her reading a letter that was spread out on the covers. The countess was so engrossed in its contents she did not spare a glance for Selena.

"Good morning, my lady." Selena came to stand at her bedside, wondering if it would be impertinent to ask about the letter. When the countess did not speak or even look at her, Selena decided to risk it. "You have had some news?"

Lady Harrowden looked up at last. "Pull up that chair, girl. I have indeed had news and, as it will affect you, I had better inform you of it at once."

Selena did as she was bid, and Lady Harrowden turned the letter, squinting at the signature at the end.

"I have had a letter from the trustee of my ward stating that there is no longer a place for her in the school in which she has been resid-ing. I can only assume from this, that Rebecca has been up to some mischief. The trustee begs to know what I will have her do next, and I am of the mind that she will come here."

Lady Harrowden sent a shrewd gaze Selena's way. "Now that you are here, you can just as easily assume the role of governess-compan-

56

ion. It will be more amusing for you to have another young lady in the house than to have nothing more to do than wait upon an old woman."

Selena kept her expression neutral. Any young lady who was expelled from school would likely be more trouble than she was worth. "Whatever you wish, my lady. I am here to be of service." She clasped her hands on her lap. "Have you decided when she will come?"

Lady Harrowden glanced at the letter again in reflection. "We had better answer this letter without delay. I am made to understand that the situation is dire, and that they must find a place for her as quickly as possible. The school is in Essex, and she can be here within two days."

"So soon?" Selena raised her eyebrows. "Is there anything you would have me do?"

"Inform Mrs. Randall at once, so she can prepare the room papered in rose. She will know the one. And as much as it goes against the grain, I suppose I shall have to inform my nephew." Lady Harrowden frowned. "We will write a reply at once, and then you will send a footman to request Richard to meet us in the drawing room."

Selena copied down Lady Harrowden's dictation in a neat scrawl, and once she had sanded the letter and folded it, wrote the direction as indicated. At the widow's instructions, she rang the bell for Mrs. Morgan to assist Lady Harrowden into her morning dress, then brought the letter with her to be franked. She promised to wait for the countess in the drawing room.

Lord Harrowden was already in the room when she entered, and she could only hope the countess would not delay her arrival, forcing Selena to be alone with Lord Harrowden for an overly-long spell. She marched forward, her jaw set. Would the earl be living on top of her for the entirety of her stay?

His clever eyes missed nothing. "You have a letter you need franked?"

Selena nodded. "It is a letter Lady Harrowden wishes to send, and she will be down to speak with you momentarily, as the matter concerns you."

"I wait upon her pleasure." Lord Harrowden's voice dripped with irony.

Selena took a seat as far away from Lord Harrowden as she could without appearing rude, and their silence lasted long enough that she shifted in her chair, anxious to be elsewhere.

"No need to be so stiff, my dear." The earl pulled a box of snuff from his hand and flipped the lid open and shut without taking any. "Did you complete the tour of the house with Mrs. Randall?"

"Yes, I have seen everything, so I shall know where to find things. I hope to learn my role quickly and be of service to Lady Harrowden." Selena almost bored herself. Margaret Winter had been right back in Bedford when she said that Selena could only get work as a companion if she had *conversation*. A companion was only useful if they could amuse one.

Selena frowned. It was amazing how quickly one lost such a thing as the art to converse when one no longer frequented Society.

Lord Harrowden stood and walked to the settee close to where she was sitting. "I have no doubt you will do just that, but I still say that this will be a dull piece of work for you." The lack of space between them made Selena tense, and she faced forward.

He sat and leaned his chin on his hand as he stared at her. "If you'd like, I can squire you to some of the local events when my aunt has retired for the night so you may amuse yourself. If you attend to her when she needs you, she can have nothing to say about what you do on your own time."

Selena could think of nothing that appealed to her less than spending more time with Lord Harrowden. He searched her face and figure in a way that seemed to take possession of it, and it repulsed her. Selena strove to answer in a way that would not give offense.

"You are very kind, my lord. However, it would not be proper for me to go anywhere unchaperoned."

He laughed softly, his expression incredulous. "Miss Lockhart, I think you will soon have to change your tune as you learn what it is to be a companion. You must wait on the pleasure of those who employ you. Do not expect to have the same consideration shown to a woman of more means."

The insult sent an angry flush to her cheeks. It could not go unanswered, but what could she say? Selena had seen firsthand how little

58

consideration a woman of small means was given. In the end, she could only struggle with her own impotence as she had no weapons in her arsenal that could constitute a fitting reply.

The countess entered the room, and Selena turned to her with relief.

"Richard, you are the very person I wish to see." Lady Harrowden took quick steps, leaning on a wooden cane that she sometimes used.

Lord Harrowden got to his feet with a show of reluctance as his aunt advanced into the room. "Why, that is a change," he said. "For you always seem to be at great pains to avoid me."

"Some conversations cannot be avoided," the countess said grimly. She turned to Selena. "Have you had him frank the letter yet?"

Selena shook her head.

"Please do so. Richard, I may as well inform you that we will be welcoming someone into this household—or at least welcoming her here until I can move to the dower house. My ward will be living with me."

Lord Harrowden raised his brows. "Your ward? I was not aware you had one. She must have a suitable trust fund if you will concern yourself with her *and* inform me of her stay. After all, you did not tell me Miss Lockhart would be coming."

"I do not tell you everything, and her dowry is none of your concern. Miss Lockhart will serve as her governess until we can find a more suitable arrangement for her."

Lord Harrowden curled his lip at Selena. "Your role continues to grow in excitement."

"Will you frank this now, my lord?" Selena asked, deciding it was best she ignore his impertinence.

The earl took the letter to the writing desk in the corner and franked it. Selena turned to the countess, eager to escape from Lord Harrowden's cynical gaze. "My lady, shall I give this to Mullings now?"

Lady Harrowden held up a hand. "Wait, and you may accompany me to the morning room afterwards. I have something I wish to say to Richard."

The countess advanced a few more steps until she was in front of him. "I need not remind you to leave my ward alone. She does not have

59

the bloodline to make you a wife, and I know how important that is to you. And she is not without protectors."

Lord Harrowden sent his aunt a calculating look. "I do not know what you think of me, Aunt. Naturally a young woman under my own roof must be protected."

Selena's jaw dropped in shock, and she quickly closed it. She couldn't believe he had the audacity to say that when he had been spouting a very different speech moments before Lady Harrowden had entered the room.

"Naturally," Lady Harrowden said with her own touch of irony. She turned to Selena. "Come. We will have tea sent."

Selena walked with her to the door, eager to turn her shoulder on Lord Harrowden.

⌁

THE YOUNG WARD arrived two days later, as Lady Harrowden had predicted. The moment Selena heard the carriage pull up, she closed the book she had been reading out loud and looked at the countess.

"Go on and see," Lady Harrowden said. "I imagine it must be Rebecca."

Selena went to the window and saw the footman opening the door of the carriage and reaching out to support the gloved hand that extended from it. "It is her, I believe," Selena said. "Shall I bring her to you?"

At Lady Harrowden's nod, Selena hurried out into the corridor. She reached the front door and exited into the blinding sunlight reflecting off the snow. She could see the colorful figure of a young woman walking toward the steps, followed by her maid, but it was too bright to distinguish her features until she got closer.

Selena stepped lightly down the stairs toward the girl, whose face was hidden by her bonnet as she examined the grounds and the facade of the estate to her right.

"I am Miss Lockhart," Selena said in a friendly voice, and the girl whirled around to face her. Selena felt the blood drain from her own face, as she stared at the very same young woman who had appeared on Sir Lucius's doorstep not a week since.

"*You*." Rebecca's face did not express the shock that Selena felt, but she managed to infuse a great deal of annoyance in the one word.

"It was Miss Woodsley, was it not?" Selena said. Her thoughts spun. Did Sir Lucius know who she was? How could *she*—Lady Harrowden's own ward—be so lost to propriety as to try to seduce a gentleman? For Rebecca could not have had any other objective that night.

Rebecca had folded her arms on her chest, and Selena strove for a degree of normalcy in this outlandish situation. "I seem to remember that was your name when we...we met." She looked around to make sure none of the servants was paying them mind. It was best she not trumpet Miss Woodsley's sins before the few servants assembled.

"I am to be your governess until you are properly out," Selena continued in what she hoped was a tone of authority. Rebecca's jaw had taken on a mulish expression, like she might throw herself into a fit—one that Selena was eager to avoid. "I will take you to meet Lady Harrowden."

"A governess?" Rebecca said, refusing to budge. "I was not told I would have a governess."

Selena furrowed her brow. "What did you imagine would occur when you were sent away from school—the circumstances of which we will discuss at another time. You must have someone to look after you." *Surely I, of all people, know how much you need it.*

Rebecca pushed past Selena to climb the stairs of the front entrance. Once inside, she stared at the banister leading upstairs, leaning back to look at the tall ceiling. "I supposed Lady Harrowden would look after me when my uncle told me she sent for me. After all, I am nearly of age."

"How old are you?" Selena would give her seventeen at most, and Lady Harrowden had not exactly been forthcoming about her ward's situation.

"I am sixteen years of age," Rebecca replied, taking in the rest of the corridor with a sweeping glance. "This is a very nice house. I do not know why Lady Harrowden has never invited me to stay before. If she had, I could have met Sir Lucius in the normal course of things. Now our paths are bound to cross."

When Selena found her voice, it was only to say, "Sixteen is still quite young."

For a sixteen-year-old girl to look so womanly, and yet be insensible to the embarrassment that should overtake her for having been caught in a compromising situation—she most certainly did need a governess. Hopefully Lady Harrowden would convince her of the need without Selena having to incriminate her.

Selena turned to the housekeeper, who had come to the front entrance. "Mrs. Randall, perhaps you could see that the footman takes Miss Woodsley's trunk to her room while I bring her to meet Lady Harrowden?"

The girl would be settled in the room adjacent to Selena's as Lady Harrowden had decided in advance. This was for the best. Despite her apprehension about her ability to reform Rebecca, Selena would still need to keep an eye on her. She led the way into the morning room where the countess was seated.

"Well," Lady Harrowden said, assessing her ward. "You've been in a bit of trouble. I hope you do not think to cause any here."

"No, my lady." Rebecca curtsied before Lady Harrowden.

"How came you to run away from your school?" the countess asked her severely.

Rebecca fingered her reticule, her pouting lips making her look younger. "I did not run away. I was with my brother for a short stay."

"Without permission," Lady Harrowden reminded her. "Where is this brother of yours? When does he come of age?"

"In six months, my lady." Rebecca's attention had started to wander, and she was looking around the room. Selena could see that Lady Harrowden would soon lose all patience with her.

"Well, he is supposed to take charge of you when he is of age, and I hope for his sake you are not so much trouble."

Rebecca turned back to the countess with wide eyes. "My brother, take charge of me? That is ridiculous. He can barely take charge of himself."

Lady Harrowden pinched her mouth tight. "Well, that is the way your father specified it in his will. And it is no surprise that the two of you are up to your ears in mischief what with bouncing around from one situation to another. I tried to suggest to your uncle to find a more stable household for you, but he didn't listen. And of course I could not take you in."

As if irritated by a hint of her own failure to take a proper hand in her ward's upbringing, Lady Harrowden bristled suddenly. "And another thing—your uncle said the school wrote of more than one illicit meeting taking place."

"No, my lady. I only spoke to the gentlemen at the assembly where we were brought to practice dancing. One of them took me into the gardens to get air."

"Foolish child," Lady Harrowden retorted. "He could have ruined you."

Rebecca trained wide, innocent eyes on the countess. "But how?" Selena resisted the urge to raise her own eyes to the heavens.

This brought Lady Harrowden up short. "Well, if you must know..." She did not seem to know how to go on.

"This is why it would be very good for you to have a governess," Selena said firmly. When she saw Rebecca's mutinous look, she glanced at Lady Harrowden and added, "Not for very long, mind you. But enough to learn the ways of the world."

Selena would have to play just as deep as Rebecca. More effective than scolding her for what had happened at Sir Lucius's house, it would be better to try to speak some sense into the girl and turn her thoughts to a more noble path—although Selena was determined to find out more about how Rebecca came to be there.

It occurred to Selena to appeal to Rebecca's ambitions. "What is it you wish for now you've left school behind?"

Rebecca knit her brow. "I suppose I should like to marry and be a very grand lady." She looked around the morning room. "And live in a grand house."

"You will contract a respectable alliance with your fortune," Lady Harrowden said. "But you must not hope for more. You don't have the birth for it."

"*Hm.*" Rebecca folded her arms and raised an eyebrow.

"Shall I bring Rebecca to her room?" Selena inquired, and at Lady Harrowden's nod, turned to her new protegée, adding, "You will wish to change your dress, I am sure."

"Oh yes, let us go at once," Rebecca said. "I have not yet worn my primrose gown, which Alice assures me is most becoming." She turned to follow, and Selena paused to speak to Lady Harrowden.

"I will get her settled in her room and will come back down to you, as soon as I may." Lady Harrowden dismissed her with two fingers and Selena led Rebecca toward the door.

They were alone in the corridor when Rebecca said in a low, petulant voice, "I suppose you mean to tell Lady Harrowden all about our first meeting."

Selena was not given a chance to answer. As they crossed over to the stairwell, Lord Harrowden exited the billiard room and stopped short upon seeing Rebecca.

"What is this? Have you arrived already, Miss Woodsley?"

How was it that Lord Harrowden knew the ward's last name when the countess had not spoken it to Selena? Surely she would have remembered it and have been better prepared for how to handle the meeting.

The earl continued. "I was not expecting to find such a charming young lady." He came over and made a deep bow, causing an appreciative glow to rise to Rebecca's face and Selena's heart to sink. Here was another tricky flirtation to maneuver her new charge safely through.

Rebecca allowed him to take her hand in his and bow over it. "You are too kind, sir. And who are you?" She pulled her hand back and smiled up at him.

"I see you will be with us for the foreseeable future, which should make my stay vastly more pleasant, I assure you. I am Lord Harrowden, at your service."

"Oh," she gasped. "*You* are the earl. You are so young."

He pretended to frown. "Not so young as all that. I am nearly twenty-six. I must have ten years on you."

She nodded simply, still smiling, and Selena wondered if it were only she who could discern the calculating look in Rebecca's gaze. He touched the ward lightly under the chin, causing Selena to clear her throat.

Lord Harrowden glanced at Selena briefly before saying, "Well, I am sure we shall entertain ourselves mightily now you've arrived. If you need anything, you have only to ask. I am the master here, and I will see that your wish is obeyed."

Rebecca giggled, and Selena took her arm and pulled her toward the staircase, offering the earl a polite nod, which he did not return. How quickly he had moved on to more attractive prey.

When they reached the room where Rebecca would be staying, Selena was surprised to see the trunk sitting on the floor by the bed with no one there to begin unpacking it. This was an unlooked-for opportunity, and Selena seized it.

"You asked if I would disclose how we met, and the answer is 'no', although I would like to know how you ended up at Sir Lucius's house, as it was most certainly by design."

Rebecca tossed her head, attempting to evade the question. Selena folded her arms, and when Rebecca saw she was waiting for an answer, said, "Well, it is only that I set my sights on him, and I knew I was pretty and rich enough to succeed if only ill luck had not brought you at that exact moment." The memory brought forth a scowl.

"But how ever did you meet him? You said you've never been invited to stay with Lady Harrowden." The circumstances of her guardian being Sir Lucius's neighbor seemed too incredible for the introduction to have happened any other way, but it had not appeared as though Sir Lucius knew Rebecca.

"Lady Harrowden? *Hmph!* No. If she ever invited me to stay here, I don't remember it. I saw Sir Lucius once in Brighton when I was there visiting my friend, and I asked who he was. Everyone knows he is a confirmed bachelor who has simply not set eyes on the right woman, so I decided to take matters in my own hands," Rebecca explained. "It was a simple matter of getting my brother's help. He hasn't a feather to fly with since he's already run through this quarter's allowance, so I promised to pay off some of his more pressing debts." She shrugged.

That was a great deal of calculating for one so young. Selena wondered if Rebecca could be brought to decorum, or if it was too late. Selena filled in the rest of the pieces.

"So your brother found out where Sir Lucius lived and hatched the scheme." Selena breathed in sharply as the realization dawned on her. "That was quite a risk embarking on such a..." She bit back the words she had almost uttered—*such a wanton pursuit*—and finished more mildly, "such a project when your guardian was so near."

"I nearly died from fright when Sir Lucius mentioned her name, I assure you," Rebecca said. "I did not know her direction since we do not correspond with any regularity. And I daresay I wouldn't have remembered it if I did. The game would have been up, though." She bit her lip. "I suppose it was best my brother came when he did."

"Yes, I suppose..." Selena's words died away. She little knew if her keeping the confidence would benefit Rebecca or not—whether the girl's character was already ruined or not. But she knew how much a good name was worth, and she would not be the one to cause the downfall of another—even if she found the girl tiresome at best and morally bankrupt at worst.

Rebecca studied her in silence, and at last, Selena said, "This is a chance for you to start fresh. I will do nothing to hinder you. In fact, I wish very much for you to have the life you dream of and will help you achieve it."

Rebecca scoffed, her face flushed with derision. "How can you help me? You're a governess. In the horridest dress. You can have nothing to teach me."

Selena breathed in through her nostrils, calling upon all her training to answer in a manner becoming of a lady. "Perhaps. But as your governess, I will give you advice on making a good match, as that seems to be your objective. I can teach you to go about it in a suitable way, and one that will give you no cause to blush for your actions. And I will do what I can to help you find a match that pleases you." Selena promised herself that she would either reform Miss Woodsley's character, or she would put a spoke in any suit that could harm a guileless young gentleman.

Rebecca smiled—a sincere smile for once. "You are determined to help me make a match? Good! You may arrange for me to meet Sir Lucius again."

Selena froze at Rebecca's words and her breath fled. Surely the sense of dread that crept over her was because Rebecca had clearly learned nothing from her recent misadventure, nor had she taken Selena's words to heart. Or Selena's heart sank because Sir Lucius would be troubled to find such a determined flirt settled a hair's breadth away.

It could not be because Selena wanted Sir Lucius's attention for herself.

9

"MRS. HOLBECK TO SEE YOU, SIR." Briggs stepped aside to allow Lucius's sister to enter the study, as she generally did not wait to be invited in. Lucius dropped his quill on the desk, splattering ink on his correspondence.

"Maria," he said, frowning at the paper and wondering if he would be obliged to copy the entire thing over. Probably. "You were never one to announce your visits ahead of time, were you?"

"Why should I when I know you will only find some excuse not to be present?" Maria untied the ribbons to her velvet bonnet. "I came to deliver the promised invitation to the Twelfth Night ball."

"Since when do I need a formal invitation to your ball? And if I did, you could have spared yourself the trouble and sent your man to deliver it." Resigned, Lucius stood to greet his sister with a kiss on the cheek.

"Come now, that would never do. I would much rather hear an acceptance from your lips than a polite refusal from your pen." She looked at the departing butler and added, "Will you order some tea? It is not warm outside."

Lucius signaled for Briggs to have tea sent. "You will have to prepare it then. I take it sparingly."

"No, I know what *you* drink in the afternoons," she retorted. "But tea is really so much better for you, you know."

"Undoubtedly. So, will this be a prolonged visit?" Lucius took a seat across from her and affected a long-suffering look that made his sister laugh. Better she think he was only joking, although in truth, he was in no mood for company.

"No, I shall leave you to your very important business, but I came to tell you that Lady Harrowden had her ward come to stay. I was just there visiting the countess today, and I met her." Maria sent him an arch look. "She's a taking young thing, apparently *quite* wealthy—the daughter of a cit, whose wife can claim some distant connection to the countess."

Lucius scrutinized his sister closely. "You are not planning match-making, I hope. Why come and tell me?"

"Well, it wouldn't be the worst match you could make for yourself. She is still young and would be malleable enough that you could make her into exactly the sort of wife you could wish for. And as much as you claim no concern over the future of Mardley, the weather these last two years—what with the cold and rain, and the early frost—it's not given us the harvest we need to maintain either of our estates in the manner we are accustomed. Imagine if it goes on like this! We shall be ruined."

"Save your histrionics for Holbeck. We are far from being ruined. Besides, I do not wish for a dewey-eyed innocent with no conversa-tion, so put that thought out of your head."

Maria tightened her lips and shifted in the chair. "Her dowry is not to be despised. But see for yourself. *I* shall not force your hand. As I said, I came to deliver my invitation, and with it the latest news, as neighbors do."

"As *gossips* do," he said brutally.

"You've been a recluse for too long. It will not harm you to have some sense of what goes on in London *or* in Hertfordshire," Maria adjured him. After a pause, she continued with the topic that most interested her. "Miss Lockhart will take charge of the ward, and I believe she'll have her hands full with this one—*so* charming, with a face that must enchant the members of the opposite sex. She appears to be eager to make her debut and will find no shortage of suitors, to be sure."

Lucius looked up at the mention of Miss Lockhart's name. "So then the ward is *not* malleable. The girl's spoilt, it seems to me. Just what Miss Lockhart needs to make her position even more intolerable."

"Why should you care about Miss Lockhart's position? She is merely a companion, and now a governess. You need to be thinking about your own marriage and securing the estate for the rest of the family. You have four younger siblings, who will be thrown to the wind if something should happen to you. And if you think you need only let George inherit, you deceive yourself. He will quickly run through the inheritance and ruin us all."

Maria had no children of her own, and he supposed that was what gave her license to think she could meddle in everyone else's lives. She certainly had no cause to worry about Mardley Estate, as she had married well enough and Lucius's estate no longer concerned her. And although he sometimes worried about his younger brother's devil-may-care approach to life, he could not bear for Maria to speak about George in such a dismal manner.

"You were saying something about this ward?" he reminded her.

"Yes. In all honesty, I do not believe she is spoilt. She does not put herself forward at all. But there is something guileless about her that is attractive enough without her supposed fortune, which Lady Harrowden said is"—Maria leaned forward with a loud whisper—"up-wards of thirty-thousand."

Lucius hid his irritation. How was it his sister still did not know him well enough to realize he did not share her mercenary bent? It would do no good to remind her, though. "Thirty-thousand is indeed an attractive prize," he said.

Maria flashed a smile of victory. "How happy I am to hear you say it. I cannot like her presence in the same house with Lord Harrowden and feel someone ought to look out for her. What a shame if she falls prey to the seduction of his title. I feel sure you will tell me that as a gentleman Lord Harrowden will keep the line—"

"I am far from being sure of any such thing. In fact, I was just in the act of replying to a letter I've received from Robertson—you remember he spent Michaelmas with us in oh-nine—and he said Harrowden had nearly ruined his brother in their early days together in London. Harrowden has always dipped deep, but some nights he seemed to be particularly lucky. He was at The Cocoa Tree the night Robertson's brother nearly lost a fortune. Harrowden was goading him into staking another bet, when Robertson's friend, Sam Buntling, asked for the dice to be changed. The insult nearly led to a duel..."

Lucius paused at that crucial moment with a cynical smile. "But surely I am boring you with what goes on in gentlemen's clubs."

Maria's eyes were rapt. "You are teasing me. Go on."

He leaned back and crossed one leg over the other. "Robertson's friend managed to avert the duel through some adroit phrasing and a good deal of humor. Robertson's luck turned at that point, and Buntling convinced him to walk away from the table at the right moment. It was a near-run thing."

"So you believe Harrowden is...what? An ivory turner? It's true he is known for flashing his wealth, although he only inherited two years ago. He has to live off *something*." Maria frowned, likely calculating how this factor might hinder her plans for Lucius's match with the ward—a fruitless endeavor if only she could be brought to reason.

Lucius's worry was not for the ward but for her governess. "I believe he is bad business and would not be surprised if the code of conduct pertaining to a gentleman does not weigh with him in the least. Robertson added a few other details that I will not bore you with, but it would not be surprising if he were on the hunt for an heiress, given his heavy dealings as of late."

He rubbed his chin as Briggs brought the tea and set it on the table between them. Maria prepared it and handed a cup to Lucius. He drank, wondering if his sister had said everything she had come to say and how long it would be before he could get back to his solitary peace. Why had his grandfather not bought a hunting box at a distance more than an easy drive from family?

"So you will visit Harrowden?" she said, at last. "And keep an eye on things? Your presence will remind Lord Harrowden that the young lady is not entirely without a protector." Maria peered at her brother from above her cup, leaving the rest mercifully unsaid. *And remind Lord Harrowden there was more than one in pursuit of her hand.*

He met Maria's gaze, his mind full of thoughts he would not share. "I believe I owe it to Lady Harrowden in any case."

~

THAT SAME AFTERNOON, Lucius arrived at Harrowden Estate and sent his card in to the countess. When he entered the drawing room, Miss Lockhart stood before Lady Harrowden next to a young lady, who stood with her back to Lucius. With the two side by side, Lucius couldn't help but compare the graceful, womanly form of Miss Lockhart to the youthful, sturdy frame of the girl, who must be the ward.

A movement to his right caught his eye, and Lucius turned to see Harrowden start toward him.

"Sir Lucius," Lord Harrowden said, not looking pleased to see him.

Lucius greeted him civilly. He could not like the fellow. He sought out Miss Lockhart's gaze, who had turned at last and raised her cool eyes to his. There was apprehension in those eyes, and Lucius tried to puzzle out what could have happened to trouble her since he saw her last. The ward turned as well, and Lucius took in a sharp breath.

Thankfully, a log in the fire cracked and rolled forward so that Harrowden was obliged to tend to it. Although Miss Lockhart must have expected it, no one else seemed to notice Lucius's reaction to seeing Miss Woodsley—except Miss Woodsley, who met his gaze with an arch look of her own. He now understood Miss Lockhart's apprehension. What a quandary! His questions came faster than he could process them.

"Good afternoon, Sir Lucius," Lady Harrowden said. "May I present my ward, Miss Woodsley?"

Lucius greeted the countess then bowed to the women. "Pleased to make your acquaintance, Miss Woodsley." He glanced at Miss Lockhart, whose smile was full of understanding, then turned to study the ward. Keeping such a determined flirt at bay, now that they were neighbors, would tax even his finesse, especially now he had promised to handle Lady Harrowden's affairs.

Lady Harrowden called the butler over and began speaking for his hearing only, and Miss Lockhart filled in the pause. "Miss Woodsley will be residing here at present, and I was just going to take her to the greenhouse, at Lady Harrowden's request, to create bundles of dried flowers to decorate the charity auction next week."

"A worthy project," Lucius said. His mind was spinning, but he came to a snap decision. He would not mention their previous encounter, especially since that might implicate him in a way that could entrap him. He was not sure how ambitious Lady Harrowden was for her ward. However, he would give anything for a private word with Miss Lockhart.

"I believe I will accompany you to the greenhouse," Lord Harrowden interjected, his eyes on Miss Woodsley. "I've been meaning to get out of doors, and it's too cold for a ride."

Harrowden had too much time on his hands if he was shadowing the women. Lucius would have to find out how things stood with him, first from the countess, and then—if he could snatch a few moments alone with her—from Miss Lockhart. Was Harrowden causing her much trouble?

"My lady, if you are not occupied, I came to see you on a matter of business," Lucius said.

"Why yes, now that you're here, you may as well give me your family's latest news." Lady Harrowden gestured to the chair beside her.

Lord Harrowden's steps had paused at the door. He was surely suffering from curiosity over whatever business Lucius could wish to discuss with the countess. *He will have to remain in ignorance,* Lucius thought with grim satisfaction.

"Was Mrs. Holbeck's visit not enough to inform you, Aunt? She was certainly here long enough." Lord Harrowden's biting tone penetrated the room before he seemed to recollect himself. "However, that is of no concern of mine. Ladies, shall we?"

When they left, Lucius took the seat beside Lady Harrowden. "I had no idea you had a ward. Is this to be her permanent home?"

The countess waved her hand toward the bell string on the wall. "Ring for something to drink if you wish. I am sure you'll want something after your ride. I want nothing."

73

"No thank you, my lady. I had tea with my sister before setting out."

Lady Harrowden pursed her lips. "You saw Maria, did you? I suppose that's what brought you here, and not news regarding my nephew."

Lucius hid his impatience. He hoped Lady Harrowden knew better than to join the list of matchmaking mamas—or guardians, in her case. She would catch cold at it. "I do have some news of your nephew, as a matter of fact, but nothing I can confirm, and still nothing concrete pertaining to your income," he said. "Do you wish to set up a meeting with your current solicitor when I bring in the accountant? It might scare him into rectifying anything that is not quite in line."

Lady Harrowden replied, "No. Find me someone new. I wish to retain what is mine, and I don't want a solicitor that must be frightened into doing what is right."

When Lucius remained silent, she tapped her fingers on the armrest. "I would like to know the state of things, and then I will know what to do—what my possibilities are."

"I'm curious," Lucius said. "Why do you not see to it yourself that the dower house is painted, so you might remove there? Surely it is your right to do so, and the dower house associated with Harrowden is larger than most and will be comfortable. There would be room for both Miss Lockhart and Miss Woodsley." And they would be out of Harrowden's reach.

"A move of that magnitude requires assistance, and I have not had any. I cannot be expected to oversee the servants' activity to ensure everything is done right. I do not have youth on my side." Lady Harrowden picked at the fringe of her shawl peevishly. "That is why Miss Lockhart's letter was timely. I have had no one to see to my interests until now."

Lucius experienced an uncomfortable jolt of conscience. He had not been available to advise Lady Harrowden right from the beginning, as he had promised her husband. He was determined to see everything through now.

"I am happy to assist you in whatever you need, my lady. If a move to the dower house will benefit you, as well as the two young ladies living with you, then your removal is not such a difficult thing to accomplish. With your permission, I will go inspect the house myself."

Lady Harrowden nodded and pressed her lips together, without a doubt refraining from giving him the reproach he deserved. "Yes, go. I suppose I was waiting until a new Lady Harrowden took up residence before removing to the dower house, but I begin to think that it will be more comfortable for all of us—myself, Miss Lockhart, and Miss Woodsley—if I were to take this step without delay. What did you find out about my nephew?"

Lucius pulled the corners of his mouth down. It brought him no pleasure to confirm her suspicions. "I am told he has had some bad dealings. He is frequently found in the gaming hells—or he was until he went on a repairing lease. I cannot know the extent of his fortune, but it appears he has sustained some heavy losses, and that might be why he has chosen to retire here."

Lady Harrowden turned pale. "A significant portion of the estate is unentailed. Surely my nephew has not run through his entire fortune— the one my husband built faithfully throughout his lifetime? He has not taken out a mortgage on the estate?"

Lucius could only shrug. All he had to go on was the letter from Robertson. "I believe it should not be difficult to find out, but nothing can be learned until we bring in the outside accountant, and even then we can only know if your own portion has been diverted to cover some of the estate's debts."

Lady Harrowden pulled herself up, her lips pinched in a frown. "All my husband's hard work...The estate was running beautifully in his hands, and he took great pains to leave it in better condition than he received it. And to think now that it is left to a *fool*." She sighed sharply. "I do not know how I will bear to be in the same room with Richard."

Lucius did not feel it an auspicious moment to inquire more specifically after the ward. Upon promising to engage a solicitor as soon as possible, and to let Lady Harrowden know when an accountant could be found to go over her ledger, Lucius took his leave of Lady Harrowden.

He did not want to come all this way and miss an opportunity to speak with Miss Lockhart, although it was probably too much to hope that he could gain a private audience with her. However, when he walked out to the stables, luck was on his side.

Miss Lockhart glanced through the window in the greenhouse as he passed by, her stiff bonnet framing a serious face. Lucius gave a small wave, then cut across the path and pulled open the wood and glass door. He found her in the process of tying bouquets to hang upside down to dry. She looked at him as he walked in, a smile on her face, and the sight stopped him in his tracks. Her smile softened her eyes. Miss Lockhart needed to smile more often.

Lucius looked around. At least Harrowden was not here. Then again, neither was Miss Woodsley. "Where is your new charge?"

"Her maid came to fetch her, saying the modiste is here, which is perfect timing for she may now take Miss Woodsley's measurements for her first ball gown. She will attend the Twelfth Night ball, since your sister was kind enough to include her." Miss Lockhart gathered some of the fresh blossoms and laid them on the table with a broad ribbon underneath.

"I suppose that means that you will attend as well, even if Lady Harrowden does not?" Lucius asked, the idea of the ball suddenly taking on a degree of interest.

"I suppose so," she answered. "She cannot go alone, but I cannot know until Lady Harrowden has told me her wishes."

"Did Lord Harrowden not come out with you after all?" Lucius fingered the end of the ribbon she held, as he studied her profile. "He said he would accompany you here, but perhaps he remembered he has an estate to run in between his numerous dalliances." He raised a brow and Miss Lockhart laughed.

"To my relief, he left shortly after Miss Woodsley did, and I can only be grateful he has diverted his attention from me, for it is most unwelcome." She pulled the ribbon from his fingers as she wound it around her bouquet.

"That is a relief. Has he then fixed his attention on her?" Lucius could only hope so, for that would leave Miss Lockhart in peace.

"He has certainly flirted with her," Miss Lockhart said, "although how fixed his attentions are I cannot be sure."

It would not benefit Miss Lockhart to have Harrowden running off with the ward, as he was likely to do if he was all rolled up like Robertson had implied. He ought, perhaps, to give Miss Lockhart a word of warning. "As much as I am convinced Miss Woodsley can handle Lord Harrowden's flirtations, you would do well to curtail his attentions if you can. I suppose he has followed her in?"

"I do not believe so." Miss Lockhart turned her clear gaze on him. "He could hardly force his way into a dress fitting. I believe she is safe enough for now, and I have plenty to occupy myself with for Lady Harrowden. I cannot be everywhere at once." Her tone had grown sharp, and her movements were brusque when she turned back to the flowers.

"You are piqued," Lucius said after a moment's pause. "I promise you, I am only looking out for your welfare. Any mischief Miss Woodsley conjures will reflect badly on you as her governess, I fear."

"Do not think I am unaware of how to handle Miss Woodsley. I may not have held a governess post before, but I certainly have had more than one governess myself. I know how to maintain the propriety of my charge." She did not look at him as she finished winding the ribbon around the stems of her bouquet and tied a knot.

"Not if she throws propriety in your face, which she is likely to do —and which she has already done," he countered, growing somewhat irritated, although it was not a rational response. It was especially irrational that he wanted her to look at him. "You are barely out of the schoolroom yourself, Miss Lockhart. You have no idea what a man like that can do to harm a young lady's reputation. *Or her innocence*, if indeed she still has any—"

Miss Lockhart whirled on him. "You are wrong. I know *exactly* what dangers a young lady faces from men who are not gentlemen, and I know it better than you ever will. I faced that very danger when I knocked on your door asking for help."

Lucius gritted his teeth as the shaft went home, but Miss Lockhart was not finished. "I also know there are expectations made upon me from all sides. Expectations from Lady Harrowden to amuse her and run her errands—not that I mind that," she added quickly, as if afraid of being overheard.

"And then," Miss Lockhart continued, "there are expectations that I will prove successful in guiding a young lady to maturity, one upon whom the necessity of behaving with propriety does not seem to leave any mark. And there are expectations to be conciliatory toward the lord of the manor, taking special care not to be a temptation to him, or make him think that because of my reduced circumstances, I am easy prey."

High color had flown to Miss Lockhart's cheeks as she faced forward again. She bit her lip and grabbed at the roses before breathing in with a hiss and examining the hole in her glove. It was tinged with red.

"Come," Lucius said gently, taking her injured hand in his. Her last words rang in his mind. *Easy prey*. "Let us go treat your wound. You should not be out here unaccompanied, even with me."

"No, I should not." Miss Lockhart pulled her hand out of his. Leaving her bundle of flowers on the worktable, she swept in front of him and out the door.

❧ 10 ❧

Selena walked alongside Sir Lucius toward the house, the cold wind nipping through her cloak. Neither said anything, and Selena wondered if she should further attempt to justify her capacity as a governess, but she decided against it. After all, what could he know about the matter? Sir Lucius led an uncomplicated life as a gentleman of means, with a large family nearby. He could not possibly understand the awkwardness attached to her situation.

Selena clenched her fists, her breath coming out in puffs. She certainly did not appreciate Sir Lucius questioning her actions. To own the truth, she had experienced some qualms when Lord Harrowden announced he would return inside directly after Rebecca had left the greenhouse. But Rebecca had been accompanied by her maid, and surely that was protection enough, was it not? Not to mention the relief Selena felt in not having to bear the earl's presence while she finished her task.

Besides, what Sir Lucius could not understand was that if Selena had been given a task to fulfill for Lady Harrowden, she was required to finish it. The countess had made it abundantly clear that the flower arrangements would have to be prepared today in order for the servant to send them to the village fair on time, and only a lady had the right touch to prepare bouquets in the proper manner that would best reflect the estate. Selena was caught between two obligations, and it was only natural that she should cede her place to Rebecca's maid, so that Selena might finish her task for the countess. How could she know Lord Harrowden would follow directly behind? It was not as if she could run after him to ask him his intentions.

How dare Sir Lucius make me question my actions. Insolent man.

"I believe I have irritated you," Sir Lucius said.

Selena's thinly soled half-boots were quiet on the snowy path, and Sir Lucius's made a crunching sound as he walked at her side.

"No, why should you think so? It is merely that I am quiet."

"Undoubtedly fatigued from having to chase after so tiresome a girl." Sir Lucius took hold of her arm in a gentle grasp, halting her forward progress.

Selena turned to face him reluctantly but avoided meeting his eyes. It would be better for her if she did not stare at him too long. His face was set in severe lines, but his eyes held such a warmth to them, she almost felt she could trust him. *That* would never do. She knew all too well how hard and cynical his face could look, since he wore that expression habitually with everyone, it seemed...except at times. But experience told her that it was only a matter of time before he would treat her, too, with indifference—or worse—scorn.

As if to further weaken her resistance, Sir Lucius studied her, a small crease forming on his brow. "I am sorry for scolding. I worry for your safety here."

Selena swallowed a lump in her throat then turned from Sir Lucius and began walking forward. She could not put her faith in him, no matter how kindly disposed he seemed right now. At what point would he, too, remind her of her lowly position and how powerless she was?

They were nearing the house, and Selena cautioned herself that their difference in station did not permit such intimate discourse, and she would do well to remember it.

That sober fact did nothing to improve her mood. Even when her family had left London's Society for Bedford's, Selena was cast aside and ignored as soon as their circumstances were made apparent to the local gentry. It was even less likely that Sir Lucius—a member of the *ton*, and a peer—would overlook such a thing. Even though he was surely aware of her straitened means, he did not know that Selena's father had died leaving a number of gentlemen's debts unpaid. Once Sir Lucius found that out...

Without realizing that she was leading a guest through a servant's entrance, Selena stepped over the threshold of a smaller door that led past the library and fed into the main corridor.

Sir Lucius ducked through the doorway and followed her into the house, and the silence prompted Selena into awareness. She had not yet answered his kind gesture or words. Inside, all the doors to the rooms with windows were shut, blocking out the main sources of light, and she stopped to face him in the dark corridor.

"Are you...will you be taking your leave now?"

Sir Lucius trained his gaze on her still. "I shall take my leave of you, Miss Lockhart, but perhaps I can speak to Lady Harrowden on your behalf? If you are truly being overworked..."

"No—that is kind of you, but I think it will do more harm than good." Selena despised being the object of pity. She looked down at her torn glove. "I will bind my finger then go speak to Lady Harrowden."

Sir Lucius turned to leave but paused before he had taken many steps. "Tell me something," he said turning back. "You spoke of Miss Woodsley's fitting. Do *you* have a dress for the ball my sister is hosting?"

"I?" Selena was surprised he would think to ask. Perhaps he did not wish her to lower the tone of his sister's ball by appearing in a shabby gown. If he had known her three years ago, he would not have questioned whether she would arrive not only in the correct attire, but in the first stare of fashion. With the advance on her salary, Selena had procured some fine cambric muslin, and she was now in the process of sewing her own dress. She was not rapid with the needle, besides being busy, but would have it finished just in time for the ball.

"I will be properly attired," Selena said, and she could not mask the haughtiness in her tone. "You need have no fear for me."

"I have no fear at all." Sir Lucius bowed and smiled warmly at Selena in a way that cut through her irritation—and her defenses. "I am convinced you are a very resourceful woman, Miss Lockhart."

Selena watched him as he left. His kindness brought her a lingering degree of comfort. *He thought her resourceful!* But the comfort did not last long. He thought Selena resourceful in...what? In the way of a governess? Could he be seeking out candidates for his future progeny?

Better to steel her heart against any comfort or hope that was sure to hurt doubly when taken away. No, Selena did not desire his notice. Any sprig of hope that attempted to blossom would wither at the first hint of frost, and in Society, the frost was sure to hit.

Selena climbed the stairs, deciding she had best check on Rebecca before reporting to Lady Harrowden that she had not had time to finish the bouquets. When she entered Rebecca's room, she stopped cold. There was Lord Harrowden in the dressing room, sitting on the brocaded chair in the corner, offering his opinion on the dress the modiste was pinning on Rebecca.

"My lord!" Selena exclaimed. "It is not at all proper for you to be here. I must ask you to leave at once. Miss Woodsley is under my charge, and it is unthinkable that she should have a gentleman in her bedchamber."

Lord Harrowden offered a benign smile. "Miss Woodsley was merely benefiting from my more experienced taste in the matter of ladies' dress. I did not see anything untoward in attending the fitting, particularly as both her maid and the modiste are here to lend propriety. I absented myself from the room when she was changing from one dress to another. So you see, everything has been done in perfect decorum."

"Not quite, my lord." Selena glared at him and held the door open wide. "I will be much obliged if you will give us privacy now."

"Oh no," Rebecca said, her lip sticking out. "Lord Harrowden has been so helpful. You see this fabric, my lord? I told you the Pompadour would become me, and so it does."

Lord Harrowden looked from her to Selena with slight amusement and stood. "Alas, Miss Woodsley. You will have to make your way without me." He came before Selena and gave a mocking bow, his eyes insolent when he lifted them to hers.

When the earl left, Selena turned to Rebecca's maid. "Alice, how could you allow him in here? I was counting on you to ensure propriety."

"Miss, I'm sure my lord meant no harm. He was the perfect gentleman." The maid held the shoes against the dress to see the match, barely meeting Selena's gaze. "And he does have an eye for the way the cloth should fold, and what color she should be wearing."

The modiste continued pinning the hem on the bottom of the dress, adding her two bits. "You need have no fears on that score, for we were all present, and Miss Woodsley was not left alone with him for a moment. The earl's advice was indeed most welcome."

Selena was sure the modiste's liberal allowance was driven by the hope of future sales from whomever the next Lady Harrowden might be. She did not think it worthwhile to argue with the modiste, who could easily be replaced. But she did see with perfect clarity that she had the unenviable task of keeping a stricter eye on her charge if Alice would not do it.

When the dress was properly fitted, Selena eyed the bodice and wondered if it should not be altered to give more modesty. It was perhaps acceptable for a young lady out for several seasons, but it was too revealing for a young maiden not yet out.

"Shall we not go see Lady Harrowden to show her your dress?" Selena asked, her voice tinged with the concern she was feeling. "I believe she would be glad to offer her opinion."

"Oh, I'm sure Lady Harrowden will have nothing to say about it." Rebecca pivoted to examine the back of the dress in the looking glass. "We've already had Lord Harrowden's word on the matter, and he said Madame Druard is known for her inventive fashions. I'm sure we shall not trouble Lady Harrowden just now. Besides, these pins are sticking into me in an uncomfortable way. Madame Druard, help me out of this now."

Selena stood by helplessly. What could she do other than grasp the child by her arm and drag her before Lady Harrowden? Perhaps she should speak with Madame Druard privately and suggest she raise the bodice to cover more—as long as the modiste would not take such a suggestion amiss. Her short acquaintance with the woman led her to believe she would.

Selena pushed down a wave of irritation that a mere girl could be so obstinate and win an argument over Selena who was three and twenty.

Selena went to see Lady Harrowden after she left Rebecca. She needed to confess to not having finished tying the bouquets and explain why. She still toyed with the idea of discussing Rebecca's attire for the ball. But to what extent should she, alone, interfere with Rebecca, and how much should she turn to the countess for help, Selena could not say.

Lady Harrowden's pale eyes were turned toward the fireplace and she seemed entranced by the flames. The corners of her mouth were turned down. Staring in moody contemplation at the fire appeared to be a common pastime for the widow. Perhaps it would be better if Selena could encourage her to move about a bit more. She was not so very infirm after all.

When Selena stepped farther into the room, Lady Harrowden looked up. "Where is the girl?"

Selena came and sat on the empty armchair at her side. "She has just finished with the modiste. Her dress will need to be hemmed, but it is almost finished."

"Good." Lady Harrowden gave a decisive nod. "I chose the fabric and pattern myself. So I know she will look becoming in it."

Lady Harrowden had chosen the pattern? Selena was nearly numb with relief. Thank heavens she had not complained about the inappropriateness of the dress. If Lady Harrowden thought it would do, then surely she must know best.

Still, the fact that Lord Harrowden had been in the room was another matter entirely, and she would be wrong not to bring it up. Lady Harrowden clearly did not trust her nephew, and if Rebecca were to find herself in any sort of scrape with him, it would be best if the countess knew everything now.

"When I went to look in on the fitting..." Selena paused, nervous about what she had to disclose. "I found Lord Harrowden in the room giving his opinion on the dress."

"What? My nephew was in the room when she was having her gown fitted?" Lady Harrowden turned to Selena, her face a picture of rigid indignation.

"Yes, my lady. I had thought her maid protection enough, so to say the least, I was concerned to find him there." Selena searched for a way to express the rest. "All three—Alice, Madame Druard, and Rebecca herself—assured me that there was nothing untoward, even that it was perfectly natural to have him there. Rebecca protested when I asked him to leave."

When the countess shot her a look of disapproval, Selena protested, "I know she is only sixteen. She does not know what is best, so of course I did not listen to her. But the modiste also said that he had impeccable taste, and Alice assured me he left the room when Rebecca was changing, and that there was nothing all that shocking about what happened. All I could do was to ensure Lord Harrowden left immediately."

"It should never have happened in the first place," Lady Harrowden said. "Why were you not there with her when she had her fitting?"

Selena felt heat rise to her cheeks, along with a flash of anger, which she swallowed. "You insisted the bouquets needed to be done today, and I knew if I helped with the fitting when there was already another woman present, I would not be able to finish the task you had given me. That is why I was not there."

"And have you finished?" the countess asked.

"No, I..." How could Selena explain this without sounding like a ninny? She was capable of doing what was asked of her—she *had* to be capable of it. Her mother and sisters depended on her earnings, and Selena did not want to return to Bedford and live in seclusion, which was the life her mother and sisters led. And if Selena were turned off from this position, she would not easily be able to get another.

There was no way around it but to say the truth. "I was not able to finish tying the bouquets because Sir Lucius came by the greenhouse and stopped to see me."

Lady Harrowden looked displeased—even more displeased than she already was, if such a thing were possible. "How did he find you? What did he want?"

Selena looked down at her hands. "I believe he merely wished to warn me against the earl's intentions. He was concerned they were not honorable." Selena took a breath. "So I returned with him to the house to check on Rebecca and left the unfinished bouquets there. I will gladly go out and finish them after I leave you."

"That's when you found my nephew in the room with Rebecca?" The countess asked, and Selena nodded.

Lady Harrowden took a breath, her jaw resolute. "Do you know how much my ward is worth?"

Selena shook her head.

"She is worth thirty-thousand pounds, and it is not tied up in any way whatsoever. There is nothing in the will that states she must be of a certain age before she can touch it. This is why it is important to keep fortune-hunters away from her, and at present I am including my nephew in that category."

"I will take greater care, my lady—" Selena began.

"I suppose you want to know what she's doing here. What my relationship is to her," Lady Harrowden said abruptly.

Selena was quick to shake her head. "I would not dream of asking so impertinent a question."

"Rebecca was my cousin's daughter. Although her husband's family had a considerable amount of wealth, they did not have the family name to lend her countenance. My cousin named me Rebecca's godmother and asked if I would mind being one of her guardians if anything should happen to them. She assured me they should not bother me if they were both alive to launch her properly in Society. I appreciated the delicacy of her manner in approaching me, and I decided to grant her request."

Lady Harrowden exhaled, a sigh of irritation. "As it turned out, my cousin died right after I made the promise, and the girl's father died a year later. I can only suppose it was Rebecca's frequent change in housing, and perhaps a lack of female guidance that led to her being expelled from school."

Selena thought about the young lady's troublesome nature. Perhaps the best thing would be to have her safely married, and as quickly as possible. She met Lady Harrowden's gaze. "Would it be such a bad thing if she and Lord Harrowden were to form an attachment? After all, she has your approval, and she comes with a large dowry."

"My hesitation is not whether she is good enough for my nephew, although I told him she lacked the birth to make him a suitable wife," Lady Harrowden replied. "I am merely aware that my nephew is not good enough for her. It's not that I have a great deal of affection for the girl. I barely know her. But I did give my word to her parents to see to her future." She pulled her shawl more firmly around her shoulders, and Selena jumped up to help her.

"I would like, at all costs, to avoid such a disadvantageous match for Rebecca. I have seen nothing in Richard to inspire me to believe he has a shred of goodness. Sir Lucius—I trust you will hold your tongue regarding what I am about to say—"

Selena nodded. Of course she would.

"Sir Lucius has promised to look into it, but I fear for the fate of Harrowden because of my nephew's gambling. The estate did not come with a huge fortune, but it was well enough in my husband's care. And in two years, Richard is showing signs of having torn down every thing my husband built. I do not want him to run through my ward's fortune as well, which is precisely what he would do upon marrying her."

Selena took a deep breath. Well did she know what ruinous gambling would lead to for those involved. The state of affairs was worse than she had imagined. She had hoped Rebecca's birth was not high enough to be a temptation for Lord Harrowden, but now it appeared the girl's fortune might be. And she agreed with Lady Harrowden. No matter how reprehensible a girl Rebecca might be, Lord Harrowden must not touch her fortune.

Having her own experience in the matter, Selena would not make it easy for Lord Harrowden to ruin someone else's life. She shoved aside the disquiet that Rebecca would court ruin on her own.

❧ II ❧

LUCIUS FOUND himself with an uncharacteristic urge to visit his sister, and he could only contribute it to a mild curiosity to know who had accepted to come to her Twelfth Night ball. He went on horseback, as it was not far, and he needed exercise to combat the restlessness that had begun to creep over him. The path leading to Holbeck's gate was lined with trees on either side, and as Lucius crossed through the open gate, the long alley opened up to the vista of his sister's manor.

Charles Holbeck was several years Lucius's senior, and they had never been particularly close. Holbeck was benefactor to more than one MP in the House of Commons and enjoyed throwing his weight around there. He was a high stickler for good *ton* and only surrounded himself with people he thought would elevate him in importance. It made him rather dull to be around. However, he and Maria seemed well-suited, and that was one less family burden Lucius had to worry about.

Maria came out of the drawing room herself to greet him when she heard his knock. "Why, Lucius, what a surprise. To think that you would stir yourself from the comfort of your house. Whatever can have brought you to visit mine?" She stopped short. "Nothing is amiss with Mother, I hope?"

Lucius removed his hat. "I have no news of Mother, but I have no doubt she is in good health." Any further speech fell off when he heard voices coming from the drawing room—familiar voices. He looked at his sister. "What, Philippa and George are here?"

Maria cocked her head. "Well, what did you think, Lucius? Of course I was going to invite our siblings to the ball."

"Who is staying with Mother then?" he asked, putting his riding crop under his arm. "I am surprised to hear she was willing to part with them for the holiday. Or that she did not insist on coming herself, so that we might form one large merry band. How unlike her."

Maria had a gleam in her eye. "I believe our neighbor, Mr. Hartley, is expressing some interest in our mother."

Lucius gave a horrified expression. "Hartley! That old man. Surely he is beyond the age of taking on a wife. And if he did, he might look younger than our mother. Every feeling revolts."

"Love knows no age," Maria said placidly.

"Love." Lucius snorted. "A very fine thing. I can just imagine them in their caps and bedgowns sharing a dish of gruel while they compare ailments. Utter nonsense. I hope you don't wish me to turn romantic now. You will be sadly disappointed."

The door opened, and Philippa and George rushed out like two colts from the pen. Philippa—whose fresh innocence belied a spirit of mischief that Lucius knew all too well could be dangerous—spoke first.

"Lucius, I am so glad you're here so I don't have to wait to ask you. I finally won Mother's approval to have a Season this year, and I will need you to host me. Mother will be there, of course. But we need your house in London. It's big enough to host a ball for me, as well."

Not having a ready answer to a request he fully intended to deny, Lucius held off and looked at George instead. "When do you go back to school?"

George returned his gaze with a sheepish look. "Oh...I was sent down for the term. So I won't be going back."

Lucius paused in the act of placing his gloves on the small table in the entrance. "You didn't tell me this over Christmas. What was it this time? Running off to see a prize fight that was expressly forbidden and getting caught climbing back in?"

George grinned and shook his head. "We dressed a local cow in the headmaster's cape and hat."

Philippa laughed, and Maria glared at George before turning to him. "Lucius, you really ought to do something. If I've told you once, I've told you dozens of times—George will come to grief, gadding about in this way."

Lucius would appreciate seeing a more serious bent to George's comportment, but he was not about to join his older sister in plaguing him. He knew all too well what that was like. "Well, George, as I know how much you will miss the books, I'll be sure to hire a tutor to keep you occupied." As he said it in his driest tone, George just laughed and folded his arms.

Philippa, always an enchanting child, but nearly grown, peered up at Lucius. She was quite taking with her sparkling eyes and hair styled in tight curls around her face. She took him by the hand.

"So when will we remove to London, Lucius? I will need you to purchase the gowns that have to be ordered. We calculated with Mama that I will need seven morning dresses and at least two riding dresses. I suppose there will be no need for a court gown now that Princess Charlotte has died."

She paused as if contemplating the idea of mourning, but he knew she was too young to be touched by it and did not even remember her own father well. Philippa went on. "But I will need several evening gowns and ball gowns, as well as gloves and stockings and the like."

She saw Lucius's pained expression and added coaxingly, "Just look at it as an investment. If you turn me off credibly, I shall find a husband in my first Season and you will have no more to do with me."

"You're more likely to find trouble in your first Season." Lucius stepped toward the drawing room. "May we go in, Maria? Or must we stand here and discuss our family affairs for all the servants to hear?"

Maria took Lucius by the elbow and entered the drawing room. When everyone had sat, and tea had been ordered, Lucius turned to Maria. "So tell me about this ball. Who is likely to come?"

"Preparing yourself, are you?" His sister snapped her fingers and indicated for George to take a seat, which he did reluctantly.

"In a sense, yes. I would like to know who to be on the watch for." Lucius set his teacup down and crossed his leg.

"And you said we will have up to thirty couples for dancing," Philippa added, her eager eyes flitting from Maria's face to Lucius's. "You promised. Lucius, you don't mean to forbid me to dance, I hope. After all, this is not London. And Mama has no problem allowing me to dance in the local assemblies."

"No, I don't intend to put a spoke in your wheel," he said. "I just ask that you behave with circumspection. I haven't forgotten how you flirted with Barnsworth when we had them to dinner for Christmas."

George, who had been lounging in his seat gave a bark of laughter. "I never saw such a poor bumbling fool. He is half in love with you already and prepared to make you an offer, I believe, but you slipped away before he could muster the courage."

"Oh as to that," Philippa said with a look of scorn. "How can you think I would be interested in someone like Mr. Barnsworth? He was just someone merely to pass the time."

Lucius stopped her with a lift of his hand. "And that is precisely the thing I am concerned about. In particular, you are to stay away from Lord Harrowden—"

"Lord Harrowden?" Philippa rolled her eyes. "Lud, whatever would I find to talk about with him?"

"I am prepared to let you enjoy the ball," Maria interjected, "but please keep your decorum and behave like a lady. Don't go flirting with all the young gentlemen there."

"You will have time enough to do that during your Season," Lucius said, smiling at Philippa's youthful impatience, and knowing that she was chafing under the combined direction of two older siblings. Fortunately, she and George were too close in age for him to add his mite.

Philippa clasped her hands together. "So you are prepared to host me in London?"

Lucius shot his older sister a look. "Surely Maria can host. Holbeck has a big house in London, and even if the location is not as easy to get to as mine, it is perfectly suited to the purpose. And you will have more invitations coming to a married woman than you will to my house."

"I think not, Lucius," Maria corrected with a pointed look.

"Oh, how can you think so? Besides, Mama will be there." Philippa put on her most coaxing face, which rarely worked with Lucius. "Of course you will get more invitations. Everyone wants to invite *you*."

"You're still a Corinthian in London, even though you're past your prime," George said with a laugh. "Everyone talks of your exploits."

Lucius about to protest, *past my prime indeed*, instead turned to his brother. "I hope you correct their misconceptions."

"No, I only fill in the missing details," George retorted, grinning broadly.

"The devil take you," Lucius replied good-naturedly.

"To answer your question, Lucius," Maria said, "Holbeck will never agree to an entire London Season, and I believe you know that. He is too busy with his political functions. As head of the family, you will have to be the one to host Philippa."

Lucius saw the future with foreboding, as the oppressive weight of an entire Season living in the same house as his family came forcibly upon him. His mother would come to escort Philippa, and that would mean bringing their two younger siblings as well, who were still in the school room. Christopher would plague Lucius to death to take him everywhere, and Louisa would bore him with her idle chatter. A sense of dread crept over Lucius. Whatever had possessed him to come visit his sister?

His thoughts had already started to stray, and he would not tarry. He had come with a vague sense of mission, however, even if he could not bring himself to ask about Miss Lockhart directly. "Who else is coming to your ball, Maria? I hope not Gregson. He's removed himself to London has he not?"

"Oh no. No such luck," Maria answered mildly. "Mr. Gregson is home for the holidays, and I couldn't very well not invite him, not without giving great offense to the rest of his family."

Lucius pointed his finger at Philippa, forcibly reminding himself of his deceased father. "Now that's someone you'll steer far from, if you please. He is only trouble." When George laughed again, Lucius pointed at him, too. "And you, as well, George. No sitting down at the card tables with him." He was beginning to feel ancient.

"Lucius, since you asked, I invited Miss Woodsley to the ball. It will be an occasion for you to further your acquaintance with her. I suppose you've had a chance to meet her?" Maria paused.

What an irony. Lucius had resisted the idea of marriage, because he feared a wife would eat up what precious little peace his life afforded him. Maria was pushing the one girl Lucius knew for a certainty would cut up his peace. However, he couldn't betray Miss Woodsley's folly to his sister, who was the worst gossip in the county. He would have to let Maria think he was considering her proposal.

"Yes, a taking thing," he said. He drank his tea in a gulp and attempted nonchalance. "And Miss Lockhart will come too, I assume? You would have given her an invitation." It was not a question, and he was not prepared for Maria to sit upright.

"Speaking of Miss Lockhart—yes, yes. I have to invite her. She is Lady Harrowden's companion, and now she has to accompany Miss Woodsley, I suppose. However, I have *news*. When I mentioned Miss Lockhart to Charles, he said he quite thought she had been betrothed to one of the members of parliament he supports. Can you imagine Miss Lockhart having been connected to such a good family?"

Lucius set his teacup on the saucer, wrestling with an irrational surge of jealousy. He could not stand to think of Miss Lockhart in the arms of another man. He wondered who the fellow was and what kind of figure he cut. Betrothed! Lucius's mind spun. It had been called off at any rate.

Maria looked at him expectantly, and he was in no temper to play into her sense of the dramatic. "Shocking, to be sure," he said in his most bored voice.

Maria's eyes sparkled, caught by the thrill of relaying gossip. "But that is not all. The engagement was broken off because Miss Lock-hart's father gambled away their entire fortune"—she leaned forward and finished in a delighted whisper—"and then drank himself into an early grave."

Lucius remained quiet, meeting his sister's gaze with a disinter-ested look, and keeping his own thoughts hidden. Maria was all too glad to fill in the rest. "Charles said the Lockharts were very particular with whom they associated at one point, which is why his friend offered for her. But that façade fell at once when Lockhart's losses became impossible to ignore. They were shunned from Society overnight."

Lucius rubbed his chin in contemplation. "Poor thing," he said, despite himself. He could not imagine what Miss Lockhart had gone through. She had kept her dignity in spite of the hardship all these years. It was a strength of character he rarely saw in Society.

"Poor thing?" Maria said in disbelief, causing Lucius to snap his head up. "Poor thing? Her family deserved it. They were living a lie and Society is not so forgiving."

"How well do I know that," Lucius said, glancing at George and Philippa, who both had their eyes trained on him. It often seemed that Maria had no heart, and he had certainly been accused of much the same. But it might not be too late for his younger siblings. "Perhaps Miss Lockhart's father deserved it, but she did not."

Maria's gaze narrowed. "I certainly hope you are not developing a *tendre* for Miss Lockhart. She is wholly ineligible. And she pales next to Miss Woodsley in beauty, vivacity, and income."

"But not in character." Lucius could not help but say it. Good Lord, it was not like him to betray himself in such a way, but he could not keep still when Maria compared the two women and thought that *Miss Lockhart* came up short.

"What do you know of Miss Woodsley's character?" Maria said. "She is charming. I plan to bring Philippa to meet her before the ball since they are close in age."

Lucius had had enough. He stood. "You must do as you deem best, Maria. George, come see me tomorrow. I may have a task for you since you now have an abundance of free time. Goodbye, Philippa."

He had the horse saddled and rode off, allowing the repetitive swaying to settle his mind. Miss Lockhart had hinted at such things—time spent in London, mixing with Society, great loss and her father's death. It had been hard for her to bear, however—much harder than he had realized. Her family had fallen quite far in Society. It was enough to break off an engagement. He wondered if she had loved the man.

After searching his mind for an excuse to ride over to Harrowden

Estate and finding none, Lucius turned his horse toward home. In any case, it was best as he had business in town that afternoon. Once he met with the accountant he had found for Lady Harrowden, he would have his reason to visit.

12

WHERE IS THAT GIRL? Selena had been searching all the likely rooms for Rebecca, and she finally cornered her maid, coming out of Rebecca's bedroom.

"Have you seen Miss Woodsley? We were supposed to go into the village early this afternoon to purchase her gloves for the ball. Lady Harrowden is waiting for us to set out, and I cannot find her anywhere."

"Oh, miss." The stout maid clutched a pile of dresses to her chest on her way to the laundering room. "Miss Woodsley said she was going for a ride. I believe she had Lord Harrowden's groom to follow her. She set out an hour ago, so I shouldn't think she will be long."

The first concern that sprang to Selena's mind was whether Lord Harrowden had gone with her. In the three days since Rebecca arrived, Selena had caught them together twice now, without any sort of chaperone—once sitting on the same settee before the fire in the library, and once coming up from the kitchen, each eating a piece of shortbread. In addition, the house had an echoing feeling to it, as servants seemed scarce. Selena did not often cross paths with one, which meant that Lord Harrowden and Rebecca were not likely to either.

Selena was worried about their increased intimacy, even though

Rebecca had once made an off-hand remark that it was too bad the earl was so young, as he would not be a suitable husband for many years yet. She went on to add that he didn't possess the worldliness of Sir Lucius, and although that didn't bode well for the hope that Rebecca had moved on from her infatuation of Sir Lucius, it did not prevent Lord Harrowden from importuning Rebecca either—something that would be disastrous to an impressionable young girl.

Lord Harrowden exited the billiard room and met Selena in the corridor, putting to rest at least one of her fears. "Well, Miss Lockhart? Have you nothing better to do?" The smirk that accompanied these words did nothing to soften the irritation that sprang up whenever she was in his presence.

"I am looking for Miss Woodsley. Apparently she has gone riding with your groom. Did you know anything about this?"

"I've told the groom to be at her disposal whenever she should wish to ride. I understand riding is a favorite pastime with her, and her mare finally arrived and is now stabled here. She does not need to ask me to take her own horse out." Lord Harrowden continued to wear a smile that he must have known would grate.

Selena said, "However, she should be asking *me* if she has permission to go out. I am, after all, her governess. Yes, she is chaperoned in this instance, but she is only sixteen."

"If you are not able to keep a rein on her, it is only natural that she will give you the slip." Lord Harrowden shrugged. "She is of such a playful nature."

Although Selena knew full well she did not have to justify herself, the words spilled out of their own accord. "I was reading to Lady Harrowden, and that is why I was unable to keep track of Miss Woodsley's whereabouts."

Her explanation only brought about another irritating smile. "As I warned you, Miss Lockhart, your position is not an easy one. Alas, there is no remedy, although I might offer you some consolation."

Lord Harrowden's insinuations alone were making her position intolerable, even without his attention on her. Selena turned without giving a reply and left to find the countess, fearing reproach. How Lady Harrowden expected her to keep an eye on Rebecca when she was at the countess's constant beck and call was a feat beyond her. She simply could not be in two places at once.

Selena relayed the information to Lady Harrowden that Rebecca had gone off, and the countess sighed and began pulling off her gloves. Selena was too uncomfortable sitting still in the drawing room with an irate employer, and she went to the corridor to wait for her charge. She sat on a small dark wooden bench next to the wall, and when Lord Harrowden strolled back into the corridor she turned her back on him rather than quit her post.

"So that's how you want to play?" Lord Harrowden laughed. He did not leave the corridor, but he did not try to engage Selena in conversation, and for that she was glad.

A quarter of an hour later, Rebecca walked through the front door, her cheeks rosy and the tips of her ears red. She looked fresh and radiant, and entirely too tempting a morsel for the earl, who had remained —it seemed—for no other purpose than to wait for her.

Selena walked forward, intercepting his path. "Rebecca, could you please let me know when you're going out riding next time? Lady Harrowden is waiting for us to go to town. Did you not remember we were supposed to set out?"

Rebecca shrugged as she pulled off her gloves. "Oh, as to that…We can set out now if you'd like. It's just that I need something to eat first. Can you order me some tea?"

Selena settled her mouth in a firm line. It was a humiliation to be treated so off-handedly, especially with Lord Harrowden standing right there.

"Go and change into your walking dress," she ordered. "I believe Alice is in your room, and I will have some bread and butter sent up. Ring immediately if she is not there, and I will make sure she is found. We do not want to keep Lady Harrowden waiting."

Selena spun around and walked toward the kitchen with a brisk step. Fortunately, she'd had time to strike up a warm acquaintance with Cook, who was only too glad to set the kettle on and prepare some simple sandwiches for Selena's charge. She found Alice at the table in the kitchen and sent her up with the tea she had prepared then hurried to the drawing room to let Lady Harrowden know they would be setting out in a half-hour.

It should have come as no surprise to Selena, though she herself was of a punctual nature, but it was closer to an hour by the time Rebecca was ready. And although Lady Harrowden's face had taken on a grim expression of impatience, Selena drove the whole party forward, knowing it was their only chance to get what they needed for the ball. By the time they had all climbed into the carriage, the hour was already advanced, and they had not much time before it would grow dark.

They arrived in town after a short drive, and Selena turned to assist Lady Harrowden after the footman helped her descend from the carriage. She turned and saw the shop where she had bought her fabric when running an errand in town.

The groom drove the carriage away, and Selena indicated across the street to the shop that was partially blocked from view by a waiting carriage. "There it is. Shall we just wait for these horses to pass? Then we may cross over."

Selena took Lady Harrowden by the arm. Rebecca was on the other side of her, examining her surroundings, her attention focused on everything but what she might do to assist her guardian. They began a slow progression with Selena taking great care not to let Lady Harrowden slip on the ice.

Another phaeton drove by, preventing them from crossing, and the large wheels splashed Selena with freezing mud. A shriek rose in her throat from being drenched in cold slush but before the sound came out, Lady Harrowden slipped and fell backward—hard.

"Oh!" Lady Harrowden's gasp turned into a grunt, and Selena could hear the pain in her voice.

She looked around for help on the nearly empty road, but the groom had already driven off with the barouche. "Rebecca, I need your assistance," she said.

To her credit, Rebecca looked somewhat concerned by Lady Harrowden's fall, but her reply was unhelpful. "What would you have me do? I cannot lift her."

Selena resisted the temptation to lash out at the thoughtless girl.

Did she care for no one but herself? "Put one of your hands under her elbow and we will lift at the same time." Selena braced herself because the road was icy, and if she could not stand, what hope was there to help the older woman?

A firm grip on Selena's arm stopped her in her tracks. "Allow me." The voice caused a fluttering in Selena's belly, but before she could turn or respond, Rebecca cried out in delight.

"Sir Lucius!"

Selena had not heard that much warmth in Rebecca's voice since she'd arrived, even with Lord Harrowden. Sir Lucius ignored her and put his hands under the countess's arms, lifting her to her feet.

"Your arrival is timely, sir," Selena said, a sense of relief stealing over her.

Sir Lucius, still supporting Lady Harrowden, met her gaze with a pained look. "You would not say that, Miss Lockhart, if you knew that it was my carriage that doused you in mud."

"Icy mud," she corrected. Selena now saw Sir Lucius's phaeton stopped a few feet away with his groom at the horses' heads. That's when she became aware of how cold she was and what a fright she must look.

"Let us not stand here," Lady Harrowden snapped. "Take me to the inn."

Selena exchanged a glance with Sir Lucius. The countess was squinting as though in pain. "Yes, Sir Lucius, can you assist Lady Harrowden? It will do her good to dry off before a fire and sit for a while."

"But what of my gloves?" Rebecca said. "I am very sorry you are injured, my lady, but this is my only chance to purchase gloves before the ball."

"The girl is right," Lady Harrowden said through her teeth. "She must have her gloves. The ball is only two days away. Selena, take her to the shop and acquire what she needs while I sit with Sir Lucius."

Selena wrapped her wet cloak around her more tightly, regretting the warmth of the fire she would not get to enjoy. "As you wish. Let us go."

She crossed the road with Rebecca at her side, taking care that no other horses were there to surprise them with an icy bath. Sir Lucius continued toward the inn with Lady Harrowden, his hand on one elbow and his other arm around her back to guide her.

The shop was surprisingly large for the small town of Woolmer Green. One of the shopkeepers came forward to the counter that stretched from one end of the shop to the other, and Rebecca discussed with him at length the different glove choices she was considering ordering. Selena, wishing to return to Lady Harrowden without delay, gave her opinion, and urged toward the choice she felt the most sensible—the long white gloves in silk that could be used for more than one occasion if Rebecca took care not to soil them. Those could be made up in short order and delivered to the estate in time for the ball. Rebecca resisted and continued to finger a pair of long green gloves that were available for immediate purchase, and that fit, but which could not be worn with her ball gown. She had not had the foresight to bring enough money for two pairs.

Selena, conscious of the time and knowing she still had stockings to purchase said, "Rebecca, you have five minutes to make up your mind before we have to meet Lady Harrowden again. I will address one of the other shopkeepers for my needs."

Rebecca nodded absently, and Selena went toward the back of the store where another assistant was free to attend her. It did not take her long to make a purchase. When she returned to the front, Rebecca was speaking to Mrs. Holbeck, Sir Lucius's sister, who had entered the shop. At her side were a younger lady and gentleman, who bore a family likeness.

"...these green ones are very pretty as you say, but what color is your dress?" Mrs. Holbeck was saying.

"Rose Pompadour," Rebecca replied.

"I believe that to be Sir Lucius's favorite color," Mrs. Holbeck replied with a smile, "but of course those green gloves will never do."

Rebecca opened her eyes wide. "You know Sir Lucius?"

The fetching young lady with a riot of curls, who stood by Mrs. Holbeck's side, laughed and said, "He is our brother."

"Oh, Mrs. Holbeck, you must introduce me to your companions," Rebecca cried.

Selena, feeling it would be rude not to make herself known at this point, stepped forward. "Good afternoon, Mrs. Holbeck."

Selena received a cold bow in return and wondered what she had done to receive such a frigid greeting. Mrs. Holbeck turned to the two standing beside her. "Miss Woodsley, allow me to introduce my younger siblings: Mr. George Clavering, and Miss Philippa Clavering. You two are nearly the same age."

Selena straightened as the insult sank in. She had not been considered worthy of an introduction.

"I believe you are right, Mrs. Holbeck," Rebecca said, pulling Selena's attention back to the matter at hand. She turned to the shopkeeper. "Please have the white gloves made up for me and sent to Harrowden Estate."

At least someone had been able to make her see reason.

"We will meet at the ball in three days' time, then," Philippa said. Her brother, dark as his sister was fair, remained quiet, and Selena was relieved to see that he didn't look particularly interested in the heiress, nor did Rebecca glance more than once in his direction.

"We will tell Sir Lucius you are here," Selena said in an attempt to move Rebecca toward the door.

"Lucius, here?" Mrs. Holbeck raised her eyebrows in surprise. "I did not see his carriage."

"He is at the inn helping Lady Harrowden recover from a fall, and we must not delay in returning to them." Selena stepped toward Rebecca to steer her to the door and escape Mrs. Holbeck's rude presence, but Mrs. Holbeck had precipitated her.

"We will accompany you." She took Rebecca by the arm and inquired more about her family. Selena fell behind with Philippa and George Clavering.

As they came out of the shop, Philippa turned back and whispered to Selena. "And you are Miss Lockhart, I believe. I am sorry for my sister."

Selena summoned a smile that fled at the rest of what Philippa had to say. "I think what happened to you in London was perfectly horrid and is not your fault." She saw George shoot his sister a warning look, and Philippa faced forward again, ending her whispered confidence.

Selena, cold and wet through, trudged onward, her heart sinking. Sir Lucius must know everything now.

The road was still slippery, but the inn beckoned to them with light spilling out of the sash windows against a darkening winter sky. When they entered, they were greeted with warmth and the smell of a mince-meat pie baking in the oven. One glance at Lady Harrowden told Selena she was already doing much better. Sir Lucius sat beside her, entertaining her with some story, and he even pulled a chuckle out of the old countess. The scene was so cozy, Selena's heart gave a strange lurch.

Sir Lucius looked up at Selena, the smile reaching his eyes. "Have you finished with your purchases?" Then his gaze fell on his siblings. "Ah. You here as well?"

"A merry family reunion." This came from Sir Lucius's brother, George, and was said in a wry tone that mimicked his elder brother's but with more playful mirth.

"George, go find Harrowden's groom and tell him to bring the carriage," Sir Lucius said, ignoring the banter. He turned to Lady Harrowden. "May I procure anything for you before you return home?"

Lady Harrowden shook her head. "Nothing. Maria, your brother came at just the right time. Don't tell me this is Philippa now, so grown."

Sir Lucius's younger sister gave a dimpled smile and curtsied before the countess. "Indeed it is, my lady. How wonderful to see you looking so well."

"*Hm.* Very proper. I assume you are still up to all manner of mischief, along with your brother, George, who has shot up as well, I see."

Mrs. Holbeck and Rebecca moved to join the conversation as Philippa and Lady Harrowden talked, and Selena stepped to the side to give them room. Too late, she realized it was where Sir Lucius stood, and it must look as though she maneuvered it. From the corner of her eye, she could see that Rebecca's attention was divided between Sir Lucius's family and Sir Lucius himself.

When he took a step nearer and turned to face Selena, she said in an undertone, "I do not know what we would have done if you had not been here to assist. I must thank you."

"What *we* would have done? Or what *you* would have done? Confess." Sir Lucius's smile was a caress. "You had your hands full because your charge would not lift a finger."

Selena peeked beyond him to where Rebecca was standing. She had her eyes on them, but Selena didn't think she could hear. Sir Lucius had his back to her, and his voice was subdued. "You are likely right," was all Selena would commit, but she returned his smile. She glanced beyond Sir Lucius again and saw that Mrs. Holbeck was also watching them. Her smile fell.

Sir Lucius studied her with such warm eyes, she could not hold his gaze. "It is beyond a doubt," he murmured. "Miss Woodsley is a trying creature. However, you know I had no choice but to stop and help, after having caused the fall in all likelihood. I had pulled over to allow a curricle to pass and didn't see you there." He gave her a rueful smile. "I am sorry to have muddied your dress."

"I have such an extensive wardrobe, one dress will hardly matter," she said in an expressionless voice.

He laughed, and shook his head. "I am quite sure you don't and beg that you will excuse me for being so careless."

"Yes, well, if I catch my death of cold, I will expect you to escort Miss Woodsley and Lady Harrowden to the ball in my stead," she said. "A swap I am sure at least one of them will be more than satisfied with."

"Oh, good heavens." He looked at her in mock horror. "I will only be getting my just deserts."

They both turned as the door opened and George entered. "The groom is pulling up outside. Lady Harrowden, may I assist you?"

"How pleased I am to see you have found your manners, young man." Lady Harrowden allowed Sir Lucius and his brother to take her by each arm. She was able to walk, but seemed a bit stiff. They helped her into the carriage, then George turned to assist Rebecca, and Sir Lucius held out his hand for Selena.

"Miss Lockhart." He bowed and assisted Selena into the carriage with a smile that seemed just for her. It tugged at her heart to be treated so kindly, and she returned the smile, only to look to the side where Mrs. Holbeck stood. She was frowning.

Selena quickly withdrew her hand and slid into the carriage, sitting back against the squabs where she was hidden in the shadows. Mrs. Holbeck's severe expression was a reminder that Selena did not represent an advantageous match for a baronet's family. It was a reminder she sorely needed before she allowed her imagination to run wild.

🙈 13 🙊

Lucius had not been able to visit the accountant until after he had bestowed Lady Harrowden, Miss Lockhart, and her charge safely into their carriage. He had only told the countess of his meeting and promised that if the accountant proved to be worthy, he would bring him to meet Lady Harrowden the next day.

At their meeting, he found that the accountant was too inexperienced to be trusted with such a delicate matter, and his senior partner would not be available for a week yet, so Lucius came to Harrowden to apprise her of as much. He was shown into the drawing room to wait for Lady Harrowden, and any hopes he might have had of spending a few pleasant minutes in Miss Lockhart's company were dashed when Miss Woodsley entered the room, alone, dressed in a riding habit with red trim.

"Oh, so you *are* here," she said, stepping into the room with a predatory smile. "I thought I heard your voice, Sir Lucius. I have been hoping to cross paths with you on one of my riding expeditions, but it hasn't happened yet. I go with the express hope of running into you."

Lucius drew back at yet another sign of such forward behavior. She had clearly learned nothing from her first thwarted attempt. "Unless it was with the aim of offering your apologies for having disturbed my peace at our first meeting, I don't see how your objective could bear any fruit."

"Oh, do you still think of our first meeting?" Miss Woodsley gave a little shake of her head and raised a hand. "I assure you, I do not. I now see that scheme would not have done at all. I am wiser—"

"It has been a little over a week," Lucius interjected drily.

"—and I do not mean to make the same mistake. Fortunately, fate has put us within easy distance of one another. Had I known it was as simple as this, I would have asked Lady Harrowden to take me in much earlier."

"I must disabuse you of the notion that fate had any hand in our meeting," he said harshly. "It was pure contrivance on your end that we met at all, and pure ill-luck on mine that I should be situated so near to your guardian."

Miss Woodsley had taken a few steps closer until she was in easy reach of Lucius where she batted her eyelashes slowly and puckered her full lips in what she likely thought to be a seductive pose. He folded his arms on his chest to resist the urge to throttle the girl.

"And let me encourage you," he added, "to allow yourself to be guided by Miss Lockhart, who is a model of decorum and elegance. As it stands, your current path will lead you to one end only, and it is not one I would wish for any young lady."

Now Miss Woodsley's mouth dropped in earnest. "You think *Selena* a model of elegance? She's a dowd. What's more—she's *old*. Besides, Mrs. Holbeck said she would particularly like to introduce you to me. She, at least, seems to think us a good match." Miss Woodsley had closed the distance and put her hand on Lucius's arm as if to coax him into an embrace.

Lucius took her hand firmly in his own and removed it from his arm. "My sister does not choose my flirts, and she never will."

Before he could release Miss Woodsley's hand, the door opened, and Lady Harrowden stepped in. Lucius took a step back and met the countess's gaze squarely. He refused to be blamed for a scene he had no part in creating. Lady Harrowden raised an eyebrow and walked forward, leaning heavily on her cane until she came to her seat.

"Rebecca, you may leave us now," she said with a wave of her hand.

Miss Woodsley's face was red, showing her to possess at least some sensibility. Lucius had begun to think she had none. She was certainly more forward than mere innocence could account for.

When he and Lady Harrowden were alone, he sat on the chair at her side, hoping he would not be called upon to explain what she had just witnessed. "I came to tell you that I found an accountant, who will be discreet—a Mr. Samuel Abbott in the village—but he is not available until a week from now."

Lucius leaned on the armrest and turned so he could see Lady Harrowden's face. "What is an even greater advantage to this particular choice is that his father worked with your husband for a time until Mr. Abbott, Sr. removed to Bath for his wife's health. After Mr. Abbott Jr.'s parents both died, he moved back to Woolmer Green. The book-keeper said he still has his father's notes tied up in bundles, and he will ask his permission to see what information remains on Harrowden. If a copy of the accounts is still there, as he thinks it will be, Mr. Abbott will be able to examine what percentage of your widow's portion is being used to cover estate expenses."

He added, "You might be interested to know that your nephew's accountant is not highly regarded by his peers. Even the bookkeeper who met with me yesterday was able to tell me that."

Lady Harrowden nodded as if she expected such a thing. "Abbott. I know the name. He worked for my husband before my nephew threw him off in favor of Mr. Chancey, saying the man came highly recommended. That may very well be true, but it is only since he took over the estate's accounts that there seems to be very little from my income to cover my own expenses. It is a shame Mr. Abbott cannot have access to all of Harrowden's accounts like he once did."

Lucius was only waiting for the word, and Lady Harrowden gave it decisively. "Very well. Bring him to me as soon as you may." She eyed him with displeasure, and he knew what was coming next. "And now perhaps you can tell me what designs you have on my ward."

"To keep her at arm's length," Lucius responded, leaning back in his seat again and crossing his legs.

"So her thirty-thousand pounds is not attractive enough for you?" Lady Harrowden gave him a disbelieving look.

"No," he answered baldly. "I have enough for my own means and would not sell myself as cheaply as that." Belatedly, he realized how it must reflect on her ward, and added, "I beg your pardon, but I must not give it to you wrapped in clean linen."

Lady Harrowden kept an eagle eye on him. "I saw you growing cozy in the inn with Miss Lockhart. Perhaps it is she who captures your fancy."

"I have no aims for matrimony at present," Lucius returned, "and I do not propose to invite you into my confidence when I do." He stood, anxious to be gone. "I will send a note when Mr. Abbott might be spared to come and discuss your accounts."

"Very well," Lady Harrowden said, dismissing him with an irritable gesture. He did not know how Miss Lockhart could live with her.

~

THE TWELFTH NIGHT ball was the next day, and near midnight, Selena was still sewing the last bit of silver trim on the bodice of her steel-blue dress—a color the shopkeeper called Mexican. He assured her it was the latest fashion, and it had certainly been many years since she had worn that. The fabric was pretty enough to make up for the fact that it was simply made.

Selena glanced at her pile of remaining trim on the small table and wondered if she should sew it into the hem. She had ordered enough of it, although she hadn't been sure if she would have the time. It would probably take another hour, but it would give an elegant touch to the dress she couldn't resist. The corner of her lips turned up. It would feel so *good* to wear something beautiful again.

Selena turned the dress, allowing the bodice to drop to the floor and the skirt to spread over her lap. She gathered the skirt and looked at it closely. It seemed as though the hem in one part had not been properly sewn, and as she examined it, she picked up the tallow candle and held it closer so she could see the stitching more accurately in the dim light.

A sudden sense of dread shot over her when she realized the tallow dish was tilted, and she looked down on the floor where melted wax pooled on the right side of the bodice.

"Oh!" Selena set the candle down rapidly, taking care not to spill more wax. She flipped the dress so that the bodice was once again in her hands and stared in horror at the melted wax that had left a dark stain on the fabric.

Hurrying to her trunk, she pulled out some old cloths she kept in there and tried to rub at the wax to remove the excess, but if anything, it only made it worse. Selena wracked her brain frantically for a solution. With the ball the very next day, Selena had neither the means to acquire a new dress nor the time to sew one.

The fatigue of the past few days of sewing in all her spare time oppressed her like a weight, and Selena laid the dress on her bed. Her fists clenched, she strode to the mantel of the chimney and grabbed it with both hands then pounded her fists on top of it. The tears did not stop flowing.

What do I do now? She had assured Lady Harrowden she knew how to dress and carry herself, that she would not put the countess to shame. And she had wanted to prove to Sir Lucius...

Selena breathed out and walked over to the bed, struggling for a solution. She squinted at the stain, willing her brain to accept the catastrophe and turn it to good account. *What can I do? What can I do?*

The wax had fallen on one side of the bodice and could not be covered up in any symmetrical way. There was not enough fabric left for an entire new bodice. But as her eyes blurred over with tears again, the stain seemed to take shape and resemble a flower. Selena blinked her eyes then drew in her breath.

That was what she could do. She could embroider something to cover the wax.

She dried her eyes and assessed the damage more carefully. The dress itself was done. True, she would not have time to add the trim on the bottom, but that was not the most pressing need. However, if she were going to turn the stain to good account by creating a flower design, she would have to start immediately. It was already growing late, and tomorrow's time belonged to Lady Harrowden and Rebecca, both of whom would likely keep her running around all day.

Selena selected the embroidery threads in a color that would set off the blue cambric—a matching blue, gold, white, and green. The easiest thing would be to embroider a peony with a small leaf and stem, and to have the stem trail down to cover the dripping wax that led to the high waist. True, it was not in fashion to have something embroidered only on one side, and it would probably look strange to have a stem embroidered down into the ribboned seam. But Selena could not allow defeat and wear one of her old gowns. She refused to let Sir Lucius see her in a dowdy old dress, and she would not give Rebecca the satisfaction of thinking she had no taste.

Pinching her lips with determination, Selena lay the threads before her on the small table and imagined the design, testing the size with her fingers, so she could produce it on the dress without an error. Perhaps it was the sin of pride that made her want to rise above her station and let people know she had not been raised to the role of a servant.

Selena threaded a needle. If she was going to be a companion, and a governess, she had better go about the idea of service wholeheartedly. However, it was unthinkable that she appear as some gauche bumpkin at the most elegant ball in the neighborhood. She would not give Mrs. Holbeck further cause to think ill of her.

It was not until nearly three o'clock in the morning that she was able to put away her needle. The candle had guttered, and Selena'd had to light a new one. The fire in her room had died down, and she didn't dare ask anyone to come and revive it. When she slipped into bed, it was some time before she could thaw enough to fall asleep, and the morning rays were not kind to her when they slipped between the curtains and lit the dimness of her bedroom.

"You do not look well, Selena." The countess studied her face more closely than Selena would have liked when she came to Lady Harrowden's bedroom with her correspondence. "You will have to do something about your appearance if we are to attend the ball tonight. You have not been seeing properly to your hair since you've arrived and must take better care to have it suitably done."

The injustice of Lady Harrowden's comment stung. "I would do so, my lady. But the maid always seems to have something more important to do. I do not feel it is my place to demand it, especially as she is carrying out the bidding of Lord Harrowden."

"So Richard is behind this, is he?" Lady Harrowden took the letters from Selena and glanced at the names. "I told him when he turned off two of our servants that there would not be enough to maintain his household, but he did not listen."

The countess spoke under her breath. "I suppose he has run through the money and does not have the means to pay for the servants. Never mind. I will speak to my maid and see that she attends to you tonight. What about Rebecca? Does she have all she needs?"

Selena smiled stiffly. "Her maid seems to get everyone below stairs to do her bidding, which is an impressive feat. I believe Rebecca is perfectly attended to."

Lady Harrowden threw off the covers and began to stand, and Selena went to assist her. "I suppose my nephew would not dare deprive Rebecca of anything, considering she has a great deal of money. He will want to be on the best terms with her."

"I believe you are right." Selena knew it would be improper to ask the countess about her reference to the earl squandering his money, but she was curious to know more. Would she have a place here for much longer?

Selena assisted Lady Harrowden, who was still stiff from her fall, over to the vanity table. As the countess sat, she bid Selena to ring the bell and have Morgan come, which she did. Lady Harrowden stared closely at Selena's reflection in the looking glass.

"Your eyes are red. You really do not look at all well." Lady Harrowden shifted the comb and powders on the table restlessly.

Selena managed a smile. "I assure you, I am quite well. It is merely that I was trying to finish my dress for tonight and did not do so until very late. You need have no fear for me."

When Selena left Lady Harrowden in Mrs. Morgan's hands, she was called to Rebecca's side to deal with the Great Tragedy. The silk slippers Rebecca had bought to accompany her ball gown—that she had thoughtlessly placed near the water pitcher—had been stained with water that had splashed over the edge of the bowl. Selena, weary to the bone, mustered all her courage to keep a cheerful face and convince

Rebecca that the champagne-colored slippers that had never been worn would do very well, and there was no need to rush off to town in hopes of finding something suitable.

The day was spent running between the countess and her ward, fetching forgotten items, soothing small irritations, and entertaining both a girl impatient for the evening to start and an older woman spouting gloomy predictions about how the weather would prohibit them from setting out. By the time they were ready to dress for the evening, Selena was worn through.

True to her word, Lady Harrowden sent Mrs. Morgan to dress Selena's hair. She was grateful for the gesture, because she was too tired to lift her hands to her head to attempt anything herself. Mrs. Morgan pulled her hair into a becoming series of twists behind Selena's head, and Selena remembered a string of white satin flowers she had that could be woven through the coiffure, and she couldn't help but smile at the final result.

She put small gold drops in her ears, the only ones her mother had managed to hide from the creditors. "Do you know if Rebecca is ready?"

"No, miss. But I will send someone to find out from Alice."

Selena was alone. She lingered to examine herself in the glass and was heartened by the picture she presented. The shade of blue she wore was becoming to her complexion and seemed to give back the rosy glow that had been lost from fatigue. The flower embroidered on one side was, well...a bit strange. She hoped it would not draw too much attention.

But never mind that. She had to look in on Rebecca.

As she approached Rebecca's room, a maid exited, out of breath. "Miss. I was coming to tell you that Miss Woodsley is not yet ready. Lady Harrowden is downstairs waiting."

Selena took in a quiet breath. "Go tell Lady Harrowden I will do what I can to hurry things along."

She was irritated with herself. She should have spoken with Alice to make sure Rebecca began dressing early, so she would be ready on time. Selena entered the room and saw that half of Rebecca's hair was still down.

She looked at the maid. "Why is Miss Woodsley still not ready?" She attempted to keep her tone even, but her fatigue made it nearly impossible. It would not do to keep the countess waiting, nor would it be good to arrive at the party long after they were expected.

Alice lost some of her usual assurance for an upper servant, her fingers faltering for a moment. "I had many errands to run to prepare for tonight. And when we did begin the *toilette*—"

"*Aye!*" Rebecca pulled the strand of hair from her maid's hands. "Never mind that. The party is not likely to start so soon, and we do not wish to be in advance. There is nothing worse than being the first one to a party."

"We are not likely to be first." Selena looked at the clock on the mantel. "It is nearing eight o'clock. The invitation was for seven o'clock, you are not finished dressing, and we still have to have the horses hitched to the carriage before we may be on our way. I will see to Lady Harrowden's needs, but I urge you most earnestly to be ready as quickly as possible."

Selena marched out the door, caught between harried and irritated. While Rebecca could appear to have a docile manner to people like the countess and Mrs. Holbeck, she was not exactly compliant. Well, at least Lord Harrowden was not in her room.

Selena found Lady Harrowden sitting in the chair, her mouth drawn down in extreme displeasure. "How long do you intend to keep me waiting?" she said.

"I—"

Selena could not finish her sentence because Lord Harrowden entered the room. He was dressed in a stiff new coat with a spotted scarf at his throat, and a Pompadour waistcoat, which seemed chosen to fit Rebecca's dress. The colorful array was partially concealed by a cape, mercifully, but that would be removed at the ball.

"I am having the carriage readied. When may we hope to leave?" His gaze drifted to Selena's bosom, and he stared at it strangely. "What is that on your dress?"

All the preparations Selena had been orchestrating in order to leave on time were suddenly of little significance as heat stole up her cheeks. She was at once very aware of her dress and ready to sink into the ground with shame. If she could not even leave her own house without comments about her unusual embroidered flower, how was she likely to fare when she got to the ball?

"This is all the rage where I come from," Selena retorted. She lifted her chin, but the whole effect was ruined by her deep blush.

"Well, you don't come from London, where no one would be caught wearing that," he said unkindly. "I suppose it does not matter for a country ball. I shall see to the horses. Are we ready to set out?"

"Do not have them readied just yet, my lord. Miss Woodsley is still dressing, and I fear it will be a while." Selena turned to the countess, who was now examining the strange design on her bodice more closely. "May I bring you your glass of sherry, my lady?"

The distraction proved to be enough, and Lady Harrowden lifted her eyes and nodded.

"You may bring mine as well," Lord Harrowden said.

Selena closed her mouth in a tight line and went over to do as he bid. How it chafed to serve one such as he. When she took this position, she was supposed to be just a companion to Lady Harrowden. How did her duties now extend to Lord Harrowden and an impertinent sixteen-year-old? But what could she do? She was completely at their mercy.

As she handed both Lord and Lady Harrowden their glasses of sherry, she decided to go up and see how she might hurry Rebecca along. The thought of climbing the steps yet again was exhausting, but she must be resolute. "My lady, I shall just—"

To Selena's shock, the door opened and Rebecca walked through it, her *toilette* completed in what could only be described as record time. Her hair was made up so elegantly that, combined with the exposed nature of her gown, she looked older than one who had been out for several Seasons. Selena stared at Rebecca in apprehension, but she was spared from having to speak.

"What is that you're wearing, girl? Why are you not wearing the dress I chose for you?" Lady Harrowden sputtered. Selena turned to stare at Lady Harrowden. So this was *not* the dress the countess had approved. Lady Harrowden pierced Selena with an angry glare. "Why did you not make sure she wore the dress I chose? She is naked in that gown."

"My lady, I—" Selena could get no further.

"*I* chose it for her," Lord Harrowden said. "You do not know what the latest fashion is, but I've just returned from several years in London. With a few tips from me, Miss Woodsley shall be up to snuff. Wait and see."

"You," Lady Harrowden derided, "are a Bartholomew baby. And you're making my ward out to be a bit of muslin. Rebecca, go up and choose a spencer to cover that bodice. We don't have time for anything else."

Immediate tears sprang to Rebecca's eyes, and she stomped her foot. "No!"

"Go," ordered Lady Harrowden. "Or you will stay home all together."

Rebecca's chest heaved, as she weighed her options for what seemed an interminable time. At last she flounced from the room.

🦋 14 🦋

AFTER DEPOSITING his phaeton with Holbeck's undergroom, Lucius made his way to the house, dressed in his best evening finery. The fact that he was early did not escape his sister's notice.

"Lucius," she exclaimed. "Perhaps we need not despair of you yet. I see your family affections bring you here, and I am gratified."

"Yes, I suppose if I am going to be here, I may as well make myself useful. Where are Philippa and George?" He searched the room, ostensibly looking for them, but hoping to catch sight of Miss Lockhart. He was anxious to see her after his visit to Harrowden two days ago had produced nothing better than a run-in with Miss Woodsley.

"I haven't seen them at all this past hour," Maria said. Lucius studied his sister more closely. She looked harried.

"I can only trust that Philippa is finally getting dressed after debating an excessive amount of time over which of the two ball gowns she should wear when we had already decided on the pink," Maria said. "George was taking a great interest in the card tables being set up, which is worrisome." She shot Lucius a pessimistic glance. "You don't happen to know the state of his quarterly allowance do you?"

"I know it was paid, and it will not be paid again until the quarter is over. He will need to take care, or he will be living frugally," Lucius replied.

Maria pursed her lips. "Yes, and I fear he will be living frugally *here*, for he cannot abide to live with Mother cosseting him at every turn, and you refuse to take too much of a hand in his upbringing." She frowned at Lucius. "Why he doesn't have more sense, I cannot explain. I know I don't lack any."

No, but you lack imagination, Lucius thought—which was almost a greater flaw. "George will come about eventually," he said and opened the door so she could precede him into the drawing room. Servants were setting up refreshments on long tables draped with white cloth and lighting the candles in the chandeliers. The candles, reflected on the windowpanes, created a warm glow. George entered, looking particularly dashing in a discreet, well-fit coat and fine pale breeches.

"You clean up nicely, George. Where did you have that coat made?" Lucius had not displayed such good taste when he was George's age. In fact, he still did not show to advantage next to his younger brother. He did not care enough to wear anything uncomfortable.

"This?" George said. "I had it made by a tailor in Oxford. He is reputed to be as good as Schultz. And I learned how to tie the ornamental." He lifted his chin, showing his perfectly tied cravat. "As you can see, I have quite the hand. It has only taken me three tries." He grinned.

"If only you had such a light touch with cattle," Lucius said.

"I only overturned once, and you refuse to let it go," George protested with a laugh.

Maria came up to them, wringing her hands. "The guests will be arriving shortly, and the ones staying here have already come down. Can one of you please go find Philippa?"

"Not I," George said. "I have promised to get the pair of cards and dice that are in my room." He walked off in brisk strides without a backward glance.

Maria was looking at Lucius expectantly, and he exhaled. "I will fetch Philippa. I assume she's in the yellow room?"

Maria nodded, her eyes widening at the thud of the front door knocker. "Hurry. She ought to be standing in the receiving line with me, and—oh, Charles. There you are. Lucius is going to fetch Philippa. You and I must—"

Holbeck bore down on his wife, his expression intent. "Maria, I just saw Downing. What in the world brought you to invite him—"

Maria hissed in exasperation. "He knows Mr. Gregson from London. Look, Lucius is here."

Holbeck became aware of his surroundings and gave a stiff nod. "Evening, Lucius." He took his wife by the elbow and led her to the entrance, and Lucius left to find his younger sister.

Philippa was coming out of her room when Lucius turned onto the upstairs corridor where her bedroom was. She stopped short and flashed a guilty look. "Am I late? I was just coming down."

"Yes. Maria is asking for you. People are already arriving." Lucius bent and kissed her cheek. "You look very nice for your first ball."

Philippa flushed. "Do you really think so? I had the hardest time deciding between two dresses."

"Yes, Maria told me."

"I know it was vexing to her, but I couldn't help it," Philippa said. "She has clearly forgotten what it's like to attend one's first ball."

"Without a doubt. Age does that to one," Lucius replied, causing Philippa to giggle. He took her by the elbow and steered her down the stairs. "Come along. If I don't convey you with all speed to Maria, there is no telling what she will do. Between you and George, she is half-distracted."

Philippa opened her mouth to retort as they approached the front entrance, but Lucius was too quick. "Maria, she was just on her way down," he said, before leaving Philippa with a small wink. If he could escape Philippa's lengthy explanation of how unjust Maria was, his evening would already prove to be halfway successful.

Lucius melted into the throng of guests mingling in the sideroom devoted to gaming tables. Standing with George was another gentleman, roughly the age of Lucius himself. He was not local, and although they had not met in London, it was fairly obvious from the faint sneer and the quality of his tailoring that he mixed with the best circles.

"This is Maria and Charles's guest, Mr. Downing," George said. "He is visiting from London for the holidays, and he has just arrived."

Lucius greeted him with a nod. "How were the roads?" *So this is the fellow Holbeck finds objectionable? I wonder why.*

"They were passable everywhere but for that stretch of woods through Hatfield," Downing said. "The Bear's Tooth Inn in Welwyn said I should be able to get through, so we attempted it. Your sister promised a most delightful ball if I could arrange to be here on time, and I remembered that Gregson was from the area, who is a particular friend of mine. I wrote to let him know I would be here."

Out of politeness, Lucius asked, "Has your acquaintance with the Holbecks been of long date?"

"A few years," Downing replied, just as politely. "We have some political dealings together." Both men turned to watch the entrance where newly arrived gentlemen poured into the room.

"The card room is filling up as quickly as the ballroom." Lucius gave a soft chuckle. Maria's plans might be foiled by her own husband's love of the dice if all the eligible bachelors were at the gambling tables. "I wonder if we'll be able to encourage any of the men to leave it."

"I promised Maria I would dance," George said, raising his eyes to the heavens. "I must, I suppose, but I'd rather be in here."

A feeling Lucius could sympathize with, although he found himself looking out into the ballroom frequently for a glimpse of Miss Lockhart. He generally only danced out of duty, but he wondered what it would be like to have her in his arms. Her waist was small, and his hand would settle nicely on it.

Downing swallowed the contents of his glass. "No dancing for me. I much prefer the cards. Less of a risk." He gave a short laugh. "Once I nearly got entangled, and I've since steered clear. I have money and mistress enough not to stumble into the parson's mousetrap."

George looked up from fingering his unbroken deck of cards and met Lucius's gaze. His eyes were full of mockery, which heartened Lucius. If his brother found Downing's affectations to be too much, there was hope for him yet.

George turned his attention back to Downing, his expression the picture of innocence. "Is that so, sir? Pray tell, what quantity of mistress is sufficient? I'm curious."

Lucius turned away before he might betray himself with a laugh.

Leaving the card room, he wandered into the ballroom as guests began to pour into it. He was feeling a bit at odds—it wasn't like him to be so restless. More than one young lady eyed him hopefully, and he knew if he did not find an occupation quickly, he would be expected to play court to several of them.

Across the ballroom, Miss Lockhart walked through the double doorway, stopping him in his tracks. She held Lady Harrowden by the elbow and pivoted back to speak a few words to Miss Woodsley. The blue tones of Miss Lockhart's dress were modish, and they set off her creamy skin to perfection. Her hair was twisted up in an elegant style with braids that criss-crossed and tiny white flowers that wove through the chignon when she turned. Her dress molded her slender figure, and the capped sleeves revealed just a hint of that smooth skin next to her long gloves. He closed his eyes, wondering if he had been bewitched. In that moment, Lucius thought he had never before laid eyes on a more desirable woman.

Miss Lockhart had not seen him, and she wasn't searching the room for anyone. She bent her head down to listen to Lady Harrowden. *She isn't looking for me.*

He took a step forward and noticed she was not smiling. Had Miss Woodsley been tiresome?—or perhaps it was Lady Harrowden who caused her grief? His gaze shot to Lord Harrowden, standing behind the countess, who was now engaging Miss Woodsley in what looked like a flirtation. Most likely *he* was the annoyance, if there was one.

Lucius knew it was his duty to greet the Harrowdens, but he was reluctant to do so, preferring to claim conversation with Miss Lockhart alone. He accepted a glass of punch from a servant who was passing a tray and stood watching Miss Lockhart, ready to step in if she should be freed from the conversation of those around her.

∿

SELENA WAS ready to drop from fatigue, and the evening had not yet begun. There were candles in every window of the Holbeck residence as they arrived, making it so that, grand as it was, it resembled a house in a fairytale. Inside, greenery was draped along the railings, and it perfumed the house with a festive scent, mixing with the various colognes of people coming in from the cold, and the tantalizing spices wafting by as servants brought platters from the kitchen. There was a variety of dishes spread on some tables and bowls of punch on others. As people paraded before Selena, the older men in brightly-colored silk jackets, and the younger men in more discreet colors, the women arrayed in all their finery, she thought London could not boast a more extravagant party.

She turned impulsively to say as much to Lady Harrowden but saw that the countess seemed overcome by the noise and the crowds. Lord Harrowden was leaning in close to Rebecca, his face lit with amusement over some private joke he was whispering in her ear.

Selena took the countess by the elbow. "My lady, do let me bring you over to the corner where there must be a bit more air. Rebecca, why don't you follow us?"

Instead of answering, Rebecca smiled up at Lord Harrowden. "No one will mind if you bring me to have a lemonade, will they?" She looked at Selena. "It could hardly be inappropriate since we are nearly like cousins."

Selena opened her mouth to object, but Lord Harrowden gave her a smirk and walked away with Rebecca on his arm. She turned to see if Lady Harrowden had noticed what had happened, but the countess's attention was drawn toward the musicians who were setting up.

It would not do to allow Rebecca to wander off in such a willful and flirtatious manner, but Selena couldn't very well leave Lady Harrowden without assistance. She would simply have to settle her in a chair, then follow Rebecca and bring her back by force. This was getting ridiculous. Not only would the girl disgrace herself, but Selena would never get another position again. Everyone would see how ill-equipped she was to instill in her charge even the most basic training in decorum.

Lady Harrowden allowed Selena to lead her over to the corner where there was a draft of fresh air sweeping across it. An older woman sat there, whom Lady Harrowden greeted with real pleasure.

Selena thought this a propitious moment to slip away and retrieve her charge. "My lady, I believe I should seek out Rebecca and keep an eye on her. Will you allow me to stay near her if I come to you regularly to see if you need anything?"

Lady Harrowden just waved her hand. "Yes. Go on."

Selena walked with quick steps across the increasingly crowded room to where Rebecca was. Halfway across the floor, she caught sight of Sir Lucius, and her breath caught in her throat. Handsome even when carelessly dressed—when formally attired, Sir Lucius was a nonpareil. His head was down, revealing thick dark hair, and he stood very close in conversation with a young woman, whose back was to Selena. At the sight, she suffered a pang that was very like jealousy. *You gudgeon! As if you have a chance with Sir Lucius. Besides, you are here as a companion, not a guest.*

The woman turned to the profile, and Selena's lips crept up into a smile, as if by their own will. It was Philippa! This was not another contender for his attention; it was his sister. Sir Lucius glanced up at that moment and caught sight of Selena's smile. He looked her straight in the eyes as he smiled in return, gave a slight bow, then leaned back down to listen to whatever interesting tale Philippa was pouring into his ear. Within a few seconds, he glanced back at Selena. She turned quickly to hide the flash of joy that second look gave her.

Selena went to Rebecca, who was displaying all her charms under the attentions of an impeccably-dressed young gentleman. His coat was the color of bordeaux and his cream breeches revealed a set of muscular thighs. His blond curls had a windswept look that didn't seem to move when his head did. A Corinthian of Society if ever there was one. Selena looked around in confusion. *Where had Lord Harrowden gone, and how could he leave Rebecca alone?*

She stepped in front of them. "Good evening, sir. I am afraid Miss Woodsley is wanted elsewhere."

The Corinthian bowed, and Selena pulled Rebecca away with a slight pressure on her arm, but they had only taken a few steps when Rebecca stretched out her hands in a different direction. Lord Harrowden was heading their way, holding a glass of champagne.

"This is to fortify you for our dance," he said, extending the glass.

Selena put up her hand in protest. "My lord, I wish you would not leave Miss Woodsley alone at the mercy of strange men. *Or* think it permissible that she drink champagne."

"Ah, but I most particularly put her in charge of Gregson—a friend of mine in the neighborhood. I knew he would take good care of her." He turned to Rebecca. "And did he not?"

Rebecca giggled. "He was most attentive. I have promised him a dance later."

"You really should not have—" Selena began.

Lord Harrowden tucked Rebecca's arm in his elbow. "So you see, Miss Lockhart. All is well. And now, Miss Woodsley and I shall take a turn about the room." He swallowed the champagne in one gulp and set his glass on the tray of a passing servant before leading her to a group of gentlemen, where he presented Rebecca.

Selena did not see how she could stop her charge from displaying herself as a most determined flirt, and her fatigue from a sleepless night and a day of running errands, one after another, overpowered her. Sir Lucius chose that moment to cross the floor.

"Miss Lockhart, I..." His gaze dropped to the embroidered flower on her bodice, and his words trailed away. Selena closed her lips, and met his gaze, feeling the heat of a deep blush steal over her.

"A new fashion, Miss Lockhart?" Sir Lucius asked softly. She lifted her chin, though it trembled slightly.

His gaze softened when he saw her expression, and he abandoned his teasing tone. "You chose well your color, Miss Lockhart. It brings a bloom to your cheeks. You are *very* lovely."

Selena did not know how to respond, or even if she *should* accept such pointed compliments from Sir Lucius when she was merely a companion. She grasped at conversation. "Your sister is in high looks. Is she enjoying her first ball? It *is* her first ball, is it not?"

"It is, and she is enjoying it immensely." He nodded in satisfaction as his sister sat with the other young ladies her age. "And thankfully, I have not had to chase anyone away yet." He turned and pointed. "My brother George is over there. You have met, have you not? He's been sent down from Oxford, so I believe we will be seeing quite a bit of him."

"I see," she said, resisting the smile that came from his wry tone—a tone she was beginning to find oddly comforting.

They stood side by side watching the crowd, and Selena could feel warmth emanating from Sir Lucius's solid arm. In the soothing silence that followed, she had a better chance to look George over than she'd had at the inn. He was a slimmer version of Sir Lucius and, with his more even features, was objectively the more handsome of the two. He was young but had probably already broken some hearts. However, Selena found Sir Lucius's rugged build and lined face more appealing.

Sir Lucius glanced back at Philippa, and his face took on a severe expression.

Selena asked, "What is it?"

"I see Gregson has found his way to my sister," he said, and Selena saw the same gentleman in the bordeaux coat that Lord Harrowden had chosen to chaperone Rebecca. Sir Lucius did not take his eyes off his sister. "He ought to know better, especially since I warned him."

Selena could understand his concern. "Yes, he was paying court to Miss Woodsley as well. He seems determined to flirt with pretty young girls."

"Or rich ones," Sir Lucius said.

"He can be quite charming—and persistent," Selena said. "It might not be easy for your sister to refuse him. I know Rebecca could not."

"Miss Woodsley does not appear to be able to say no to anything," Sir Lucius said, turning his gaze back to Selena, his eyes flashing a droll look she could not help but respond to.

"Miss Woodsley is only sixteen. Perhaps she is simply very young and inexperienced and..." Selena did not really believe what she was saying. "I fear success of this nature goes to her head."

"Philippa is only seventeen and might be tempted by the same thing. However, as you will shortly see, she will soon give Gregson the go-by." Sir Lucius turned expectantly back in his sister's direction, but instead of tossing off an unwelcome suitor, she laughed and blushed rosily as Gregson plucked a drink off a passing tray and presented it to her with a bow.

"The devil," Sir Lucius muttered, striding toward them.

Selena bit her lip and hoped for his sister's sake it would not create a scene that drew the attention of busy-bodies, of which she had already spotted a few. Mrs. Holbeck came to stand at her side, her gaze also fixed on Philippa.

"It seems you are finding your own entertainment despite being a companion, Miss Lockhart," Mrs. Holbeck said. "You arrived with Lord Harrowden, and now I see you talking to my brother."

Mrs. Holbeck turned as Rebecca swung by them, laughing loudly with Lord Harrowden during one of the country dances. "I believe my brother is at the stage of his life where he will be seeking a wife. He has all but said as much."

Selena did not know what response was expected, so she remained silent. Mrs. Holbeck faced her squarely, forcing Selena to meet her gaze. "I believe you will do well to spend *less* time in my brother's company and more time training your ward. He is of too generous a nature to let you know he is not interested in you."

She could not allow Mrs. Holbeck to continue with her insinuations that Selena was *casting her net*. "I assure you, I am not seeking his interest."

Mrs. Holbeck went on, as if Selena had not spoken. Her gaze was trained on Rebecca as she changed partners and executed a perfect figure on the dance floor. "I believe Lucius has set his sights on someone with more to offer."

Selena turned her gaze to Rebecca as well. She was looking very grown-up and attractive. If someone did not know what she was capable of, she might understand the appeal. But Sir Lucius *knew*!

Mrs. Holbeck turned back and rested her hand on Selena's arm. "Do what you came for and continue to teach propriety to Miss Woodsley, who still has much to learn. If you do, I'll see that you get a good recommendation when you leave Woolmer Green." She patted Selena's arm and gave a patronizing smile before leaving.

❧ 15 ❧

SELENA CLENCHED her teeth and tried to control her breathing to hide the surge of rage that had come over her. She moved blindly in the direction of the retiring room, hoping for some moments of peace after the humiliating lecture she'd received from Mrs. Holbeck, who apparently thought Selena was at the ball with the intention of snagging the greatest matrimonial prize the county had to offer. *Ha!* As if life had not taught her better than that. She would not be so foolish again.

What was particularly misery-inducing was the fact that there was a grain of truth to Mrs. Holbeck's insinuations. Selena *did* find Sir Lucius attractive, and she liked how she felt in his presence—both restful and...and alive, if such a thing were possible.

She liked the crease in the middle of his forehead and the severity of his mouth, which fit his sardonic disposition so well. And she liked his irony, particularly when he included her in the joke. Not even her former fiancé had respected her intelligence enough to do that. She liked Lucius's straight hair, the color of which was of such a glistening dark brown, it seemed to hold hints of silver. Most of all, Selena liked the sudden smile when it flashed across his face. It should have been ill-fitting for such a cynical man, but instead it called to her like a beacon of happiness.

And for some inexplicable reason, Sir Lucius seemed to care for her. He lost no opportunity to seek her out, and she felt protected and cherished when he was near. That was perhaps the worst of all. It led her to hope.

"Where did that girl run off to?" Lady Harrowden's voice nearby plucked Selena out of her thoughts and stopped her in her tracks on the way to the retiring room. She had forgotten all about Lady Harrowden in her distress and now counted herself lucky that the countess seemed to think she had walked this way with the intent of returning to her side.

When Lady Harrowden's question penetrated, Selena stopped short, and she became aware of her surroundings. She had completely forgotten about Rebecca, too. She searched the room with quickened breath. What mischief could the girl have gotten into in that short time?

Selena nodded toward the dance floor. "Ah. There she is, my lady. She is dancing with Mr. Gregson it appears. Though I told her not to."

After a brief pause where Lady Harrowden watched the couple but did not respond, Selena took the empty chair at her side and decided to be straightforward. Perhaps she might receive some help. "Rebecca is not very pliable. In fact, I fear she cannot be moved to do anything she doesn't want to do, despite being only sixteen. I hope we need not fear her doing something scandalous."

"I should certainly hope not." Lady Harrowden reared back with a sharp look at Selena. "This is why she has a governess to look after her. It is your responsibility to see that she comes to no harm. It shouldn't be that difficult. You are her elder by several years, after all."

Selena kept her eyes trained on Rebecca as she danced, carrying on a lively, flirtatious conversation. Well, that would be the last time she tried honesty. She was not sure if she could continue to hold her peace after many more tongue-lashings such as that, however. Could one simply leave a post because it was too demanding? Selena had to admit the sober truth. No. One could not, not when she was as poor as Selena.

Another lady approached the countess to speak with her, and Selena stood. "I will see to Rebecca, my lady."

She made it partway through the throng of people when she felt a hand on her arm. Selena looked up and was overcome with relief—then guilt, thanks to Mrs. Holbeck—to see Sir Lucius. No, she could not think of him as *home*. She could not think of him at all. He was above her in station and wealth, and she may as well be a scullery maid for all the chance she had at earning his regard. Selena attempted a smile, which was pained, and Sir Lucius studied her intently with a slight frown.

"I was going to try to retrieve Miss Woodsley before the next set begins," Selena explained. "She is dancing with Mr. Gregson, although I did not recommend such a course of action, and even removed her from his presence."

"Troublesome chit," Sir Lucius said, his eyes still searching her face as if there was more. Sir Lucius glanced in Rebecca's direction. "Apparently there are two determined upon ignoring advice because I had a like conversation with Gregson. Come, I will go with you." Sir Lucius took Selena's hand and put it on his arm.

As much as Selena tried to remain unaffected by his attention, it was a fortifying experience not to admonish a silly girl to see reason all on one's own, especially a girl who was determined not to listen. The music came to an end as they reached the couple.

Sir Lucius put his hand on Gregson's shoulder. "You have a short memory."

Gregson whirled around. "What?" Then understanding dawned. "No, really, Sir Lucius. This is too much. I did not think your disapproval extended to dancing with every maiden at the ball."

"It does if Miss Lockhart does not countenance such an action." Sir Lucius turned to Rebecca. "I recommend you to follow her example and not thwart her authority every chance you get."

Rebecca scowled, and Selena wondered if, perhaps, the magic of Sir Lucius's charm had worn off on the girl. That would be more than she could have hoped for. Selena turned as Sir Lucius's brother joined their party.

George bowed before Selena and Rebecca, then turned to Mr.

Gregson. "I believe someone is waiting for you in the card room for the game you promised?" He smiled at Rebecca. "If you've quite finished with your dance." She smiled back at him, her scowl magically erased, and Sir Lucius exchanged a wary look with Selena.

Turning back to Mr. Gregson, George added, "I understand the enticement of such a partner, but Downing said he's waited for you long enough."

Mr. Gregson laughed, but Selena's blood had turned to ice. "Mr. Downing?" she asked, her voice little more than a whisper.

Mr. Gregson heard her and turned from George with a smile still on his lips. "Matthew Downing. A friend from London I had the pleasure of running into here. Do you know him?" He studied her curiously, and Selena couldn't entirely hide her dismay, although she tried with everything that was in her.

"I...I do not know. I think not," she said. Sir Lucius's eyes were on her, and although she did not dare to meet his gaze, she could sense his curiosity. For once, she did not want his kind look. She did not want to see it turn to pity—or disgust, for engagements were rarely broken without just cause.

George and Mr. Gregson walked off toward the card room, leaving Selena alone with Rebecca and Sir Lucius.

"Who am I to dance with now?" Rebecca said. "You've turned off all my dance partners. It is most unfair."

Philippa came through the main entryway on the arm of Lord Harrowden, and Selena glanced at Sir Lucius in time to see his jaw clench. This was another acquaintance he would not countenance for his sister and, as she knew all too well, he was right not to do so.

"There is Lord Harrowden," Rebecca said, standing on her toes. "Perhaps he will ask me to dance. Surely you can't object to that since he is my guardian's nephew." Rebecca was about to go to the earl when Selena put a restraining hand on her arm. She had to try her best to instill some sense of decorum while she could. While she still had a position.

"Can you not see that Lord Harrowden is walking with another lady? You cannot interrupt his conversation. You must wait until he approaches you." Selena spoke with as much authority as she possessed, but apparently Rebecca was immune to it.

"That is why you are still a spinster. You won't take a risk." Rebecca was about to walk off, but Sir Lucius's words had the ability to make her pause.

"And you, dear girl, will be known by all the world as fast beyond redemption. For the moment, only Miss Lockhart and I are aware of the extent of your folly, and the fact that we have kept it to ourselves is a kindness you do not deserve. However, if you continue in this vein, even we cannot save you from yourself. You will be so lost to decency you will not be able to show your head in Society. No one will welcome you. Trust me on this." Sir Lucius had spoken these quiet words near her ear, but there was no mistaking the threat in his voice.

He stepped back. "Now, if you'll both excuse me. I have no wish for my sister to remain in the company of someone I can only think of as..." Sir Lucius seemed to recollect himself, as he glanced at Rebecca and finished on a murmur. "Excuse me, Miss Lockhart."

Selena watched him walk over to his sister, gently take her hand from Lord Harrowden's arm and put it on his. It seemed he was rescuing one person after another this evening. What a tiresome ball it must be for him. She turned to Rebecca, expecting to see another calculating look—or to see her disappear altogether, having run off after some gentleman she had not yet had the benefit of flirting with. Instead, Rebecca's face was very red and her lip trembled.

Selena's gaze softened. She had to remember that Rebecca was still a girl. "Come. Let us walk over to the window and get some air." She put her arm through Rebecca's, and as they made their way across the room, Selena darted her eyes among the crowd, fearing to see the one face that would overset her more than any other. The crowd blended together, and she could not discern any distinguishable feature over another.

She led Rebecca to the alcove where she knew they would be revived from the fresh air pouring in over the sill—and where she could not be discovered by Mr. Downing. It seemed incredible that he was *here*, and she could only hope that she had misunderstood. Behind the curtain, Selena had a chance to calm her turbulent reflections and hide her emotions more neatly.

"Is what he said true?" Rebecca asked, her voice penetrating the near-darkness. "Could I lose my place in Society and not be received by anyone?"

Selena opened her fan and applied it to Rebecca. It was not just Selena's emotions that had been thrown into disorder. However, Rebecca's words brought hope. Perhaps the girl really did possess an ability to think through consequences.

"In a second," Selena warned her. "You can lose your reputation that fast. A reputation is a fragile thing in Society, and once lost in the eyes of the *ton*, it cannot be recovered. This is why I've been urging you toward being more circumspect in your dealings with gentlemen. There is a protocol a young lady must follow, and I know somewhere deep inside you must know it."

"I *don't* know it," protested Rebecca. "Margaret Shirly at the Paisely Seminary told me that without birth, only my fortune would succeed in winning me a husband, and what a shame it was that I could never tell whether a man truly liked me, or whether it was my fortune he wanted. She advised me that the only way I could know for sure was to choose what man I wished to pursue and make him fall for me, which is what I set out to do."

"She is wrong," Selena said gently, wondering whether Margaret Shirly was equally as ignorant as Selena, or if it was a vicious plot to ruin a weak character. "The best path is to let yourself be guided by those who have more experience and let *us* chase off the fortune hunters. But first we have some work to do on training you in decorum and in a lady's accomplishments. Perhaps we can start work on that tomorrow."

Rebecca sniffed and wiped at her eyes. Selena had not seen the tears fall in the dim light. "I really did like Sir Lucius best of all, ever since I saw him in Brighton, walking with his mother on the Steyne. All the ladies there wanted to speak with him, and he was polite, but he never favored one woman over another. I thought Sir Lucius might favor me. Do you think *he* would show an interest in me if I were to behave more properly?"

Selena's heart beat painfully at the thought. She did not want to answer, but she had a responsibility to see Rebecca creditably married off. "I do not know, but I do not think it impossible. If you truly change, Rebecca—truly change on a heart level—*anything* can happen."

Even without her having been stretched to the point of exhaustion, not much more would be needed to seal the end to one of Selena's most depressing days ever. And then there was the threat that lurked. Matthew Downing. There could only be one, but surely not here. And even if it were *he*—the small amount she had eaten for dinner sat like lead in Selena's stomach—there was still hope their paths would not cross. She was, for the moment, well hidden behind the curtain of an alcove.

Selena wondered how she could convince Lady Harrowden and Rebecca to leave straight away. Her mind turned the possibilities over and found none that would work without telling Lady Harrowden all. But surely there were enough people to prevent their paths from crossing? And George said Matthew would not leave the card room...Selena came to a decision. She should be sitting in the corner beside the countess. That would be safe enough.

"Shall we—"

Her words were interrupted by a loud shriek and a movement beside her that was so frantic, Selena could not imagine what had come over Rebecca. Scream after scream pealed out, and Selena tried to make out what was happening in the dimness. Suddenly her vision was flooded with light. Rebecca had ripped open the curtain and stumbled through, clutching her dress and lifting it, shrieking and screaming in panic.

Selena snapped to attention. "Calm yourself," she urged as quietly as possible. The music had stopped and the entire ballroom stood transfixed as Rebecca continued to scream. "*Sh!*" Selena said. "Stop it. What is happening?"

"*Ooooh.* There is something clawing at me. Something bit me. Look. I have a scratch. There is a demon."

A movement caught the corner of Selena's eye, and she watched as a mouse scurried from the alcove along the wall. Rebecca must not know of this and be thrown into a greater panic if Selena hoped to avoid even more of a scene.

"Rebecca, enough! You must calm yourself," she adjured.

~

WHEN LUCIUS HAD PUT some distance between Philippa and Lord Harrowden, he began his scold. "Is this not precisely what I warned you about?"

"Lucius, you give me no credit," Philippa replied in a hushed voice, and he thought he detected hurt. "I could scarcely tell Lord Harrowden *no*—not when I had already danced with other men."

"You most certainly could," Lucius retorted. "It's what—"

The sound of piercing screams reached his ears, and he instinctively scanned the room looking for Miss Lockhart. It should have come as no surprise when he saw the curtain to one of the alcoves twitch open, with Miss Woodsley setting up such a racket as to stop everyone in their tracks. Miss Lockhart, at her side, was searching the sides of the room and her eyes were wide with what looked like fear. Lucius started forward and Philippa trailed quickly in his wake.

When Lucius reached them, Miss Lockhart was attempting to soothe her charge, but to no avail. Although Miss Woodsley had stopped screaming, she was lifting her skirt and looking at her ankles, exclaiming, "It must have been some rodent. How distressing. I don't feel safe anywhere in this house now."

Charles Holbeck moved in their direction, and as he passed the musicians, gestured for them to resume their music. His face was set in grim lines, and Lucius wondered if that would cool Maria's ardor about Miss Woodsley being an acceptable wife for him.

"Are you quite well?" he asked Miss Woodsley, darting a quick glance at Miss Lockhart. But Miss Woodsley only dissolved into tears.

"A mouse, I think," Miss Lockhart whispered. She put her arm around Miss Woodsley.

The room had not completely settled down to its usual din of conversation, and some of the men were still outside the card room where they had congregated when the commotion broke out. Lucius moved in front of them to cross paths with Mr. Holbeck and apprise him of what had happened. He came to an abrupt halt when he heard a voice call out, sharp with surprise.

"Selena!"

The voice came from the entrance to the cardroom, and Lucius turned quickly in that direction, his eyes widening in outrage. *Selena* was Miss Lockhart's Christian name. Who had dared to use it? Others turned toward the source as well, and Sir Lucius now saw it was Mr. Downing.

Miss Lockhart stood frozen, her back to Lucius. She had not yet shown any response to having been addressed. Lucius could see from her rigid posture that she was distressed. What connection did she have with Downing that he made free use of her Christian name? The answer fell on him like a weight when he remembered his conversation with Maria. Who else, besides family, would use her Christian name but her former fiancé?

Lucius moved closer to Miss Lockhart, stopping a couple feet away. He could not bring himself to break the silence. Miss Lockhart turned at last to face Downing. She was deathly pale, and her lips were resolutely shut. Downing dropped his gaze to the embroidered flower on Miss Lockhart's bodice, then looked at her.

"What are you wearing? Your sense of fashion appears to have suffered a decline." Downing laughed, and the sound echoed harshly, particularly so as the crowd was silent, all eyes trained on Downing and Miss Lockhart.

"I never thought to see you in Society again, even in such a small town as Woolmer Green," he continued. "But I see I was wrong. I suppose Society is more accepting than I had imagined."

Although Miss Lockhart looked lost and vulnerable—alone—she lifted her chin.

Brave girl. Lucius was holding his breath. Should he intervene? He hesitated. This was her battle, and to stand at her side might cause even more tongues to wag.

"Perhaps not everyone is as deeply prejudiced as you are, Mr. Downing," she answered in a firm voice. Her eyes flicked over Downing, and Lucius saw the disdain in them.

"Perhaps not everyone is as discerning," Downing retorted. "As for myself, I have a minimum standard to uphold, as you once knew—and agreed upon. That was why we thought ourselves to be well-suited." Downing looked around, but his eyes just as quickly snapped back to Miss Lockhart, a smile hovering on his lips that conveyed his scorn. "I must know. Whose guest are you at this party?"

Maria had heard the source of commotion and came to stand at their side. "She is no one's guest, Mr. Downing," she answered in a ringing voice. "She is Lady Harrowden's companion—and also governess to Miss Woodsley. I had not known you were acquainted."

Curse Maria's meddling, thought Lucius uncharitably. He knew very well she had orchestrated this. Holbeck's conscious look confirmed it.

Downing's eyes grew incredulous. "A companion-governess? Well, that explains your presence here, at least."

Miss Lockhart's chin fell a notch.

Lucius's gaze flitted back to Miss Lockhart, and he was troubled by a sense of agony at her predicament. The war raged within. If he stepped forward, it was as good as declaring himself, something he could not do. If he stood up for her, even from an altruism that was foreign to him, she would be one more person who laid her charge at his feet expecting more from him. He could not do it.

Downing then glanced at Miss Woodsley, who was, for once, quiet —submissive even. "I suppose it is no surprise that a charge of yours would screech in such an unholy way. It appears I am not as prejudiced as you seem to think, Selena. Or at least not shockingly so. What I am, however, is *discriminating*. Not that I ever regretted breaking things off when I did—" Downing stopped short as the rapt attention of the crowd finally succeeded in silencing him.

He gave a feeble laugh and went on in a more subdued tone. "This only shows I may trust my instinct, not that I ever doubted I might do so."

Philippa had come to stand beside Maria and was watching the interaction with a frown. She eyed Lucius reproachfully.

Downing transferred his gaze to Philippa at Maria's side, and his eyes flashed with interest. He inclined his head in her direction, and Lucius wanted to pummel him. All around them, the crowd listened still, waiting for more morsels of gossip to turn over at the breakfast table the next day. Miss Lockhart stood stiffly, her forehead and the top of her cheeks crimson.

Mr. Downing addressed the crowd. "I don't believe there is anything more to see here. Gregson, why don't we get back to our game?"

"You are the one who left it," Gregson replied, "and I can only think it was because you were on a losing streak. I am more than happy to resume."

Apart from a few glances Miss Lockhart's way, both pitying and malicious, the crowd began to form another set as the musicians put their bows to the strings and began a lively introduction. Mr. Downing paused on his way to the card room.

"Mrs. Holbeck, would you kindly present me to this charming creature?" He gave a small bow before Philippa.

Philippa answered before Lucius could step in. "I assure you, no introduction is necessary. Lucius, we were speaking, and I believe we had not finished?"

Any of the usual irritation Lucius might feel toward his family vanished in the pride he had in his younger sister at that moment. She had set Downing back in his place, the toad.

"No we have not finished. Come then."

Downing tightened his jaw before turning abruptly and entering the card room, and Lucius looked back at Miss Lockhart, who still stood frozen in solitude. The crowd cleared a wide berth around her. Not even Lady Harrowden had come to her aid. Lucius wanted to go to her, but Philippa was tugging on his sleeve, insistent for his attention.

Lucius turned and left the ballroom with Philippa, as a sense of numbness came over him. It was utterly wrong to leave Miss Lockhart, but to make some sort of public gesture was equally impossible.

Selfish? *Yes!* Lucius admitted it grimly, and he despised himself at that moment. But he could not commit himself to leaping to her defense publicly when they had no understanding. He'd not even had time to ask himself if he *wished* for an understanding with Miss Lockhart. Lucius was turning over in his mind what was to be done, when George crossed his path on the way to the card room.

"George," Lucius called out. His brother caught his urgent look and walked forward to meet him. Leaning in, Lucius whispered, "Go to Miss Lockhart and help her."

He had to leave quickly, or he could not be sure of what he would do. The urge to rush to Miss Lockhart's side was growing to where he could not ignore it. Better to leave now and give himself time to think through the best course of action before he took an irrevocable step.

Lucius exited the ballroom in the hope that he would be obeyed.

16

SELENA STARED bleakly in front of her, and her sense of isolation was profound. She had not one friend in the entire room.

The conversation around her had resumed, and there were some whispers coming from women giggling behind their fans. It brought to mind forcibly the ball she had been foolish enough to attend just after her family's humiliation became public. She had thought her friends were better than that—that they would not care for such things, but she had been wrong. And though Bedford had been a fall from grace on a smaller scale than London, the result was the same. Selena could not escape her past.

Her next thought was to flee. But she had some dignity left, never mind that she could not go anywhere without Lady Harrowden. She became dimly aware of Rebecca, who did not seem to know what to do and fidgeted at Selena's side. The uncertain movement reminded Selena of Rebecca's youth, as she took slow steps toward the countess and turned to watch Selena with wary eyes. Selena, burning from head to toe with shame, walked to Lady Harrowden's side as well. What else could she do?

The countess stood, using her cane as support. "Get my things. We are leaving." She did not stop to see if Selena would obey or look at what state she might be in before moving toward the door, her cane making a thumping noise at her side on the wooden floor.

Selena turned to Rebecca. "Come. Lady Harrowden is ready to leave."

Rebecca looked uncertain. "And Lord Harrowden?"

Selena had forgotten about him, but as he had not ridden alongside the carriage, but inside with them, he would have to be consulted. If he chose to stay, at least it would be because he had an alternative. Selena was about to consider how to exchange words with him without entering the card room—she could only assume that was where he was—when Sir Lucius's brother, George, came up to her.

"Miss Lockhart, how may I be of service?" George, young though he was, was looking at her, his eyes full of compassion. It brought Selena to the present, and she resisted the urge to search behind him for a sign of his older brother.

Where was Sir Lucius? And what did he think of the whole affair? He had only registered on the periphery of her consciousness when she had been confronted by Mr. Downing, but there was now more tenderness to be found in the compassionate gaze of his brother, George, than there had been in Sir Lucius's. All she could remember was that he'd looked stunned.

The courage that had stiffened Selena's spine throughout the whole affair nearly deserted her now. Sir Lucius could not bear to be around her, she was sure of it.

"I thank you," she replied, looking up at George with real gratitude. He was not a friend, precisely, but he had come to her. "I need to get word to Lord Harrowden that his aunt wishes to leave. Can you do this for me? I do not know where he is."

"I will do so right away, ma'am. I believe he has not left the card room." George inclined his head to Selena and entered the room.

Selena became dimly aware that Rebecca had stayed near her rather than follow Lady Harrowden, and she said, "I must get our wraps. Lady Harrowden is waiting for us by the door. Why do you not meet her there and let her know I shall be along shortly."

With a consideration that astonished Selena, Rebecca started

forward, saying, "I will get the wraps, and I will meet you at the door."
She walked off before Selena had time to reply.

Upon reflection, perhaps it was not so considerate after all. Selena
was the one who was forced to stand in place under the gleeful stares
of the crowd and wait for George to bring Lord Harrowden to her. She
took two steps toward the card room but did not dare enter it, so she
leaned against the wall, out of the way of people milling on the
outskirts of the dance floor. George came out minutes later.

"Harrowden says he will accompany you. He has no other means of
getting home this evening." George grimaced and added, "He said you
may wait upon him, as it will take ten minutes to finish his game."

Selena shook her head. "Lady Harrowden will not like that."

George gave a rueful smile. "I daresay not." He paused for a
moment before extending his arm in a gallant gesture. "Would you do
me the honor, Miss Lockhart, of taking a turn about the room with me
while we wait upon Lord Harrowden's pleasure?"

Selena could only imagine it would enrage Lady Harrowden further
not to have Selena rush to her side, but she expected to be turned off
anyway, and George was offering her a small degree of comfort.

"I would be glad to do so." She glanced up at his youthful face.
"Thank you for offering."

George switched sides, so that she was mostly hidden from the
prying eyes of those in the room, a gesture she found incredibly
thoughtful for a man so young. "You came to my rescue very gallantly
just now. It was uncomfortable for me to stand alone."

George shook his head. "I cannot take credit for the idea. It was
Lucius who sent me to you. He was walking with my sister, Philippa,
and I believe it was his intention to come to you if her business was
not urgent."

Unruly hope took flight in Selena's breast, and she damped it down
quickly. If Sir Lucius had been intent on saving her from disgrace, he
could have come to her much earlier when Matthew had humiliated
her so thoroughly. He could've stood at her side, or taken her defense,
or...Selena trained her eyes on the ground as they walked. *Sir Lucius is
likely a coward*, she thought with a sudden sting to her eyes.

She blinked the tears away. No. What did she expect? It was not his battle to fight. He never gave her any reason to believe she meant anything to him.

"You are quiet," George said, "but I believe this evening has been particularly trying. I'm terribly sorry for the pain and humiliation you have undergone. Downing is no gentleman."

A mantle of despair settled over Selena. They were almost at the door where Lady Harrowden was waiting with Rebecca, and she stopped and turned to George. "Thank you for your kindness. Thank you for everything. I wish you will tell your brother I said goodbye. I am sure I will be leaving tomorrow."

George furrowed his brows. "I understand if this whole business has been distasteful to you. But truly, must you leave? Do you have somewhere else to go?"

He could not have asked a question more capable of reminding her of the bleakness of her situation. Selena allowed her gaze to drop. She was so weary. "If I am given my salary for the amount I have worked, I will have enough to return to my mother's home. I can only hope Lady Harrowden will not withhold that."

"If she does, she is nothing better than a *harridan*." George laughed suddenly at his own cleverness. "Lady Harridan. Why did I never think of that before? It is so fitting." His face grew serious when he glanced at Selena and saw she did not smile. "If it's money you need, Lucius will provide it for you. I know he will. You need only send him word."

Selena tried to summon a smile as he glanced at her. *I will not ask Sir Lucius for a farthing.* "I hope it shall not come to that," she replied.

They had arrived at where Lady Harrowden and Rebecca stood by the door. Showing an innate grace that Selena wondered if Sir Lucius was aware existed in his younger brother, George kept up a conversation of idle chatter with Lady Harrowden, so Selena could be still and rest her weary mind. Rebecca was surprisingly subdued throughout the entire thing. She didn't even try to flirt with Sir Lucius's brother. Selena darted a glance at Rebecca and wondered. Perhaps she was finally considering what it was to have a damaged reputation.

Lord Harrowden appeared more than ten minutes after he had promised, and Lady Harrowden turned to him in rigid indignation.

"At last, you have come, Richard. You have certainly kept us waiting upon your pleasure. Our coach is outside. Pray—let us not delay any longer." She acknowledged George with a dip of her head and led the party outside in her stiff gait.

As soon as the doors to the coach were closed, and the carriage rumbled off, Lady Harrowden could not refrain from speech any longer. "Whoever had the temerity to invite that gentleman to this party? Surely Maria Holbeck could not have known of the association or she never have allowed it. I must have a word with her."

Without waiting for an answer, she continued. "Selena, if this is the kind of entertainment I might expect with you as my companion, I assure you, your position here will be short-lived. Your mother was very sparse on the details in her letter. Of course I knew your father had disgraced himself, gambling away the family fortune and drinking himself to death." She punctuated the words angrily, and each one was a blow. "I suppose I should have surmised that your position in Society could not survive such a thing. But to be *humiliated* in such a way—and my good name by association—I cannot countenance such a thing. I am not accustomed to having the Harrowden name tainted in any way by scandal."

Selena opened her mouth to speak and bit back the angry words she had been about to utter. *Well, you should have exercised your intellect before engaging my services, for how could you think to avoid such a thing when you knew my circumstances?* There was no point in arguing anyway—her employment would indeed be short-lived. Before she could say a word, whether wise or hasty, Lord Harrowden shifted on the seat next to the countess.

"I found it most entertaining, if you must know, Aunt." With a malicious glance at Selena, he added, "I was under no illusion that your companion would elevate our situation. If you had sought my advice —"

Lady Harrowden gave a huff of disgust. "Sought your advice, indeed! As if I need anyone to *advise* me on what course to follow."

Rebecca, for once, did not utter a word, and Selena listened to them bicker back and forth for the whole ride home. She had lost all interest in trying to defend herself or contribute to the conversation and merely looked out the coach window at the dark countryside.

When they reached the estate, Lady Harrowden stepped forward without Selena's help, so she stayed behind to walk with Rebecca.

Rebecca took the broad stone steps with a measured gait. "I knew you were poor, but I had no idea you had been shunned from Society. I now know that it is not what I want for my own life." She met Selena's gaze. "I would never want to end up like you."

Selena faced forward as they entered the house. Rebecca had not meant to wound with her words—Selena knew that. If anything, it was done in a spirit of complete and utter self-focus. She supposed she could be glad at least that Rebecca would learn a lesson from what happened to her and, perhaps, temper her own behavior.

Selena accompanied Rebecca up to her room, parting ways with Lady Harrowden and her nephew without another word. She had nothing left to say, and it seemed had no further business here. She brought Rebecca to her room where her maid was waiting for her then turned to her own bedroom.

Alone at last, Selena sat on the bed and thought through the evening's events. She had not been hurt by Matthew—not really. Selena was so vastly different from the person she was three years ago, she could not look upon a marriage with Mr. Downing with any sort of pleasure. She supposed she had been shallow then, although she could not have known it until it was all taken away. Balls, dresses, and conquests were all she knew back then. It was only now she saw that what had seduced her in her youth no longer held any interest.

What hurt was not Mr. Downing's public raking down—no! What hurt was that Sir Lucius did not come to her aid. She had grown accustomed, in their short acquaintance, to him being there for her, even rescuing her. Public humiliation was not a greater danger than being lost in a snowstorm, but somehow it felt just as desolate. There was truly nothing to keep her here.

❧

LUCIUS FOLLOWED Philippa out into the fresh air of the entryway then into the library. His mind was consumed with the vision of Miss Lockhart's stricken face, and his conscience was ringing quiet alarms that he had perhaps been wrong. He was so used to building up walls, to not getting involved.

His mother had leaned on him ever since his father died, and Lucius had been too young to bear all her burdens or squire her about. Maria used him for her own ends, usually to even out her numbers and attract the right kind of society by having her titled brother attend all her functions. Even Charles had attempted to get him to throw his weight into politics, so he could gain another ally that might sway the votes.

And George and Philippa, endearing though they were, were always in some scrape or another. George seemed only to get himself into trouble, and Philippa could wear down stone with her persistence, all while displaying a tendency toward wildness. It was never beyond the lines of propriety with her, but Lucius worried if someone didn't keep Philippa in check—and his mother was too indolent to do so, Maria too heavy-handed—he would end up having to rescue her reputation through a meeting at dawn or some such drama.

The last thing he needed was to have to defend the reputation of a woman who was not even related to him.

But Miss Lockhart had begun to creep past the barrier of indifferent acquaintance into something resembling attachment. He didn't know how it had happened, but her quiet dignity calmed him. Her poise attracted him, particularly when the rest of his family seemed to possess none. And when she flashed him a sudden, rare smile at something he said, it caused his heart to beat painfully as if he were a lad experiencing his first crush. He tried to ignore these facts, but facts they were.

"Lucius," Philippa said, calling him to attention. "It was terrible what happened with Miss Lockhart. Could you not have done something?"

Lucius evaded her gaze. "It would have been a very delicate thing to do, for it would have given rise to speculation about the nature of our—"

"Who cares about speculation?" Philippa demanded. "Imagine if it were me receiving such backlash from a man like Mr. Downing. What right had he to treat her in such a way, especially after he jilted her? *He* should be the one who gets a tongue lashing for being so fickle. It was entirely unfair that Miss Lockhart had to endure that—and all under the stares and whispers of the guests. I cannot believe Maria invited him here."

Lucius shook his head. "It could not have been innocently done. I suppose I should not be able to believe it, but I do. Let us not talk of this, however. What is done is done. I will do what I can to spread it about that Downing is the villain in the scenario."

Philippa studied him with unnerving attention until she came to a conclusion. "But you will do so at no cost to your own reputation or comfort."

Lucius turned to her, exasperated. "I cannot imagine that this is what you came to talk to me about. To ring a peal over my head—you, a mere chit of seventeen years?"

Philippa shook her head. "It's about Lord Harrowden. You were starting to scold me for dancing with him, and indeed I did not see how I could refuse. However, he asked very particular questions in the short time we were together. Questions that were entirely too personal to be idle."

She had Lucius's attention. "Has he importuned you? What sort of questions did he ask you? I will wring his neck."

"No, Lucius. Don't jump to conclusions," Philippa said with a weary patience that suddenly made her seem more mature than her years. "He did try to find out how much I was worth, which is such a silly thing to do when he has the subtlety of an ox. He must think I have more hair than wit not to see what he was about."

She met Lucius's gaze. "But he also tried to find out how much time you are spending with Miss Woodsley, and whether you might have some interest in that direction. He even tried to ascertain what sort of interest you might have in Miss Lockhart, asking if she had been invited to Maria's residence or yours—I suppose it was to see if she is being treated with the courtesy of a lady, a companion, or...or something else. It was really rather clumsily done, I must tell you. I am surprised he thought I was that naïve—that I wouldn't notice."

Lucius narrowed his eyes. What was the end to all Harrowden's questions? It only took a minute before the answer was obvious. He was looking for a fortune, and perhaps a mistress, and he was scoping for potential rivals for both.

"I overheard Maria talk to him about your interest in Miss Woodsley." Philippa laughed when Lucius turned to her with an expression of disgust. "I am quite sure that is what prompted his questions to me. I must confess though"—Philippa smiled, and two deep dimples appeared on either side of her cheeks— "I exaggerated your regard for Miss Woodsley."

"I have no regard for Miss Woodsley," Lucius snapped.

"Don't bite my head off. *I* know that. Well then. I *created* your interest in Miss Woodsley." Philippa had the grace to blush.

"To what end?" Lucius asked, staring at her blankly. Either he was obtuse or Philippa was growing more devious with age.

"I wanted to throw him off the scent," Philippa replied with an innocent look. "I did not want him to notice that you were interested in Miss Lockhart."

"What?" Lucius whipped around to face her fully. "Who has told you such a thing?"

"Nobody had to," Philippa said. "I have eyes in my head, Lucius. You mustn't think that because I'm only seventeen years old, I'm a baby. In fact, sometimes I think I have more sense than you do when it comes to matters of the heart."

"I am not sure Mr. Barnsworth would agree," Lucius said wryly.

Philippa giggled. "I told you that was idle flirtation—" They both turned when the door opened, and George entered the room.

Lucius walked toward him, impatient for news. "George, have you seen to Miss Lockhart's needs?"

George returned a succinct nod. "I believe she has just left, accompanied by Lord and Lady Harrowden and Miss Woodsley." George took a breath and leveled an accusing glare at Lucius. "I think you might have seen to her yourself."

Lucius repressed a desire to deliver a cutting retort. George's words hit a little too close to home.

"Well, as I don't intend to be lectured by my younger brother—who was sent down from *school*, I might remind you—you will have to keep such reflections to yourself. When you've grown a pair of side whiskers and live within your means, you may think about lecturing me. Although I don't promise to heed it."

George folded his arms, not at all repulsed by the rebuff. "Miss Lockhart told me to bid you goodbye."

Lucius's brow creased. "Goodbye? She is not leaving Woolmer Green, surely?"

"Are you so surprised?" George shrugged. "She has no friends here. She was humiliated, and no one stood up for her—not her family, distant though they may be, and not...anyone else." He pressed his lips together, his gaze penetrating.

Lucius shifted uncomfortably. This was not a discussion he wanted to have. He needed time to sort through what he was feeling and what course of action he should take. It appeared he would not have as much time as he would like. He would have to see Miss Lockhart first thing tomorrow morning. Perhaps before breakfast. Surely she would not leave at the crack of dawn?

He inhaled suddenly, remembering. "George, there's something I want you to do. I need you to go to London and find me a solicitor who can look into the particulars of Lady Harrowden's jointure."

George smiled. "It will be no hardship to go to London, I assure you. But why—"

"Also," Lucius continued, "I'd like you to ask discreetly in the clubs —I'll give you a few names of gentlemen you can talk to—tell them I sent you. Ask where Harrowden's affairs stand and how much he is in debt. I believe the noose is tightening around his neck, and that his affairs are far from being in order. I want to know just how desperate he is. Can you leave as early as tomorrow?"

Philippa had been listening quietly, and now she turned to George and added her mite. "Lord Harrowden was asking a lot of questions about me, my dowry, Miss Woodsley, Lucius's interests—"

Lucius held up his hand. "And this must be done with the utmost discretion. I am asking the same of you, Philippa—not even a word to Maria, if you can manage it."

"Of *course* I can manage it," she replied, indignant.

George, listening quietly, met Lucius's gaze. "I can do it, of course, but may I ask what interest you have in the affairs at Harrowden? I cannot see how they concern you at all, and it is most unlike you. Does this have something to do with Miss Lockhart?"

Lucius refused to answer that, although Miss Lockhart's presence had made keeping his promise to the former Lord Harrowden a matter of importance at last. "I am fulfilling an old promise," he said. "I should go myself, but I don't like to leave just now."

He saw Philippa and George exchange a look. Since he, himself, was not entirely sure whether his decision to remain had as much to do with Miss Lockhart's presence as he suspected it might, he did not wish for impertinence from them.

"I will leave tomorrow," George said.

"Very good," Lucius said. "I will give you a note to bring to my banker to fund your trip. Just try not to get into trouble while you're there. And George?" His brother paused on the way to the door, and Lucius leveled his gaze at him. "Thank you for seeing to Miss Lockhart tonight."

George flashed him a smile, and he was gone.

17

SELENA HAD HAD ENOUGH of sitting idly in fruitless contemplation. She pulled the pins from her hair with leaden movements. What would wait for her in Bedford? Likely a marriage to the squire, whose intelligence was not above average and whose physical appearance she regarded with something akin to disgust. Had he not been intent on pursuing her, she probably would have liked him a little bit. She certainly would not have noticed any of his shortcomings. But to think of being tied to him—of him laying his hands on her...Selena shuddered. She would have to bury any hopes of passion, or even intelligent conversation.

It did not occur to Selena until she was packing her trunk, carefully laying one dress above the other without the benefit of silver paper, of which she had none, that she had no idea how exactly she was to return home. She supposed she would have to approach Lady Harrowden for her wages and beg a ride to the station where she would have to purchase a ticket on the stagecoach. She went over to the window and stood looking through it. A sliver of moonlight lit a patch on the darkened, snowy landscape.

Should she leave in such a hasty manner? Was that the best? Or should she ask Lady Harrowden whether she wished for Selena to stay on, at least until someone new could be brought in?

The next morning brought little counsel, and she decided she would not make a final decision until having first spoken with Lady Harrowden. Selena went to the breakfast room with the desperate hope she would not have to meet Lord Harrowden there, but her wish was not granted. Despite his frequent late nights, he seemed oddly averse to missing his breakfast.

"You are up early," Lord Harrowden said before stuffing the last bite of breakfast in his mouth. "I would have thought you would still be abed trying to recover from last night's humiliation."

Selena paused, eyeing him with unveiled disfavor. She did not know if she should tell him she was planning to leave Woolmer Green. After a second's consideration, she decided not to do so since it was none of his affair anyway. She filled her pink flowered Limoges plate from the sideboard without a word and sat as far from him as she could. It didn't matter that he fixed his gaze on her in a way intended to provoke her to a hasty retort. It wouldn't work.

"So you have nothing to say for yourself then?" he said. "You might try for some conversation, since it appears you have few other resources to turn to."

Selena was goaded beyond her limits by the accusation that she had no conversation. The impertinent mushroom of Bedford Society had said the same of her.

"I am not so deprived of company that I need to engage in conversation with someone who is of absolutely no interest to me." Selena clutched her napkin under the table, too edgy to take a bite.

Lord Harrowden's cutlery clattered on his plate. "If Downing's reminder was not enough to take down that pride of yours a notch, I daresay *time* will do the trick. You should have accepted my *carte blanche* when it was offered to you. Before long you'll be firmly on the shelf, any claim to beauty long gone, unable to get a position, and sinking further into poverty. That ought to humble you, and I have no doubt that *that* is what your future holds." His face had lost all semblance of civility. How flimsy that mask had been.

At last they spoke without pretence. Selena pressed her lips together before answering. "You are trying to frighten me by dashing my hopes, but it is difficult to disappoint one who holds no expectations. I have neither wish to marry, nor do I have great need of a position. I have someplace to go. I still have family. You may fling as many barbs as you wish my way, but I am not quite the defenseless creature you think me."

"You have a mother and sisters, I believe." Lord Harrowden peered at her under narrowed lids. "Your father drank himself into a grave, and you have no brothers. There are no men to defend your case, and therefore you *are* a defenseless creature. A *poor*, defenseless creature." He inclined his head with a cruel smile. "Are you not?"

Selena tried to swallow down the spasms that had risen from such vicious and *true* words when the door opened. Mullings stepped inside. "I beg your pardon. Sir Lucius Clavering is here to see you."

"What the devil does he want with me?" Lord Harrowden wiped his mouth with his napkin. "Tell him I am unavailable, as I am having my breakfast."

Selena's heart sped up at the sound of Sir Lucius's name, but she willed herself to be calm. She obviously meant nothing to him, so there was no point in allowing her heart to take off the way it did. Unfortunately, her heart did not seem to listen to reason.

Mullings's next words set her pulse racing again. "It is not you, my lord, that Sir Lucius wishes to see. It is Miss Lockhart."

Selena rose from the table, hoping the nervous flutter that had taken over her insides was not obvious. She walked toward the door that Mullings held open, conscious of Lord Harrowden's penetrating glare.

"Perhaps I should accompany you," Lord Harrowden said. "It is not seemly for a woman in my household to be alone with a man."

Selena did not look at him. "Do not trouble yourself, my lord. I will ask Mrs. Randall to stay with us." She swept out before he could answer her.

Once in the corridor, she smiled at the butler. "Would you mind please? I would feel more comfortable if Mrs. Randall remained with us." He went off in search of the housekeeper, and Selena waited outside the drawing room for her to appear.

Mrs. Randall walked down the corridor with her brisk step, and Selena gave her a nervous smile. "Thank you for coming."

"Think nothing of it, Miss Lockhart." Mrs. Randall opened the door in front of her and entered first with Selena trailing in her wake. "Sir Lucius. It is always good to see you at Harrowden. Might I bring you some refreshments?"

Sir Lucius shot a glance at Selena that she had not the faintest hope of interpreting. It looked a cross between guilt and pleading. He returned his gaze to Mrs. Randall. "I would be much obliged. I have come without having any breakfast."

"Very well, sir. I shall return directly." Without another word, Mrs. Randall left the room, and Selena was alone with Sir Lucius.

So much for having Mrs. Randall as chaperone. However, alone with nearly any man was preferable to enduring more of Lord Harrowden's insufferable presence. Selena came to stand in front of Sir Lucius, and he bowed, his eyes raised to hers as he stood. Sir Lucius's growing sense of unease did not escape her, and when the silence between them stretched, she decided she must break it.

"Will you sit?"

Sir Lucius nodded and waited for her to take her seat at one of the armchairs facing the fire. He chose one snug at her side, rather than the one placed at a more respectable distance.

Selena sat at the edge of her chair, her spine stiff and her hands clasped on her lap. She was fairly confident her posture did not betray the turmoil of emotions she was experiencing within, and she made an effort to keep her fingers loosely clasped. She was not sure if she should be heartened or worried by the fact that Sir Lucius seemed exactly the opposite. He looked as though he had not slept. His clothing was just as careless as ever, but there were lines under his eyes that were not usually there. And his hair was more disordered than usual, as if he had run his fingers through it more than once. She lifted her gaze to his, waiting.

"George tells me you are leaving," he said at last.

"Yes. I see no reason to stay now." Selena returned her gaze to her clasped hands. It was too unbearable to look at him for long. She had not been aware how much her feelings for him had grown until she decided to leave and would not see him again. Mixed with his indifference last night, the pain of misplaced longing was acute.

"But Downing will leave," Sir Lucius said. His tone was severe, and there was that crease between his brows that had become dear. "He will not trouble you here. Woolmer Green is a quiet place, one where you can escape Society's censure."

Selena shook her head. "I cannot escape it anywhere. I thought the same when I went to Bedford, but as soon as news had reached there of my father's demise, the whispering started, and the mockery. The invitations stopped. This was the reason I decided to come here and start fresh, but this time with no expectations of being received anywhere as anything but a companion. Still, it has happened again."

She picked at her skirt in a nervous gesture until she realized what she was doing and folded one hand over the other. "And it is likely to happen wherever I go."

"If that is so, then why leave?" Sir Lucius insisted. Selena looked up then, examining his face. *Why would he care?*

"Why not face it here in Woolmer Green since you must face it at all." He leaned toward her, and his knee brushed hers in what was probably a careless gesture, but she was so unused to such nearness, she felt as though she would jump out of her skin.

Then the anger came in a rush, and Selena whipped around to meet his gaze. "It is easy for you to say, Sir Lucius. You may go where you please, and nothing even close to vicious rumors need ever trouble you. Nothing disturbs your very *orderly* existence."

"I..." Sir Lucius did not answer right away and stared at the floor. He drummed his fingers on the armrest, and Selena waited, her nerves taut. At last, he put an elbow on his knee and brought his head close to hers, his face inches away, and his eyes boring into hers. "*You* disturb my very orderly existence."

Selena thought she would faint from exhaustion—from the well of emotions Sir Lucius had stirred. It was all so fatiguing, and she put her hand to her cheek, creating a barrier of protection. He wore away at her dignity. To turn a blind eye to such heartless behavior as he had shown last night—if she had meant anything at all to him—would mean she was the most spineless of creatures.

He leaned back, which she'd thought merciful, until he continued his assault. "What I am trying to say in a hopelessly inadequate way is that I do not wish for you to leave. I want you to stay."

Selena could not have been more surprised if Sir Lucius had leaned over and pushed her off her chair. She turned to face him, expecting him to break into laughter or mockery, or to recant what he'd said. He did none of those things. His gaze softened, beseeching, and in it she could see longing, but he did not move closer again. She forgot how to breathe.

"How am I supposed to respond to that?" Selena's hands were now tightly clenched on her lap, anchoring her, surely, from flying off the chair, powered by such turbulent emotions. After all these years of sinking further and further from Society. After last night...it was too much to hope that he had any proper intentions toward her.

"Say you will stay, Miss Lockhart," Sir Lucius said.

Selena felt tears prick at the back of her eyelids at the tender manner in which he spoke her name. "Under what guise?" She could not meet his gaze any longer. It had become too weighted. Instead, she watched the flickering flames in the fireplace, hoping desperately that Mrs. Randall would not reappear until this painful conversation—this painful, *wonderful* conversation was terminated.

But the weight of reality pressed at her as the memories of last night flooded her vision. She spoke in a near whisper. "You did not see fit to speak of this last night before I made a hasty departure. Nor did you see fit to connect your name in any way with mine by stepping forward when I was the target for Mr. Downing's mockery." She skewered him with her gaze. "Those actions do not belong to a man who has the right to make a request of any nature."

"I know it." Sir Lucius leaned forward and covered his face with his hands, rubbing it fiercely. "I did not come to your aid. It was wrong of me. I cannot explain fully—not yet."

Abruptly, he sat up and reached for Selena's hand. "I am being very forward—impossible even. Because I cannot ask you for...for what you should have every reason to expect after I've requested you to stay. I simply need time. I only ask that you give us that time to deepen our acquaintance while I sort things out."

Selena's heart grew cold, even as she hid her sudden desire to weep. What was he offering her? She could hardly say. He certainly was not offering her marriage. Surely it could not be yet another *carte blanche*? As if he thought she would accept such a thing. He must be a fool indeed. But Sir Lucius was no fool.

Perhaps *she* was the fool if her longing to see where things might lead with Sir Lucius kept her from rejecting him outright, despite his lack of gallantry.

She was most certainly a fool—and a pitiful one at that.

"I have already been giving much thought to my situation," Selena said. "I will stay a short while longer because it is wrong to leave Lady Harrowden without allowing her to find a new companion."

When relief flashed over Sir Lucius's face, she warned, "Lady Harrowden might not even wish me to stay. She certainly had plenty of reproaches to throw at me last night. I may have no choice in the matter but to be on the first stagecoach."

"That was very wrong of her." Sir Lucius's brow creased again. "Although I think you might be surprised when she makes no mention of your leaving. Lady Harrowden blusters easily enough, but she really does need a companion, especially now. And Miss Woodsley still needs a governess. I'm asking you to stay while we find a replacement."

Selena felt a ludicrous sense of disappointment, even as her chin came up. "It is for their sake you ask this of me?"

"No, it is for mine," he returned.

She looked away, suppressing any feelings of promise that rose in her breast. "If I stay, it is only for Lady Harrowden's sake."

"For now, it is enough simply that you stay." Sir Lucius took her hand in his and raised it to his lips. He pressed a warm kiss on her bare hand, which made Selena feel faint.

Mrs. Randall entered, carrying a tray, and closed the door firmly behind her, her back turned to Lucius and Selena. She seemed to take her time in doing so, and Lucius used it to lean back away from Selena. Both were silent as Mrs. Randall came forward, setting the tray on the table near them. She served them coffee and little cakes.

Then she went to the other side of the room and took a seat near the window, giving them both a small degree of privacy.

"I hardly know what else to say, Sir Lucius. I make no promises," she whispered.

"Please just..." His voice trailed away and he began again. "I know I am not being fair, but I am not dallying with you, Miss Lockhart. I promise."

Selena sighed. "I do not know what I will say to Lady Harrowden today when I see her."

The coffee and cakes sat between them untouched. Lucius said, "Tell Lady Harrowden I have gone to visit the dower house, and it will be a simple matter to move in. She will be able to have the parts of it painted with very little trouble to herself while she is in residence. Tell her I will assist you in all the details. She may remove to it as soon as she pleases and will not need to stay here, where I suspect her small income is partially used to assist with the expenses of this big estate. Lord Harrowden will have to carry the expenses on his own."

Selena darted a glance at Mrs. Randall, wondering if she were listening. In any case, it would soon be known throughout the staff if Lady Harrowden were to remove to the dower house. True, Selena did not desire to live under the countess's sharp tongue longer than was needed, but Lady Harrowden would surely need her to help direct matters if they were going to move. And Selena did need the income. Perhaps she would also find that, away from Lord Harrowden's influence, she, Rebecca and Lady Harrowden would get along much better.

Perhaps she might even learn to harden her heart to Sir Lucius. He had not put her interests above his own at the ball, despite the olive branch he seemed to be offering her now. If she could just keep that detail at the forefront of her mind, then it should be possible to stay to suit her own purposes while keeping Sir Lucius at arm's length. It was certainly worth a try.

She gave a nod. "Very well. I will stay at least as long as the removal to the dower house and until a new companion may be found."

"That is good enough," Lucius said. "That's all the time I need." He smiled at her, and it set her stomach fluttering.

Selena looked away. She may be a pathetic fool, but she would not be foolish enough to let him see it.

~

LUCIUS BID FAREWELL TO SELENA, but he was far from feeling at ease. For the first time in his life, he regretted not stepping forward when he'd had the chance to defend her. Watching his parents' marriage growing up did not inspire him to think that felicity was found in the bounds of matrimony. But Lucius was beginning to be hard-pressed to imagine his life without Selena. And the fact that he left her as recently as last night, alone and surrounded by a pack of hungry wolves brought on by his own sister—he was heartily ashamed of himself.

Selena must not have known that it was his sister who had invited Mr. Downing. He would have to tell her, of course, and hope that she did not hold that, too, against him. It was time he went about things differently. As Lucius crossed the billiard room, he saw Harrowden inside, sitting close to Rebecca and whispering in her ear. She flushed and giggled, starting up from her seat when Lucius walked by.

"Sir Lucius," she exclaimed. "What a pleasure to see you here. Were you coming to visit me?" She looked at him with such optimism, he found it hard to disabuse her of the notion. He also did not think it would help Selena's cause if he told Rebecca exactly what he thought of her a second time.

"I came to see Lady Harrowden, but I learned that she is still in bed. However, I am always delighted to see you."

Lucius saw too late the eager look that lit up her eyes at such a practiced compliment. He'd been distracted by Selena, and this was the first compliment he had paid Rebecca. Until now, all he had done was to keep her at arm's length, almost to the point of rudeness, and rake her over the coals for being such a difficult charge to Selena. Paying even a modicum of address to a young, impressionable girl was perhaps not the wisest thing he had done.

Harrowden was looking at him with undisguised irritation. The man had something up his sleeve, and it likely had to do with keeping Rebecca close by, probably with the intention of seducing her if things did not go well with his financial affairs. Lucius hoped George would not tarry in coming back.

He bowed before Rebecca. "I was just on my way out. I bid you good day."

"Have you already called for your horse? Can you not stay a little longer? I can sit with you if you like." Rebecca took a step forward.

Lucius darted another glance at Lord Harrowden's face, which was glowering. "That is very kind of you, but I must be off. I will walk to the stables. I am not entirely a stranger to this estate, having come here since I was a boy."

Lord Harrowden stepped up to Rebecca's side and took her elbow in his. "You would do well to remember that this estate is no longer owned by the former earl. You cannot roam freely at will any longer."

Lucius lifted an eyebrow. "Noted."

Rebecca slipped away from Harrowden and put her hand on Lucius's arm. "Perhaps I may walk with you there."

Sir Lucius looked at the thin fabric of her dress. "I do not know that it is a good idea. You are not dressed for it, and I'm in a bit of a hurry."

Rebecca's face fell. "Very well," she said, surprisingly docile. It seemed she was making efforts at taking his advice to heart. "But will you come visit again soon?"

Lucius thought of Selena, her slender collarbones that were just visible under the neckline of her dress. He thought of her creamy skin and her elegant nose and lips that, despite being prim and fit for a governess, invited one to press one's lips on them. His one consuming thought was to see her again as soon as possible.

"I will be sure to come soon," he said. Before he turned, he caught the exultant look that flashed over Rebecca's features. He could not declare himself to Selena soon enough.

❧ 18 ❧

AS LUCIUS LEFT HARROWDEN, his conversation with Selena continued to weigh heavily on his mind. He remembered the quiet look of reproach she gave him. He had not shown her how much he had begun to value her, and he was determined to start now.

At least he had convinced her not to leave. Or...not. She had made it clear her staying had nothing to do with him. But unless the countess sent her packing before the move to the dower house, Lucius had time. He was going to prove to her he was worthy of her.

His first step must, of course, be to visit his sister and see what other activities she had planned for the entertainment of her guests, and to see if she would be inviting the countess to any of them. He also needed to dig and find out why she had acted so spitefully by inviting the man who had jilted Selena, although this must be handled delicately or she would know the matter was important to him and perhaps be led to do irreparable mischief before he could secure Selena's hand.

Lucius kicked his heels for another hour, knowing Maria would not be up and about yet. If he went now, he would be more likely to run into Downing, whose neck he wanted to wring. When he thought it was time enough, Lucius had his horse saddled and rode over.

Maria was once again in the corridor when he arrived, and he suspected she spent her days peering through the windows waiting to see who would visit. "Lucius, you are here a mere day after our ball. How gratifying—have you come to discuss last night?"

"Of a sort." Lucius followed his sister as she turned directly into the drawing room. "I'd like to know what other activities you have planned while your guests are here to while away the winter days." He sat on the brocaded chair across from Maria and tossed one leg over the other, trying to look disinterested.

Maria's eyes widened. "I knew you would come to your senses and start wishing to join Society. The time is ripe for you to settle down, and this just confirms it." She gave Lucius a knowing look that almost had him bolting from the room were it not for his purpose in coming.

"And for whose sake are you interested in these gatherings?" Maria tapped her chin with a small smile. "I know you will do nothing unless it serves your own interest. Is it Miss Butler?" She gasped. "Or have you at last taken an interest in Miss Woodsley?"

"I have an interest," Lucius said carefully, "but you must not be surprised if I don't share it with you. Suffice it to say that I'm keen enough in the guests you have gathered to join in more of your excursions, parties, and the like."

Maria could not hide the exultant gleam that leapt to her eyes. She could imagine whatever she wanted. "Well! It's nice to see you are finally thinking about settling down. By the way, where did you send George off to? He didn't give me any details, but I don't like to think of him traipsing around London to no purpose."

Lucius looked up as Philippa walked in the room. He stood and gave her a kiss on the cheek when she presented it, and she sat down to join them. He wondered if Maria had noticed that he hadn't kissed her in greeting.

"It won't be to no purpose. I have a matter I wanted George to look into, and it doesn't suit me to leave Woolmer Green at just this moment. He will be fine. I sent him with some letters to give to friends, and I know they will keep an eye on him. In any case, he is no longer the boy we sometimes treat him."

Maria didn't answer but turned her gaze to Philippa. "I see you are none the worse for wear after last night. You handled yourself mostly well at the ball, but there are a few things we ought to speak about if you are to be ready for your Season."

Lucius leapt after this thread of conversation. "And that is precisely why I am not fit to host Philippa in London. She will need a woman to guide her, and I have none in my life."

Maria sent him a look heavy with irony.

"No suitable woman, I should say," Lucius added to provoke her. The pleasantry did not sit well with him, however. He could not laugh at Maria's expense when he had so brutally neglected Selena.

"Why, Mama will be there to do that, of course," Philippa said, unconscious of Lucius's troubled—and guilty—train of thought. "You need only open your home."

Lucius rolled his eyes. "That is precisely what I do not wish to do. To have my normally peaceful townhouse overrun with people in and out of the schoolroom."

"Lucius, you know you won't deny Philippa," Maria said. "No matter how much you appear to be difficult and unwieldy, you know what is owed to your family, and you never fail to do your duty."

Lucius stared at the flowered patterns in the rug. He had not yet launched into either of the purposes of his visit, and he needed to come to the point. "Maria, just what did you mean by inviting Downing here? You did not warn Miss Lockhart. Did you know of his former attachment with her?" *So much for going about it delicately.*

Maria puckered up, and he thought he saw a twinge of defensiveness in her attitude. "Of course I knew. Downing is an MP and Charles is one of his benefactors. Charles told me all about the failed engagement, remember? Downing did very well to end the engagement when he did. Do you think he would have been elected to the House of Commons with *her* as his wife? I assure you, he would not."

"Very well," Lucius said. "The engagement ended years ago. Why allow her to be humiliated once again, and at your ball. I had not imagined you to be so cruel."

Maria stood in impatience and walked across the room to fiddle with papers on the desk. "*You*, Lucius. You were the reason I invited Mr. Downing at the last minute. I knew he would be at ease with the other guests and that he would accept the invitation, provided he had no other plans. With Charles as his benefactor, how could he do otherwise? But your attentions to Miss Lockhart have been too marked to be missed. Others have noticed as well. Even Lady Harrowden thought there might be something there. And, well"—Maria turned and took a few steps toward him— "now you know she is not suitable. I did not wish for you to be deceived as to her situation."

Philippa had been watching the discussion, but wisely kept silent. Lucius took a steadying breath before replying. "Anyone can know of her situation," he said. "You need only see that she is engaged as a companion to know she has fallen from elevated circles. There is no reason to drag her name through the mud on top of it."

Maria stood, arms akimbo, her eyes glittering. "It is one thing to be simply impoverished. It is quite another to leave behind unpaid vowels to such a *large* number of gentlemen as to be *quite* shocking the way Lockhart did. And then to drink himself to an early grave? The disgrace has fallen on his family, and it remains there."

Lucius forced himself to stay seated instead of storming from the room, as he had not yet achieved his other objective in coming. When he spoke, it was in a carefully modulated voice that anyone less obtuse than Maria would have been cautioned by. "Very well, Maria. But to allow her to be shamed publicly—and in your own home—was very badly done."

She served him a pointed look in return. "And yet, you did not leap to her defense, did you, Lucius? You may preach all you like, but you are not any more favorable to courting such damaged goods than I am in promoting them."

Lucius swallowed. The knowledge that his behavior spoke volumes —and not to his honor—combined with the cutting words 'damaged goods' filled him with an almost irrepressible desire to lash out, preferably at someone he could actually hit. The bulk of his anger, however, was directed at himself.

It would not do to answer Maria now. He could not win this argument until he had proven himself to Selena—and to everyone else— that she took precedence over his own comfort.

He adopted a neutral tone when he changed the subject. "You've not specified your proposed plan for the entertainment of your guests."

Maria's eyes lit with the victory of having won this round. "I have planned dinner and whist two nights from now. I wasn't intending to open it up to more than just our guests staying here, but of course I would be delighted if you would come. You are always a welcome addition to any gathering," she added, graciously.

At last, his goal. "Would you be equally delighted to invite Lady Harrowden and her household?"

The smile hovered around Maria's mouth. "You're taking my words to heart, I see. I am glad to hear it. I suppose that can be arranged. I will have an invitation sent off today."

Lucius stood. There was no point in remaining now that he had achieved what he came to do. "Very good. I expect George back that same morning, so he might be in attendance as well."

~

SELENA STARED through her bedroom window, thinking of Sir Lucius. *You disturb my very orderly existence.* She wondered what it would have been like had he leaned the few remaining inches and kissed her. She rested her fingers on the small square windowpanes, which were cold to the touch. Her breath steamed the glass.

Lord Harrowden came into view as he walked on the snowy ground below, and by instinct, Selena drew back behind the curtain and out of sight. She peeked down again and saw that the earl was agitated about something. His face was hidden under his hat, but his breath came out in clouds, as he stalked forward, head down and clenching his fists.

Just then, Rebecca ran outside after him with only a light cloak around her. So she was out of bed already. Lord Harrowden turned and lifted his face to Rebecca, and Selena saw a smile appear. She ducked behind the curtain again, but when she looked out, he had taken Rebecca by the arm and was leading her back indoors. He leaned in to give her a peck on the cheek, and Selena frowned. Something must be done to stop his advances.

It was eleven o'clock, and Selena could avoid it no longer. She exited into the corridor and began walking, the sounds of her slippered feet muted on the wood floor. Her thoughts churned fruitlessly as she traced the steps to Lady Harrowden's room. She may as well find out sooner rather than later what her fate here would be. Selena wasn't sure if she minded a sudden end to her position, though it would mean a loss of income, and perhaps future positions if she could not gain a reference—if Lady Harrowden still harbored those feelings of disgust she had alluded to last night.

And then there was Sir Lucius and her implausible future with him...Selena picked up her pace and drew in a breath. She could not dwell on that fact. It was the lot in life of women like Selena, who had lost their station. Hope died too.

She tapped three times on Lady Harrowden's door, as was her habit, and stepped inside. Mrs. Morgan glanced up, out of Lady Harrowden's sight, and sent Selena a sympathetic smile. It was an unexpected relief to have an ally in that corner.

"Have you brought my correspondence?" Lady Harrowden asked Selena. Gone was the irritation from last night. It came as such a surprise, Selena almost dropped the platter. It was as if nothing had happened.

"Yes, my lady," she said, stepping forward. "I have also seen Sir Lucius this morning, who has some news for you."

Lady Harrowden glanced up at Selena in between rifling through the letters that were handed to her. "And when will he come back to give me this news? Did he say?"

Suddenly the situation appeared awkward to Selena. She wondered if Sir Lucius had thought through the implications of asking her to relay the news to Lady Harrowden, rather than bringing it himself. It would look as if he were conferring some unusual favor on Selena, a mere companion.

"I believe he did not want to delay the news and feared not to come back early enough to give it to you, so he asked me to pass it on to you."

Lady Harrowden opened one of the letters with a small knife, her movement an aggressive jerk of the hand. "He knows I rise at eleven o'clock. If he was impatient to give me the news, he should've waited until I was up to make his visit. Very well then. Let us have it."

It was not a promising beginning, but at least Lady Harrowden did not seem to have any suspicion of what else Sir Lucius could have come to speak about.

"He said that the dower house is ready, and that any painting to be done may be accomplished while you are in residence. You may remove to it as soon as you wish, and he has offered to assist you in whatever you need." She forced herself to meet the countess's gaze. Would Lady Harrowden say she needed Selena's help as well, thus prolonging her stay?

Lady Harrowden set the letter in her lap. "That is very good news. At least he has done me a useful turn. I had planned on having you begin your lessons with Rebecca today. If last night's ball taught me anything, it is that she is totally unfit to be presented in Society as early as this Season. With her fortune, she has the chance of making a good match. But if I present her now when she is just an ill-bred thing with no manners at all—even if she is lovely to look at—it will not reflect well on me and will waste my time."

Lady Harrowden stood and signaled for her maid to bring the dress she had laid out. "Now I see we shall have to revise our plans, but perhaps only a very little. The packing for the dower house must start immediately. I will direct the servants to begin packing the linens and dishes that are mine—if there are indeed any servants left. I see less and less of them these days. And you"—she lifted her finger to Selena — "you will also help, but I am of the firm belief that your priority is to spend a couple hours a day teaching Rebecca proper deportment. Test her on the skills a genteel woman must possess to see what she lacks and begin teaching her those skills."

Selena began to think that perhaps Lady Harrowden had no intention for her to leave at all. And although she wasn't sure if she should put ideas in the countess's head, it surprised her so much she couldn't refrain from asking. "My lady, after your words in the carriage ride home last night, I had understood you wished me to leave. I have been in expectation of my immediate dismissal."

Lady Harrowden turned as Mrs. Morgan buttoned the back of

her dress, conveniently avoiding Selena's gaze. "I was, perhaps, too harsh with my words last night. I do not like surprises. But Mr. Downing showed an appalling lack of manners by attacking you in such a way, and you did not deserve such treatment." Adopting her usual acidic tone, she added, "If there are no more incidents like this, I suppose I can overlook it. I cannot make this move to the dower house without assistance, and Sir Lucius knows that. Do go find Rebecca and see that she is up so she may begin her lessons at once."

"As you wish, my lady." Selena gave a small curtsy and left. She did not bother to tell the countess that this incident would likely happen again, especially if they were to take Rebecca to London for the Season, where everyone knew her. She was too surprised at the countess showing any sort of softening.

As Selena descended the stairs, she considered that it might be prudent to build up a savings, then find a new position before the trip to London would take place. That way, she could not be accused of cruelty toward Lady Harrowden, who needed her during the move, but she would not have to bear this situation much longer either. In any event, it was bound to be more bearable at the dower house than at the estate where Lord Harrowden lurked at every turn.

Selena sought out Mrs. Randall and sent her up to Lady Harrowden, who had decided to direct some of the affairs from her spacious bedroom. Then she went to find the ward.

Rebecca exited the drawing room with Lord Harrowden at her side, and Selena was behind them, so she had a view of their behavior together, which was more intimate than was proper. Rebecca's head was bent next to his, and she laughed at the things he was telling her.

Selena narrowed her eyes. Lord Harrowden could make himself attractive and charming when he wished to. But he was one who hid his teeth. With Rebecca's wealth, she would never be made to feel Lord Harrowden's darker side. That is, until he'd spent all of it down to the last penny.

"Rebecca," she called out, and they both turned. "Lady Harrowden has sent me to find you. She wishes us to begin training in deportment, so you may be ready for your London Season." Selena would leave it to

Lady Harrowden to break the news that the Season would not start quite so soon.

Rebecca sighed loudly. "How boring. Why am I to do such a thing now? I'll have enough practice at the balls like last night."

"Lady Harrowden hopes to turn you out well for your Season—perhaps as an Incomparable," Selena added, not quite truthfully. "She believes you would benefit from some training in the arts of a young lady, and she suggested we start working on that now." Selena was eager to get her away from Lord Harrowden. "Shall we go then?"

Rebecca turned and followed Selena without arguing, although she sighed again. Loudly. Lord Harrowden took a step forward, as if he was going to join them, but with a glance at Selena, he turned abruptly and left through the door that led to the stables. Selena hoped he would go for a horseback ride and lose himself in the woods.

She opened the door to the sitting room. "I believe we can be comfortable here. Lady Harrowden is, as we speak, directing the servants to prepare a move to the dower house."

"Move?" Rebecca exclaimed. "I have no interest in moving. I like it here. I've always envisioned myself in a grand estate like this, and it suits me very well to live here. Although," she said reflectively, "I would not mind settling for a smaller estate if I married Sir Lucius."

There was so much to address, Selena did not know where to begin.

"Rebecca, if you wish to make a good marriage and be mistress of an estate like this, you need training. There are no two ways about it." In her most coaxing manner, Selena added, "No young lady likes training—or perhaps there are very few who excel in such arts. There are many more of us who wish to have an adventure, or wish to do something else rather than hold ourselves perfectly straight, or sit and force a needle into fabric, or wrack our brains to remember how to conjugate French verbs. But it is something we all must do."

Selena ended with a breathless huff. She hadn't realized how much of her own frustration was coming out, especially since she *had* done all these things and where had they led her? Straight to the role of governess-companion to two of the least grateful women she had ever had the privilege to meet. At the very least, she could torture

Rebecca with the same training. The thought gave her quiet satisfaction.

At the same time, she was cognizant that allowing her frustration
to win out—if it became habit—put her at risk of becoming a bitter
old woman. Then she would be little better than the countess.

Selena's voice of authority seemed to have penetrated Rebecca's
mist of selfishness, because after considering for a moment, she asked,
"Do you really think this will help me to make the match I wish for?"

"I can make no promises, but I do believe it will help." Selena
replied, glad that her charge seemed to have caught on at last.
"Remember what Sir Lucius warned you against at the ball. *This* is
what we are training for."

"To gain a marriage contract with Sir Lucius?" Rebecca clarified.

Selena immediately realized her mistake and taxed her ingenuity to
address such obstinacy. "You are still thinking of him, and him alone?
But you have already received much attention, and this was just a small
assembly. Imagine how much success you would have if you were to go
to London," Selena said. "Don't you dream of making a splash there,
where the world is at your feet? You could make a very good match, if
that is your mission." She felt a twinge of guilt at appealing to Rebecca's shallower tendencies, but she shoved that aside. It was pure
survival at this point.

"I suppose so," Rebecca said. "But I have never seen such a handsome man as Sir Lucius, who has perfect address, who is titled and
already wealthy. And it would be *such* a conquest to turn his head. All
my former classmates would be so jealous. Plus, I'm not sure another
such man as Sir Lucius exists."

Selena privately agreed and could not argue. But perhaps, with
time, Rebecca's head might be turned by another young man. "Very
well, if that is what you wish for, let us work on making you a suitable
wife for him," Selena said.

It caused her a pang, but she tried to convince herself that she
meant it, too. As it stood, Sir Lucius had given Selena no indication,
other than a smoldering look and a request to stay, that he considered
her a potential candidate. She may as well carry out her unenviable
task of training Rebecca to satisfaction.

Selena's words worked like a charm, and Rebecca suddenly became much more complacent. She began listening attentively and even seeking praise for her efforts. Selena had her demonstrate her walk and her speech, then instructed her on what needed improvement. She had Rebecca exhibit what she knew of watercolors, which was even less than Selena. Her charge knew absolutely nothing of French.

"What were you learning in that school?" Selena asked her in puzzlement. It seemed Rebecca had not picked up on any of the womanly arts.

"Oh, I did not pay much attention. I did whatever I felt like, and I believe as long as my trustees continued to pay, the school mistress was happy to let me do what I wished. It was only when I left without telling them where I was that they decided the reputation of the school might be compromised." She rolled her eyes. "That's when they decided they wished to send me away. Very poor spirited of them, I must say. I am sure many of the girls admired such a bold move as I had made. They are probably still there being forced to learn their lessons, and look where *I* am!"

Selena was not amused and couldn't resist a riposte. "Yes. *You* are here—forced to learn yours. So you see, it all comes to the same thing. If you know what you want, you must apply yourself to gain it. Come, let us stop and have some tea."

19

LUCIUS PACED BEFORE THE WINDOW, a sign of agitation he permitted himself when he was alone. His servants likely suspected something was amiss since he had responded to Finn with impatience when the groom brought news that his gelding had contracted mud fever.

No, he was not his usual complacent self. But tonight was the night of Maria's dinner party, and George had not returned, and Lucius could not move forward with pursuing Selena until he had set everything to rights at Harrowden. He owed it to Lady Harrowden to make good on his promise to her husband, and he owed it to Selena to offer her a marriage that would not come at the expense of others. Lucius had even gone so far as to inquire after a suitable replacement for Rebecca's governess from chance words that Maria had let fall. He would waste no time in suggesting that to Lady Harrowden, once he had secured Selena's hand.

Lucius trusted his brother would come without fail and hoped he would bring news of Lord Harrowden that could shed light on his situation. How ironic it would be if the earl had gambled away his fortune, and the cavalier treatment to which he had shown Selena would be brought down upon his own head. That was what came of all the criticism and prejudice Harrowden had thrown Selena's way—it would come back to haunt him.

Lucius sat in his armchair and looked at the empty one to his right. He leaned his chin in his hand. She had looked back at him at the ball, when he had been talking to Philippa. She smiled at him from across the room and their gazes held, and when he could not resist looking back, her eyes were still on him. That's when he knew she'd felt something for him. The next morning, he'd kissed her hand in the drawing room, and her hand fit perfectly in his. But it wasn't enough. He wanted more than anything to pull Selena into his arms.

He looked at the empty chair again, a smile hovering on his lips. When she was Lady Clavering, she would not be sitting in *that* chair. She would be sitting in *his*. On his lap and in his arms.

He leapt to his feet and began pacing again. He needed to be moving but refused to go riding, although he had an ardent desire to see Selena. He wanted to be sure she would be present this evening. But he couldn't leave when he knew George would come. And sure enough, he was just crossing over to the shelves to find some book to read—of which he would likely stare at the pages with his mind far away—when the sound of the front door opening reached his ears. *George*. No one else would come in unannounced and without knocking.

The door opened, and Lucius turned to walk forward. "I knew you would come without fail. What news did you bring?"

George laughed boyishly and removed his hat and gloves, handing them to Briggs who had followed him in. "Offer me some ale if you would. I have just returned directly from London and have not stopped at Maria's yet."

Lucius indicated for Briggs to obey his brother's request then gestured forward. "Certainly." He led the way to the chairs near the fire, where he motioned for his brother to sit.

"Well, I've been waiting for this news," he said. "Out with it."

"Lucius, you're becoming a regular bear. All right. You were right. Harrowden has engaged in some wild speculation. Something about a cotton mill in Glasgow. He'd already had an unfortunate gambling habit, which you knew of, and there are several IOUs unpaid. That is why he can't show his face in London. But some of his cronies at The Cocoa Tree had spoken of a sure thing, and all that can be said is that Harrowden showed a mighty interest in the project, asking a number of questions in front of others until he perhaps realized he should be more circumspect. He followed Williams out of the club, deep in conversation."

George met Lucius's gaze. "London is abuzz with talk that the speculation failed. Something about a typhus epidemic that wiped out half the workers, and if that weren't enough—the mill went up in a blaze a couple weeks ago. It's news because a few gentlemen had put their hopes in it. It was said to be a sure thing, although I'm not sure all of them would have invested to the extent that I suspect our neighbor has. His gambling debts had become very pressing. Almost everyone I spoke to—all in great confidence, of course—believe the same thing. Harrowden is in over his head."

Lucius leaned back as the news sank in. "Hm. I suppose it comes as no surprise in the end. It won't take long for news to reach here. I owe it to our family relations to assist Lady Harrowden in whatever way I can, but there might not be much I can do. If Harrowden has mortgaged the unentailed portions, the estate will have trouble supporting itself. Did you manage to find a solicitor?"

"Yes, I went to see the two names you gave me. The first was in India, but the second man said he had a peer who was located in Hertfordshire not far from here, who might be a better fit. So I have brought his direction and name to you. What will happen to Lady Harrowden?"

"Her jointure should provide a modest living for her, and she can probably afford even a servant or two. But it will not at all be what she is accustomed to, especially if she must leave Harrowden estate and will no longer have access to the dower house. I do not know what property is entailed and what is not. As much as she can be a difficult old woman, I would not wish it on her—not at this stage in her life."

George shook his head. "Nor I."

Lucius looked up when Briggs opened the door carrying two tankards. "Ah. The ale you've been waiting for. Here—then I imagine you'll want to go back to Maria's to refresh yourself? And I will go see this solicitor. Just so you know, there is a dinner party tonight, and I plan to attend."

"Trying to get rid of me already? Much thanks I get." George took a deep swallow, then looked at Lucius with interest. "You're coming back to Maria's so soon? What do you hope to achieve by going?"

"It's none of your business, young cawker." Lucius laughed as George pulled a face. "However, since you troubled yourself to go to London for me, I'll tell you. My hope is to right a past wrong and relegate Miss Lockhart to a position of dignity. I believe Downing is still there, and I made sure an invitation would be sent to the Harrowdens."

"You hope to redeem yourself in Miss Lockhart's eyes," George said and smiled knowingly. "Good. May she be willing to overlook your gross lack of chivalry and not have you tossed out for the presumption as you deserve."

"As you say." Lucius would let his brother tease. In any case, he deserved the reproach.

~

SELENA STOOD IN THE CORRIDOR, listening. She turned in a full circle, but saw no one. No one carrying a tray, or standing at the door, or ducking out of sight when she passed by. How strange that she didn't notice the servants' activity until the absence of it overwhelmed her with its silence. Could it be possible they were all upstairs assisting Lady Harrowden with the packing?

A knock sounded at the door, and Selena waited, but no one came rushing to answer it. After a moment's hesitation, she went to the door and opened it.

Standing on the other side was a tradesman, or a servant of some sort, and Selena looked at him questioningly. He pulled off his cap and bowed before her. "Excuse me, miss. I was told to speak to the cook."

"I believe you will find her at the servant's entrance," Selena replied, slowly. A tradesman at the front door? "You are not aware of how to reach it, perhaps?"

"I knocked there, but no one answered. And Messir Anton, the butcher, said I was to deliver the message come what may, begging your pardon, miss. He said as to tell you there warn't be any more meat delivered until his bill is paid."

Selena knit her brows. Surely such a basic bill could not be over-due? She had suspected there were some inconsistencies with Lord Harrowden's manner of living and the allowance the estate provided, and Lady Harrowden had hinted as much. But meat was such a basic item. Surely there must be some misunderstanding?

"Wait here. I will bring the cook to speak to you." Selena closed the door and hurried down to the kitchen. She met the sight of Mrs. Randall with some relief. There were still servants at Harrowden after all.

"Mrs. Randall, I believe you must be busy at the moment, for I know Lady Harrowden requested your presence, but there is someone at the door—"

"Yes, it is just as you say, Miss Lockhart. I am unable to attend to the person at the door. Perhaps you could see Mullings? Ah, no. Mullings left this morning. Or..." Mrs. Randall's voice trailed away, and that's when Selena noticed just how harassed she was.

Selena looked at the housekeeper in concern. "Now, it is a very odd thing, but there are no servants about. Not a one. And now there is a tradesman at the front door saying there will be no meat delivered as promised until the bill is paid." Selena looked around. "Where is Cook?"

Mrs. Randall began to wring her hands. "Some of the servants have chosen to abandon their posts today, and I do not know what to do. Their wages have not been paid in some months. Cook is one of them."

Selena's throat began to close in a familiar mounting of panic. It had started in this same way when her own household began to disinte-grate, and as much as she found it arduous to like Lady Harrowden, it would be much more difficult for the countess to recuperate after such a loss than it had been for Selena, who was young and surrounded by family. Lady Harrowden was a widow.

Selena pushed past the lump in her throat. "I will attend to the tradesman. Do we not have any household savings? Can I not pay the bill and have meat sent for tonight's supper?"

Mrs. Randall shook her head. "I do not know how we will manage. The earl has been elusive about the estate's finances, and I dared not question him further. But it has been some time that we've been living on credit, and we are no longer able to pay the bills when they come in. It's been difficult to get candles and the most basic supplies for the household. And now we have only a handful of servants remaining. I've been here my whole life, but those who have no loyalty to Harrowden left today."

Selena's thoughts raced as she fixed her gaze on Mrs. Randall. The first person she thought of who might be able to advise her was Sir Lucius, but that was ridiculous. What had he to do with Harrowden's troubles, even if he did have a promise to fulfill to Lady Harrowden. Perhaps based on that promise, she could speak with him about this matter. He did say she could send for him if she needed him.

The thought of seeking out Sir Lucius's counsel made Selena's pulse quicken. She mounted the stairs, turning the idea over in her mind, and went to the door where the tradesman was still waiting. "I am not able to find the cook at present, but we will send someone to pay the bill as soon as it may be contrived." The tradesman gave an awkward bow and left without another word.

Selena did not know why she needed to tell such a fib. If they did not have the money now, they would not have it later. Perhaps it was to save her own face and not have to relive the trauma of being dunned by tradesmen. Or maybe she wished to spare Lady Harrowden—she could not discern the workings of her heart. But she simply could not tell that man they had no money when she still hoped it might be found.

Selena took a deep breath and turned to go inside. She had to consult with the countess. Selena climbed the steps quickly and rapped on the door. When she heard the call to enter, she did so and found Lady Harrowden directing one of the servants to pack the collection of embroidered linens that had been laid out for her perusal.

Selena stepped forward and waited until the countess turned her attention. "My lady, might I have a word with you?"

Lady Harrowden snapped her fingers at the maid who seemed to be moving too slowly for her taste. "Hurry up, girl. We will soon need to get ready for tonight's dinner party at the Holbecks. You are moving much too slowly. The sooner I can remove to the dower house, the better it will be for me." She then turned to Selena. "Must you interrupt me now? Cannot you see I am too busy. What did you do with Rebecca? Have you finished your training today?"

Selena gathered her courage. "My lady, it is a matter of great urgency that I must speak with you alone. Please."

At last, Lady Harrowden turned her full attention on Selena, although a look of fresh irritation crossed her features. "Very well. Everyone leave the room."

When the maid and footman had left, Lady Harrowden sat with a groan. She was surely unaccustomed to so much activity, even though she had not left her own chambers.

"Well, out with it," she said. "What seems to be amiss? Did you get Rebecca ready for tonight? You understand you are not to go with us this time. I believe that horrid gentlemen will still be there, and I do not want any more embarrassment, either for you or me."

"Yes, I understood that," Selena said, "and it accords perfectly with my own wishes. I am happy to comply."

Selena took the chair across from her. She needed to be eye level with the countess. "My lady, Mrs. Randall has just informed me that many servants have walked off today because their wages have not been paid in months. People are beginning to suspect they will not be paid at all."

Lady Harrowden pinched her lips so tightly, the lines around her mouth turned white. Although Selena feared for Lady Harrowden, she thought it best to say everything.

"And when I was in the entryway, there was a knock on the front door. I opened it because there were no servants there to do it, and it was the apprentice to the butcher, who came to have his bill paid. He knocked at the front door because no one answered at the servants' entrance, and he was told that he could not leave until he had delivered his message. He said there will be no meat brought to this house until we have paid the bill. It has been several months since they have received anything from us."

"That is impossible," Lady Harrowden snapped, but she had gone pale, and her eyes were wide. "You must be mistaken."

Selena shook her head. "I had it directly from his lips, and I met Mrs. Randall in the kitchen. She appears to be in a bit of shock."

Lady Harrowden lifted a shaking hand. "Call Mrs. Randall to me. And tell Morgan to prepare something for me, for I am feeling faint."

Selena rang the bell then took her place at the countess's side. Lady Harrowden stared blankly in front of her before seeming to come to a decision.

"This is what we are to do, Selena. You will go in my stead tonight, and you will tell the Holbecks that I am unwell. Tell Maria to send Sir Lucius to me, if he is not there for you to tell him yourself, and you will keep an eye on Rebecca. I don't care if my nephew goes or not. That is not my concern. But we must keep up appearances as long as we are able. We must fix this mess before things go too far, if such a thing is possible."

Mrs. Randall entered, her face pinched in worry, and Selena stood. She would see Sir Lucius this evening. Then again—she would likely be forced to see Matthew Downing. Pleasure did not live without pain in the world of a Lockhart.

"Very well, my lady," she said. "I will do as you say."

🦋 20 🦋

SELENA LEFT Lady Harrowden's presence and went in search of Rebecca. She found her in her room with stacks of dresses strewn about—as if each one had been pulled out for her inspection. Alice was holding a dress up to her mistress, and they both turned to look at Selena when she walked in.

Rebecca huffed in frustration. "The modiste has not brought the silk gown she promised for tonight. She sent someone with her apologies, but she must not think I will be using her services again. Now what shall I do? I have absolutely *nothing* I can wear."

Selena stepped forward, eyeing the mounds of dresses that covered the bed and armchairs. Rebecca had more gowns than Selena had ever possessed, even during her London Season.

"I am certain you will find an appropriate dress from this pile. You have plenty of choices. It is not as if people will see you in something you've worn before; you have not been here long enough." She eyed the one Rebecca's maid had held up and gestured to that one. "This will do very well—the color suits your complexion. I have come to see to it that we are on time. Lady Harrowden will not be joining us tonight at the Holbecks. She has asked me to accompany you in her place."

Rebecca took the news without question but fretted and mourned the loss of the dress that would not arrive. Selena did not have the patience to coax her into a better humor. "Alice, please ensure that Rebecca is ready by eight o'clock."

Selena left and made her way to her own room. She had two hours to dress and prepare herself for the unpleasantness of seeing Mr. Downing again. It was fortunate they had been invited to dinner. It might delay Rebecca's suspicion that all was not well at the estate.

As Selena unwound her hair and brushed it before tying it up again, she wondered where Lord Harrowden was and whether he would go tonight. She had not seen him all day, which was as unusual as having a house empty of servants. His absence was an improvement, but it was nevertheless worrisome. Something was not right, and Selena felt as though she were waiting for a storm to break.

She took a look at her own stash of dresses. All the ones she had arrived with were worn. There was one serviceable dress she had managed to make up in slate bombazine, in addition to the unfortunate ball gown. She would have to wear the slate dress, which was rather informal for evening wear but was the best she had. As for the ball gown, she never wanted to wear that again.

At five minutes to eight, Selena went downstairs in search of the one remaining footman, who she eventually found in the kitchen with Hazel. He leapt to attention when Selena entered.

"Please have the carriage brought around, as we are going out tonight," she said.

He bowed. "Yes, miss."

Selena watched him go and wondered why he had chosen to stay when all the others had left, then glanced at Hazel's blushing face and thought she had her answer. Selena was grateful he'd continued to treat her with a mark of respect. Although this catastrophe was not her own affair—unlike the first one—it still hit too close to home for her to be comfortable.

Alice, to her credit, had Rebecca turned out and downstairs at eight o'clock on the dot, and Rebecca looked charming in the dress she'd chosen. She must have known it, for she was in a complacent mood.

The groom brought the carriage around, and Selena wondered if even at the last minute Lord Harrowden would appear and join them, but he did not come. She felt free under the absence of his mocking regard, although she knew that other challenges awaited her at the dinner that night—ones that would be even less comfortable.

As the groom brought the carriage up to the front entrance of the Holbeck's estate, everything was quiet outside, unlike their formal ball days earlier. Although the windows were lit, and they could hear sounds of voices from within, there was no receiving line or guests in the entryway. The Holbeck's butler brought Selena and Rebecca into the room where the other guests were gathered.

The first set of eyes that turned her way were those of Mr. Downing's, and it took everything in Selena not to quail and run back to the carriage. She looked away.

Mrs. Holbeck stepped forward and clasped one of Rebecca's hands in hers. "It is most delightful to have you back at our house, my dear." She glanced at Selena, then turned back to Rebecca. "But where is Lady Harrowden? The other invitation was specifically for her."

Rebecca looked at Selena, hesitantly. She had not asked in the carriage why Lady Harrowden was not coming, as it likely had not occurred to her.

Selena answered. "Lady Harrowden is not well, and she requested that I chaperone Miss Woodlsey in her place." Mrs. Holbeck returned a tight smile, then left Selena and Rebecca to themselves and went to join a conversation with other guests. One of the young women standing with her mother nearby commented softly on Rebecca's dress, and Rebecca turned to her, leaving Selena alone.

Sir Lucius entered through a door in the drawing room. When he spotted Selena, he started toward her with a smile, which she could not resist returning, although she hoped it might not be noticed.

"You've made it," he said. "Maria had just told me minutes earlier that you would not be coming, as you had not been invited. I was about to leave."

Selena's eyes widened. She could not mistake his meaning, and it made her heart beat loudly in her chest. "Sir Lucius, I must have a word with you."

He leaned forward and put his lips close to her ear. "*Lucius*, if you please."

Selena darted her gaze to the side and saw Mrs. Holbeck watching them. She turned to Sir Lucius. "Lady Harrowden is under great duress. It appears several bills have not been paid at the estate, and many of the servants have quit their posts because they have not received pay in some months. A tradesman came to the door today, and he said there would be no meat delivered until the bill was paid."

She saw her concern reflected in his eyes and felt insensibly better. She did not have to share this worry alone. "Lady Harrowden was so shocked she stayed to her bed this evening, which is why she is not here."

Sir Lucius pursed his lips. "I must tell you, this comes as no surprise to me, although he must have been borrowing from the estate almost from the time of his inheritance for things to progress this quickly. My brother, George, returned from London this morning, where he made inquiries about Harrowden's situation. It turns out he speculated wildly on some scheme that failed, and in addition to his own disastrous gambling habits, I fear it will not be long before he comes to ruin."

A frisson of fear stole over Selena. "What will that mean for us? Will Lady Harrowden still be able to move to the dower house?"

Sir Lucius bent his head close to Selena as he spoke. "I will be bringing both an accountant and a solicitor to meet with Lady Harrowden tomorrow, as it happens, to look into her jointure and the accounts that pertain to her. I don't know whether the dower house was entailed along with the rest of the estate, but in all events, the consequences of Harrowden's actions will result in pain for the countess, because her name will be attached to the scandal. There is no way to avoid it."

Selena glanced around the room and was reassured that people were not paying her too much attention, despite how closely she and Sir Lucius stood. Perhaps this evening would go more smoothly than she had feared. Then she chanced to look again at Mrs. Holbeck, who had her eyes trained on them, and revised her assessment. The woman could stare daggers.

She was still unwilling to end a conversation that brought her comfort in an evening otherwise fraught with tension.

"It was distressing to have a tradesman at the door," Selena said. "He came to the front entrance because he'd knocked on the servant's entrance, and no one was there to receive him. The cook had walked off by then. The tradesman said he'd been ordered to deliver the bill by any means necessary, and apparently that meant knocking on the front door."

Sir Lucius brushed his arm against hers in their nearness. "This is not a storm of your brewing. You are just a companion to the countess. You need not suffer for Harrowden's folly."

A sudden surge of tears welled up in Selena's eyes, but she quickly blinked them away. "I believe you cannot fully understand. It is too reminiscent of what happened in my own family, and it opens up fresh wounds. Knowing what it is to have undergone such scandal, I could not wish it on anyone, even if Lady Harrowden is not always particularly kind to me."

"You deserve better, Selena." Lucius's voice was deep, and he said her name like a caress. "I will come see Lady Harrowden tomorrow. And you—" He waited until she looked up at him. "Make sure you accord me a few minutes of your time as well." Lucius took her hand in his and pressed it, and Selena again found herself glancing at his sister, whose face was rigid.

"I will," Selena replied breathlessly. He had used her Christian name, and she found herself without the strength or desire to object.

Mrs. Holbeck had begun pairing people up for the dinner table according to some prearranged plan of hers. "Lucius, take Miss Woodsley into the room," she ordered.

There were no other eligible gentlemen when it came time for Selena, and she followed the couples into the dining room and sat in the only chair available. It was to the left of Mr. Downing.

Selena's heart sank. This was what she had feared. Apart from glancing at her once, Mr. Downing did not acknowledge her and turned to his partner on the right for the first course. Selena ate in silence, as it appeared the older man to her left was deaf. But when the courses changed, Mr. Downing served himself some poultry and turned to her.

"I did not expect that you would return here, " he said. "I thought you'd had enough after the ball the other night. It was quite a reunion of sorts. To own the truth, I never expected to see you again when you left London."

"I did not have a choice in the matter," Selena replied. "Lady Harrowden fell ill at the last minute, and I needed to chaperone Miss Woodsley tonight. It was not my intention to come, believe me. I'd had my fill of you the other night."

He laughed in much the same way she remembered. How could she ever have thought his laughter held warmth? "I can imagine so. It was such a shock to see you, Selena—I could not help myself. You look every bit as beautiful as you did when we were engaged. And, if I may pay you a compliment, you have not lost your proud bearing even as a paid companion. You've held up well."

Selena lifted an eyebrow and managed to keep her hand steady when she lifted her fork to her mouth. She did not think it necessary to thank him. And although the errant thought of bringing the tines of Selena's fork down on his hand—*hard*—crossed her mind, her training led her to continue a conversation as though they were not enemies.

"I have not followed your career. Did you achieve the position in parliament you wished for?" Selena chewed the food in her mouth, which was as dry as sawdust.

Mr. Downing took a sip of wine and answered in his Elected Official voice. "Yes, I was elected into parliament three months after our engagement was at an end."

Because our engagement was at an end, you meant to say. "I know that was always one of your ambitions. How wonderful for you that you were able to realize it."

Mr. Downing fingered the stem of his wineglass on the table. "Now I suppose it is left to me to find a wife. I had not thought to do so, but seeing you again has made me realize that it was once my ambition, and it is not a bad one as far as ambitions go. It will portray me as a serious gentleman who can advance in politics. Without a family, there is a risk that I am seen as too young."

"Well." Selena gave a tight smile. "There is nothing hindering you from finding a wife now, is there?" When would the course change, so she could be freed from this tormenting conversation?

"Your charge seems to be full of spirit." Mr. Downing directed his gaze at Rebecca across the table, and Selena followed it. "I thought her a bit fast the other night, but one must admit she has many graces."

"She is beautiful—that is very true, Mr. Downing. And although there can be no objections to you pursuing her, Lady Harrowden has determined that she will not be presented this Season, but the one after that."

"I have heard she is in possession of thirty-thousand pounds." Mr. Downing peeled his gaze off Rebecca and turned back to Selena. "Perhaps I will continue my visits to the Holbecks, so I might steal a march on the other gentlemen in London. It is not often that one finds such a beautiful face attached to such a pretty figure."

His words sparked a flash of temper in Selena, who replied, "By *figure*, I can only assume you mean her income. By all means, pursue her. But as you are lacking a title, I don't believe you will find her so easy to tempt."

Across from them, Sir Lucius laughed at something Rebecca said, and Selena thought she saw a strain around his eyes. Or perhaps she had merely imagined it. Apart from suffering more of Mr. Downing's presence in Hertfordshire, the last thing Selena wished for was to watch Rebecca flirt with Sir Lucius.

The words came out before she could stop them. "You may find that someone else has already stolen a march on you." She indicated Sir Lucius with the tilt of her chin. It was more from spite toward Mr. Downing, than conviction that she added, "I believe his sister would like to see this match prosper. So if you intend to use this as a place to stay while you pursue Miss Woodsley, you may not have an ally in that quarter."

Mr. Downing returned an indifferent answer, but Selena knew his wheels were turning. They had not spent a year in courtship without her learning the extent of his ambitions. It would be too much for him to let thirty-thousand pounds slip through his fingers without making a push.

Eventually the interminable dinner ended, and Selena made her way to the drawing room where whist tables were being set up.

Mrs. Holbeck was directing the affairs. "Philippa, I did not count you in our number. We have enough full sets excluding you." She glanced at Selena but did not consider it necessary to tell her that she, too, was excluded. Selena turned to the settees on one side of the room, and Philippa came over to join her with a shy smile and a remark on how much she hated whist.

～

LUCIUS LISTENED with half an ear as Rebecca regaled him with her stories over dinner. His thoughts were on Selena, sitting close to Downing. That must have been a last minute alteration of Maria's since she never would have put Lady Harowden next to him. Her only design could have been to increase Selena's discomfort. He would have to have a strong word with his sister.

He played one round of whist, while discreetly watching Philippa in conversation with Selena. They looked upon easy terms, and he was glad that not all his siblings were as prejudiced as Maria. When the thirteen tricks had been tallied, and Lucius's partner excused herself from playing another hand, he went over to the window alcove, debating on whether he should interrupt Philippa's conversation, or if it were better that the two should become acquainted.

Downing appeared at his side, greeting him with a nod. "Sir Lucius."

"Downing," Lucius returned. They stood silently for a moment, and Lucius folded his arms, while Downing studied the enamel lid to his snuffbox. The air was thick with tension. It was so ridiculous Lucius wanted to laugh—as if the two men were about to face each other in the ring. He could hear the quiet strains of Selena and Philippa's conversation to his right. Lucius would not speak first, but he was curious why Downing had chosen to seek him out.

"I am told you're pursuing her." Downing nodded in the direction of the room where Selena was sitting.

Lucius wondered what interest the man could possibly have in who

Lucius chose to pursue when he had already abandoned all claims to Selena. "Who gave you such information?" he asked.

Downing took out his snuff box, eyeing Lucius as he took a pinch. "Selena did," he said shortly.

Lucius drew back in astonishment. Selena told her ex-fiancé that Lucius was pursuing her? That seemed an awfully bold move on her part, unless she wished to make Downing jealous. Perhaps the unthinkable was possible. Perhaps she still had feelings for the man, although he had treated her abominably. Lucius thought about it. No, it was more likely that she wished for Downing to know she was not wearing the willow for him.

"It is true," Lucius said carefully. "I am hoping she will become my wife." *There! I've done what I came for.* Lucius would no longer remain silent where his feelings for Selena were concerned. He would tell the whole world and defy them to criticize his choice.

"I might have some interest in that quarter too," Downing replied in just that pompous, arrogant way, as if they were discussing horseflesh for purchase at Tattersall's. Lucius could scarcely credit his ears.

"I regret to inform you that you had your chance long ago. You gave it up, and that is your own loss."

Downing scrunched his pale eyebrows together in confusion. "I've only just met the girl. How can you say I've already had my chance?"

Downing glanced at Selena where Lucius's eyes were trained, and understanding dawned. "Oh, are you now referring to Selena? Yes, I had my chance and was clever enough to pull out before I was irrevocably tied. That would've been ruinous for my career. But with Miss Woodsley, I will acquire a charming social hostess at my side and, if I may speak freely between gentlemen, her dowry at my disposal."

Lucius's mind was reeling, for as much as he'd planned to declare his intentions toward Selena publicly, he hadn't intended to wear his heart on his sleeve without provocation. He looked about the room as he fiddled with his pocket watch, needing a minute to gather his thoughts. So Downing had not been talking about Selena. He was now intent on pursuing Miss Woodsley? Well, he could join the list of people who had their eye on her fortune. Lucius couldn't care less about that.

Now that he'd committed himself, he may as well go the whole way. "You may do as you like. I was not referring to Miss Woodsley for myself. I was referring to Miss Lockhart."

Downing's eyes opened in astonishment. "You are interested in Selena? But there is a scandal attached to her name, of which I am sure you are aware."

"I could hardly have remained in ignorance after you publicly humiliated her at the ball. But unlike you," Lucius replied, "the scandal affects me not in the least, as it was not of her making but her father's, and he is no longer alive. I don't need the income of a wealthy bride. I have only to please myself in choosing a wife." He faced Downing squarely. "And I will thank you to address her as Miss Lockhart from now on."

"Until she becomes Lady Clavering, or even then?" Downing sneered. His eyes on Selena, he added, "She can be a bit of a shrew. I suppose you've not become acquainted with that side of her, but it will surface, given enough time."

Lucius could not retaliate. He had no way of knowing if what Downing said was true—he'd not had enough time to know her deeply. And the fact that Downing knew Selena better than he did incensed him. However, now committed, he refused to give Downing the last word.

"I have seen Miss Lockhart in difficult straits, but nothing has given me cause to feel anything but esteem for her. I can only suppose your lack of gentlemanly conduct has been behind any untoward behavior you imagine her to have displayed." Lucius worked his jaw, trying to keep his temper in check. "I thank you for having thrown her over all those years ago. Although I would not like her to have suffered such humiliation, it suits my purposes, exactly."

Then, because Lucius could not bear another moment in Downing's presence, he walked over to where Philippa was still sitting with Selena. He paused before addressing her.

"Miss Lockhart," he began, attempting a light tone to cover the irritation that still coursed through him. "I hope you are instructing my ne'er-do-well sister on proper decorum. I begin to fear it is lost upon her."

Selena smiled and blushed prettily, darting a glance at Philippa. "No, she was telling me all about your antics when you were little. I have learned so much."

Lucius raised an eyebrow and allowed a smile to lift the corners of his mouth. "She could not possibly know anything about me. She is years younger."

"No, it is only what I cobbled together from George—and Finn when he's saddling my horse for me. He lets things fall." Philippa's eyes twinkled in amusement, and Lucius opened his mouth to speak.

"Lucius!"

He looked around as Maria called his attention, then turned back to Selena and Philippa. "It looks as though I'm going to be called into another game of whist. I will come and see you tomorrow, Miss Lockhart, where I hope to undo all the falsehoods Philippa has poured into your ear." He gave her a wink and left.

❧ 21 ❧

THE NEXT DAY Lord Harrowden strolled into the breakfast room, looking as though he had not slept or bathed in two days. It was clear to Selena he had spent the night carousing.

"What. Is this all there is?" he asked, examining the collection of dishes on the sideboard. There was coffee and chocolate in silver pots, and there were rolls with butter and jam in small dishes. But there were none of the kippers or sausages or any of the other breakfast foods that generally graced the sideboard.

Selena met his gaze directly. "A tradesman came from town demanding to be paid for the butcher's bill. He said until it was paid, there would be no more meat delivered. In addition, a great number of servants abandoned their posts yesterday."

Lord Harrowden averted his eyes, and she delivered the home thrust. "The estate cannot continue to function in its usual way until some of the bills are paid, and measures have gotten rather desperate."

It was all she needed to say. Lord Harrowden had a wild look about him—she'd never seen him appear so panicked and unkempt. He dropped the saucer he had picked up, and it clattered on the wooden sideboard. He turned without a word and walked out the door.

We're in for it now. She needed to send a letter to her mother to let her know she would be returning home, but she wasn't sure she could even expect her wages. Had Lord Harrowden's folly touched the countess in some fiscal way? How would Selena get home if she were not to be paid?

She left the breakfast room and met Rebecca coming downstairs at an unseasonable hour. Selena had decided to continue her work as if nothing were amiss until the estate could no longer support her, so she seized this chance.

"Rebecca, I did not look to see you up so early, but I'm glad you are here because we have much work to do. Why do you not go into the breakfast room and eat something, and then we may begin."

Rebecca exhaled through puckered lips. "Very well then."

Selena went to the stairs, but a knock on the door brought her up short. She no longer expected anyone to answer the door unless the lone footman happened to be nearby. As Selena headed to the door, she saw Rebecca disappear into the billiard room instead of the breakfast room. Rebecca must have seen Lord Harrowden there, which did not bode well. The less time they spent in each other's company, the better.

When Selena opened the door, Sir Lucius was standing on the other side of it. His eyes widened in surprise when he saw her.

"What, are you answering the door now? They have not given you a third role, I should hope."

His teasing brought a reluctant smile to Selena's face. With him she could almost feel that the world was not falling apart at the seams, although the deliberateness of his gaze made her nervous. "Why yes, indeed. Please come in—what has brought you to Harrowden?"

"You." Sir Lucius stepped inside, inches away, and she turned her eyes up to meet his. A smile hovered on his lips. "The solicitor and accountant will both arrive shortly, but I came ahead of them so I might speak to you alone. May we have private conversation in the drawing room?"

Selena's heart began to beat wildly, and she turned to hide her confusion. "Certainly. Follow me."

The drawing room was empty, and her footsteps echoed as she walked across the floor. Through the window, she saw mounds of white snow, which had not melted, although they'd had a warm wind in the past day that would bring on a temporary thaw.

Selena turned to face Sir Lucius, who was standing at arm's length. His normally severe expression held a tender look. She could not explain it to herself, but she craved his nearness. Breathless, Selena gestured to the seats before the fire, which brought to mind the intimacy—and pain—of their last conversation.

"Would you like to sit down?"

"I would like to marry you," he said.

A flush sprang to Selena's cheeks. "What? Why? Surely..."

Lucius closed the remaining distance with one short stride. He inclined his head, a slight crinkle in his brow. "You must have known what I was hinting at when I asked you to stay."

Selena shook her head mutely. "I didn't know why you asked me to stay. I didn't expect that."

He took her hands in his and held them to his lips. "But you are not opposed to the idea?" he asked.

For the first time in their acquaintance, Lucius looked nervous. Selena's gaze dropped to the folds of his cravat, and he brought their clasped hands to his chest, waiting. Her heart was too full to speak. She had never wanted anything more than she wanted now to say yes, but the thought of what it would mean—the thought of facing Society with its mockery and derision—made acceptance impossible.

"Selena, ever since you walked through my door, I have been undergoing...changes." Lucius took a deep breath, and spoke quickly, as if trying to get all his words out. "I think of you constantly. I think of your life here at Harrowden and am unsettled because you are not spending it with me. It's the first time I've ever wished for such a thing. Apart from the family obligations I deem my duty to fulfill, I've never considered another person's comfort above my own. That is..." Lucius paused. "That is until the night of the ball when I refused to speak out in your defense. I hadn't known my own mind then, and I did not dare make any kind of public declaration—not when I hadn't made a private one in my own heart."

He reached up and traced his finger along the line of her jaw, tilting her face up to catch her gaze. Selena shivered under his touch, still mute with the wave of long-suppressed feelings that surged up.

"But I have heartily regretted that foolish decision at the ball. It brought my selfishness to light and made me hate the man I'd become. It made me long to be someone new. So I'm asking you—will you have me?"

Selena glanced at the door, fearful that someone would walk in at that moment, and at the same time, hoping for it. She was not prepared to give an answer. What had brought about this change of heart? How could she be sure it was long-lasting? If Lucius could turn away from her in front of everyone at the ball, what's to say it wouldn't happen again—or worse! That he would regret having married her?

Every journey to London would entail a risk, as she would surely be met with censure and scorn. He would be reminded of her low position at every turn, causing him to doubt— then regret. He would finish by relegating her to some country estate while he went to London to meet his mistress. Had he not treated her with scorn at their first meeting? And everyone spoke of his reputation. A man did not come by such a thing innocently.

Selena shook her head, her eyes now trained on the floor. She could not meet his gaze. "I do not think I can. I do not think I will marry. You don't know how superficial the *ton* is—I will never be welcomed in it."

"Selena." Lucius held her hands in his firmly, and she was yoked to him, tethered mere inches away. "I am part of the *ton*. I know how it operates. But it's made up of people, and each person acts according to his own conscience. Mine tells me you will make me happy. Only say that you will be my wife."

Selena bit her lip and refused to answer. Perhaps it was childish of her, or fearful, or foolish. Perhaps she was being unreasonably stubborn. But it did not seem possible that the feelings he professed to have for her would last.

"Selena, look at me," Lucius commanded.

She raised her eyes slowly to his, and with a gentleness she did not think he could possess, he placed his fingers on both sides of her face, caressing her cheeks with his thumbs. Her breath came unsteadily, and she could not move. She could not think.

"I'm going to kiss you," he whispered.

He waited, his eyes searching hers, and although every objection should spring to her lips, Selena could voice none. None of them fit. The longing to connect to him and to be loved by him was too great.

Lucius leaned down and pressed his lips on hers, his hands sliding back to cradle her head. The sense of excitement, and of coming home, crashed and coursed through her simultaneously. Faint with longing, Selena was ready to agree to anything. Lucius deepened the kiss and slid one hand around her waist to pull her even closer. Time stopped, and Selena could only feel the intimacy of his arms pulling her against him and his lips exploring hers.

"Selena!"

She came to her senses with a jolt, her breath coming in gasps. What had she been doing? Heat infused Selena's cheeks, and she wanted to pull away—to turn to see who had called her, although in her heart, she knew—but Lucius held her fast. He was looking over her shoulder.

"You traitor," Rebecca shrieked.

Selena heard Rebecca's voice through the pounding of her pulse in her ears, but she could not see her until she had extricated herself from Lucius's grasp. She turned toward the door, but by then it was too late. She took two steps after Rebecca, but Lucius was too quick for her. He pulled on her hand and held her fast.

"Let her go. It will not do her any harm to realize that not every man on whom she sets her eyes will make her the object of his attention."

Stricken, Selena still looked toward the door, and he continued. "If she had opened her eyes much earlier, she would have seen that I thought you were worth ten of her from the very beginning. Now that I have come to know you better, there can be no comparison." He gave a gentle tug on her hand, and she turned back to him. "But you and I have something to finish."

Selena whisked her hand from his grasp. "Not the kiss, I implore you."

Lucius knit his brows. "But why not," he asked softly. "If we are to become man and wife, our first priority will be to each other and not your charge."

"We will not become man and wife," Selena said. "It was foolish and weak of me to have allowed it to go this far. I do beg your pardon." She turned her face to the window, and although she willed her feet to move, they seemed stuck to the floor. She could no more end this conversation than she could give him a favorable answer.

"Why? I know you feel for me as I do for you. No one who returns my kiss with such eagerness can claim to be cold toward me."

Selena was flooded with shame. She had no excuse to kiss him the way she did, and she forced herself to look at him. "Your sister doesn't like me. And every time someone like Mr. Downing, or some other former London acquaintance should chance upon our circle, they will treat me with disdain. You will be reminded of my disgrace and will wonder whatever possessed you in a moment's weakness to have offered for me. And I do not wish to do that to you."

"Selena." He ground out her name in frustration.

She shook her head and turned to go. "I must find Rebecca."

❧ 22 ❧

SELENA HURRIED from the drawing room. She needed to find Rebecca before she did something drastic.

And oh! That girl must not flee to Lord Harrowden. She would probably spill everything into his ears.

"Where are you running in such a frenzy?" Selena turned at the sound of the earl's voice and nearly stumbled in relief. He was not with Rebecca.

"I..." Selena paused. It suddenly occurred to her that it would not be prudent to let him know Rebecca had run off upset because he would ask the cause—that, or he would run after her. She was saved from having to answer by a knock on the door.

Again! And no footman. Lord Harrowden looked at her, and she knew there was no point asking him to answer the door. He was above her in station. She walked over and pulled it open.

"Excuse me, ma'am." One of the gentlemen assessed her quickly and seemed to have judged her position was not that of a lower servant. "We have an appointment to meet Lady Harrowden, and I believe Sir Lucius Clavering as well. Here are our cards."

"Ah." The solicitor and accountant Sir Lucius had spoken of. The awkwardness of the situation struck her at once. He was still in the drawing room, and she would be forced to see him again. "Please come in," she said.

The earl stepped forward. "Good afternoon. I am Lord Harrowden. How may I help you?"

The same man exchanged a look with the other, then bowed. "Good afternoon. We are here to see Lady Harrowden."

"On what business? I will relay your intentions to her. She is my aunt," Lord Harrowden said at his most haughty. Selena thought she saw fear underneath.

The door to the drawing room opened, and Sir Lucius stepped into the corridor. "I thought I heard sounds of your arrival." He favored Selena with a slight inclination of the head. "Miss Lockhart, would you kindly give these cards to Lady Harrowden and tell her I am here as well? She will be expecting us, as I sent a note ahead."

"Of course," Selena said and escaped before the situation could become any more uncomfortable. Let Sir Lucius fend off Lord Harrowden's curiosity. And let *her* flee from Sir Lucius's presence, which overset her in such a way she almost could not recognize herself.

Lady Harrowden was dressed and prepared for the meeting, and Selena fled as soon as she was able to search for Rebecca. She did not find her, and her mare was gone, so she knew that she had gone riding again, as she often did for hours at a time, especially when in a pique. This time there was not even a servant to go with her.

Selena spent the afternoon in what could best be described as hiding from Lord Harrowden, hiding from Sir Lucius for when the meeting came to an eventual end, and peering through the window, looking for signs of Rebecca's return. Eventually, she heard the sounds of the meeting adjourning and stayed hidden until Sir Lucius and the gentlemen left.

Lady Harrowden did not have need of her but asked for Rebecca, and Selena promised to bring her as soon as she returned from her ride. She continued to keep an eye outdoors, and when she spotted Rebecca riding toward the estate, Selena bundled in her pelisse and walked out to the stables where the stable lad was unhitching the horse.

"Rebecca," Selena said, approaching her. "We must talk."

"I do not wish to talk to you." Rebecca pushed past her and headed toward the exit.

Selena hurried behind her. She felt foolish, and guilty, and not the role model she was supposed to be. True, Sir Lucius had asked her to marry him, but she had not agreed to it. In fact, she had said no. And therefore, she had no excuse to have been kissing him, especially in such an abandoned manner. It was most awkward. She finally gathered her courage and grabbed Rebecca's arm.

"Listen to me. What you saw was a mistake. I am not going to marry Sir Lucius."

Rebecca eyed her shrewdly. "Well, now. That makes it harder for you to moralize, doesn't it? Does Lady Harrowden know about this?"

Selena shook her head. "She knows nothing about any attachment." She scrambled in her mind to try to save the situation, even if it meant hiding behind an altruism whose foundation was deceit. "Of course, you can tell her if you like, but that will not exactly endear Sir Lucius to her as a suitable husband for you."

Every word she spoke was like pouring vinegar on a wound. The thought of giving Sir Lucius up and handing him over to someone like Rebecca was painful, though she could not imagine Rebecca's pursuit would truly prosper. There was every chance that Sir Lucius would *not* choose Rebecca, and indeed it did not seem as though he would—but Rebecca would not lose her chance because Selena stood in the way.

Selena might still have hope for a future position as a governess. Perhaps one day a family would love her so much they would keep her on, and she would care for even the grandchildren. One thing she knew for certain; she could not marry Sir Lucius. She was not worthy of him. And she could not bear to see the look on his face when at last he'd decided he had made a mistake—when at last the prejudice that Society, including his own sister, held against her proved too much for him to bear. Even his business dealings would be tainted by association with her. She could not do it.

Rebecca turned without a word and began walking toward the house, and Selena followed. "All this time and he could have kissed me," Rebecca said as she marched forward. "He shows a complete lack of taste if he chooses to pursue you instead. You are so *plain*."

Selena trailed behind her. "Do not form a hasty judgment, Rebecca. There is still time for you to make a perfect match." She did not even pretend that the perfect match was with Sir Lucius. "Come. Lady Harrowden has been requesting your presence, and I did not know what to tell her. She's been waiting to see you these two hours and more."

Rebecca whirled around and faced Selena. "And that was uncomfortable for you, wasn't it? I am glad. I hope every day is uncomfortable for you, and I intend to make it so." She stomped toward the house.

Selena's heart sank even further, but she did not have the energy to argue. Fortunately, Rebecca did go straight to the drawing room, where the countess was sitting and staring in rumination through the window.

Lady Harrowden turned on her, and the peevishness of her tone revealed her mood more than anything. "At last, you've seen fit to present yourself. I do not like this notion of you running about whenever your fancy takes you. It is not proper for a young lady."

Rebecca folded her arms, and when Lady Harrowden turned away, rolled her eyes, but she replied meekly enough. "I am sorry, my lady." Selena was weak with relief that Rebecca had not betrayed her—yet.

Lady Harrowden gestured. "Sit, child," and waited until Rebecca sat across from her. Selena took the chair farthest from the fire. "We have much work to do before you are ready to go to London, and I have made a decision. Miss Lockhart here will begin training you "

"*She*," Rebecca interjected. "What can she possibly have to teach me? She is a poor, paid companion."

Lady Harrowden replied firmly, "But she was trained as a lady, and that is something you still lack. It is time to rectify your upbringing."

Rebecca shot a malicious glance at Selena. "She was trained as a lady, but I don't know that she always behaves as one."

Selena's heart beat in her throat.

Lady Harrowden continued as if there had been no interruption. "And that is why you will not be presented this Season. It is only two months away, and there is not enough time to prepare you. You will be presented next Season. This year, you will remain at the dower house with me, and you will work on your French, embroidery, your diction, your posture, deportment, your manners, and—"

With such an artillery of disciplines, it did not surprise Selena in the least that Rebecca leapt to her feet. "You wish to make me a prisoner here! And that is just what I won't accept. I am independently wealthy, and I can do as I wish."

"Women can never do as they wish," Lady Harrowden said. "Now, you'll do as I wish because I am your guardian, and when you get married, you will do as your husband wishes. That is the way of the world."

Rebecca stopped and put one hand on her hip. "Yes, but a husband I can twist around my finger."

Selena held her breath as Lady Harrowden gathered herself in indignation. "At the rate you are going, girl, you will not find a husband. No one will have you, for you are much too fast for your own good."

"Excuse me, my lady. I must change out of my riding habit." Rebecca turned without another glance and left. It was incredible to Selena that she could so disregard the respect due to the countess. It seemed Rebecca had been born without any sense of what was morally right.

There was silence as the door shut behind Rebecca, and Selena remained where she was. She was sure the countess wished to speak to her.

"That girl." Lady Harrowden's face was pinched in displeasure. "I am tempted to cast her off. I shall not do so, though she sorely deserves it." She sighed, audibly, then looked at Selena, a martial light to her eyes.

"Sir Lucius has come through at last, and although my accounts are in order—apart from a few changes that will need to be put in place—the Harrowden estate does not appear to be." Lady Harrowden turned to Selena, who was struck by how feeble she suddenly looked.

"There is a scandal brewing," Lady Harrowden continued. "Richard has put the tenants at risk with foolish schemes and shameful gambling. And now this ward of mine is completely out of control.

Something must be done to scotch any hint of scandal where she is concerned. I am counting on you to keep her in line."

Lady Harrowden turned her head, signaling an end to the conversation. Selena let out her breath silently. "I will do what I can, my lady."

~

LUCIUS LEFT Lady Harrowden not dissatisfied. She had met with the accountant and solicitor, and after examining her accounts, and the details of her jointure and portion, they determined that although she had been bearing a disproportionate amount of the household expenses, her income was largely untouched. The dower house was part of her jointure, so she would be able to remove to it. She would have a place to stay, and she would have an income, but Lucius sensed a frailty to Lady Harrowden regarding the looming scandal and knew it wouldn't be easy. And now, it was time to secure his own future.

He was oddly cheerful, despite having been turned down in marriage. He knew Selena loved him. She could not have melted into his embrace in such a way if she were cold toward him. But her fear of rejection was holding her back, and if Society's rejection was a hovering threat, his sister's was an immediate one. Maria's interference was one thing he had the power to stop cold—and as for the opinion of the *ton*? Well, it mattered not at all, and he would see that Selena was shielded from it.

It was time to pay Maria a visit.

He was shown into the study, where Maria sat with Holbeck, and she stood in surprise. "Lucius, I did not tell Cook there would be another plate for dinner. We were not expecting you."

Advancing into the room, Lucius gave a nod to Holbeck and replied, "I'm not staying for dinner. My mission will be brief. I have come to tell you that you will have to host Philippa this Season because I am getting married."

Maria dropped to her chair, as if stunned, and clasped her hands together. "That is such good news. I assume it is Miss Woodsley? I saw the two of you at dinner the other night."

Lucius took a seat in the only remaining armchair. "I wish you will rid yourself of the notion that I have any interest in Miss Woodsley. Would it change your mind to know that she came to my house, unaccompanied, with the object of seducing me? That is why she was sent home from her school. Apparently, she saw me once and determined that I was the one she wanted. Is that the kind of wife you would choose for me?"

Maria darted a glance at Holbeck, who evaded her gaze. "Well, she *is* young. She simply lacks adequate training, which she is now receiving with Miss Lockhart. And she has made it apparent that she is attached to you..."

Lucius looked at his sister in exasperation. "Is her fortune so important to you that you would overlook such behavior? You must have windmills in your head if you think I can. No, it is not Miss Woodsley."

Realization struck, and Maria cried out, "For heaven's sake, Lucius. Not Miss Lockhart!"

Lucius narrowed his eyes. "As a matter of fact, Miss Lockhart is my choice, and that is what I came to say to you, Maria. You will welcome her with more warmth than you have yet shown her. You will receive her in Society with all the graciousness of a sister-in-law, and you will tell Mother that you are thrilled for our engagement," he said severely. "You will show your support to this match publicly, or I will never set foot in this house again."

He glanced at Holbeck. "And I will withdraw all support to Holbeck's policies and bills and encourage my friends to do the same."

Maria flushed, protesting, "Lucius, you are out of your mind."

But Holbeck lifted a hand and silenced her. "Now, Maria," he said, "the Lockhart scandal was some years back. You are always saying you hope for Lucius to be married, and he finally has a wish to do so. I say leave him be. He's old enough to know his own mind."

Maria glared at her husband then folded her arms across her chest. Lucius studied her, hiding his amusement. He had been nearly certain of Holbeck's support once he touched on political affiliations and financial gifts, with which he had been generous. Maria would come around.

"Very well," she replied—and very much in the manner of one being goaded beyond what she could bear.

Lucius did not care one jot.

23

REBECCA DISAPPEARED for the rest of the day, and Selena did not seek her out. She would grant her charge this one day to overcome her fit of temper before attempting their lessons again. This also gave Selena time to regain her own composure, but after such a tumult of emotions that included a heady kiss—and an audience—*that* was not easily done.

When Mrs. Randall brought a simple supper to the dining room that evening, she informed Lady Harrowden and Selena that Rebecca was not feeling well and had requested Alice to bring a supper tray to her room. Selena did not believe it for a minute, but she was grateful for the reprieve. At least for tonight, she would be spared blatant hostility and barbed innuendos. Lord Harrowden was not in the habit of joining them for dinner, and she had not seen him after the morning visitors either, although she had been too absorbed in her own reflections throughout the day to spare him a thought. And Lady Harrowden had nothing original to contribute.

Needless to say, dinner conversation that evening was dull.

Selena went to bed thinking of that kiss. She could still feel the soft touch of his lips on hers when she closed her eyes, and her nerves tingled, her senses screamed, from the memory of being pulled up against him in such a tight embrace. She had the sensation of falling.

What would it be like to say yes? What would it be like to be kissed in such a way any time she felt like it, and to have Lucius look at her with such tenderness? To be cherished, and protected, and tucked away from the world. *To sit with him at that small table near the fire and take supper together, discussing mundane subjects without a care in the world.*

Selena curled up in a ball on her side as her pragmatic nature dragged her back to reality. A tear leaked out of the corner of her eye and pooled in her ear. What a ridiculous dream to have. A cozy dinner with Lucius by the fire? That was his hunting box, where he went to *escape* from women, not set up home with one. And there would be no such idyllic escape from the world. Evading Society was impossible for a titled man such as Sir Lucius, and she would not keep him from the *ton* by agreeing to such an unequal alliance. She could not do that to him.

It was a long time before Selena fell asleep that night.

She awoke much later than her usual time the next day. She dressed, brushed her hair numbly, and went downstairs, where she took her plain breakfast in a stillness that seemed to pervade the entire house. For once, Lord Harrowden was not there to disturb her complacency. But the lack of servants and activity was unnerving. It was time for Selena to find Rebecca and begin her lessons, even as she wondered whether she could ever have any credibility with the girl again.

Alice burst into the breakfast room. "There you are, miss. I have not been able to find you. Miss Woodsley is *missing*." Her eyes were frantic, and Selena rose to her feet.

"Please slow down," she said. "Start again. What do you mean she is missing? Did she not go out for a ride?"

"Her smallest trunk is missing, and so is she," Alice said, gasping for air. "I had hoped she merely went for a ride, although I was surprised she wouldn't ring for me to dress her. I was downstairs in the kitchen having my breakfast. When I finally went to her room to wake her, I saw that she was not there, and some of her clothes are missing."

The food Selena had just eaten sat like a weight in her stomach. Her first thought flew to Lord Harrowden and where he might be, but she did not know who to send to inquire after him. It occurred to her for the first time how odd it was she'd never met his valet. Perhaps he didn't have one?

"Can you find the footman and see if he is able to locate Lord Harrowden? Perhaps the earl has some idea of where Rebecca went. He seems to be more aware of her riding schedule than I am."

The maid gave a nod and rushed off, and with deep foreboding, Selena hurried to Rebecca's room. There she found the usual disorder, except that it appeared her brushes and toiletries were missing. And her placard was open and in disarray.

Selena left the room and searched frantically throughout the house, expecting—hoping—to run into Rebecca at any moment. Where had that girl gone off to? She attempted to foster an expression of serenity when she passed Mrs. Morgan on the way to the stables, however the maid stopped her.

"Lady Harrowden is looking for you, miss."

Selena paused. She did not know if she should question Mrs. Morgan as to Rebecca's whereabouts. She didn't want to create unnecessary panic, nor did she want to admit to having lost Rebecca. Lady Harrowden had given explicit instructions. Under no circumstances was Selena to allow Rebecca to wander off on her own or get into any sort of trouble—a mandate nearly impossible to obey. What position could Selena find after this, if she did not come with a recommendation? None! Her fate would be sealed.

"Tell Lady Harrowden that I'll come without delay," Selena said. If only she could buy a little more time, she might be able to fix this mess. But where could she look now? She couldn't begin to think about taking out one of the horses and searching the countryside. If she didn't find Rebecca, she might have no choice.

"My lady was very specific and said you must hurry," the maid urged. "She has an important task for you."

With that, Selena changed course and turned her steps toward Lady Harrowden's room. She might as well go now. Five minutes couldn't make a difference in searching for Rebecca, and there was still hope for a plausible explanation for her trunk and that she had simply gone off riding.

Selena knocked on the countess's door and waited until she was bid to enter. "You called for me, my lady?"

"It is past eleven o'clock," Lady Harrowden said. "You are to present yourself at eleven without fail. Your main duty is to me and that troublesome girl. I cannot imagine what is keeping you from being on time. I ask so little of you."

It was as if any inroads Selena had made into Lady Harrowden's good graces could be undone in just one brief slip. True, she had not paid attention to the time. But there was something of greater importance that she needed to see to. Perhaps she could quickly serve the countess and be sent on her way to continue her search without anyone the wiser. "I apologize, my lady. What may I do for you?" She saw that the countess was not yet dressed and hoped that that would buy her some more time to check the stables. If she ran, she could do both.

"I would like you to help me answer some of my correspondence before I rise from bed. There is the stack of mail with invitations that will need replies. You may begin with the invitation on top."

With a sinking feeling, Selena went over to the pile and took it in her hands. She paused, debating whether she should say something, but she could not put it off any longer. Rebecca's flight was of too serious a nature, and it affected the countess as well.

"My lady, I have some troubling news, I fear. I cannot find Rebecca. Alice says one of her trunks is missing—"

After a mere second's astonishment, Lady Harrowden threw off the covers and began to stand. "What is this? How could you have lost my ward? You have only one responsibility. Do you not rise before her?"

Desperate protests sprang to Selena's lips. She could defend herself if only she had the time. And couldn't Lady Harrowden see that Selena had been given an unfair burden? She had two roles instead of one. Selena strove to remain calm.

"In general, I do rise before her, but I did not see her at breakfast, and we did not cross paths in the house. I looked in her bedroom, and she was not there. I cannot work miracles, my lady."

Lady Harrowden accepted this without further reproach. "And my nephew—have you seen him?"

Selena shook her head. "Then again, I've not had time to look. I asked Alice to send a footman to find him, but..." She did not want to say she feared the worst.

"Ring for my maid, and tell her to return at once," Lady Harrowden said. "We have no time to lose."

The countess's intensity propelled Selena toward the door, needing no further encouragement. She pulled the bell for Mrs. Morgan on her way out and took hasty steps toward the staircase. At the bottom of the stairwell, she turned to the side entrance, which was the fastest route to the stables.

She had gone two steps when the sound of the knocker echoed through the house. This could be news of Rebecca! Without waiting for anyone to come, Selena ran to the door and opened it.

Lucius's face lit up when his eyes fell on Selena. The white cravat tied with more care than usual highlighted the gleam of his white teeth and bright eyes. Selena's breath always seemed to leave her in his presence.

"Selena," he said.

"Rebecca is missing." The words came spilling out of her.

Lucius's smile fell, and he stepped forward. "Might I come in? Perhaps I can assist in some way."

"I will take you to the countess at once," Selena replied, then stopped. "No, she is not dressed. I will tell her you are waiting upon her in the drawing room."

"I can find my own way. Let Lady Harrowden know I'm here, and if you can, come and speak with me before she arrives."

Selena did not wait any longer but rushed up to the countess's room and knocked. Lady Harrowden was still in a state of undress and her hair had not been done. The maid was only tying her stays.

"Sir Lucius is here, and wishes an audience with you. What shall I tell him?"

"Did you find the girl?" the countess asked.

"No," Selena said, despair overtaking her. "I began looking, but then Sir Lucius arrived. I cannot be everywhere at once."

"Try harder," the countess snapped. Selena set her mouth in a firm line, and Lady Harrowden added after a moment, "Tell Sir Lucius I will be right with him."

Dismissed, Selena hurried down the stairs, her heart beating from fear as much as exertion. She rushed into the drawing room, where Lucius stood, peering at the snowy landscape through the window. He had not sat but turned when she entered and held out his two hands, as if to invite Selena to rush forward and place her hands in his. It was a tempting proposition, but she could not trust herself.

Instead she took two steps forward. "Lady Harrowden said she will come directly."

She thought she saw a flash of disappointment on Sir Lucius's face as he dropped his arms to his side. "Tell me, what has you in such a panic?"

"But I've told you," Selena said in astonishment. "Rebecca is *gone*, and it is my fault."

"How is it your fault?" Sir Lucius asked, his voice rising a notch. "What have you to do if a flighty damsel will not stay put?"

He did not understand. Selena's frustration sent tears to her eyes, which she blinked away, digging her fingernails into her palms to make her tears stay put. She must not show weakness. And if he did not know that it was his kiss that sent Rebecca off in a jealous rage, she certainly did not wish to spell it out for him.

"Of course it's my fault. I will be blamed for everything, and I will not be able to secure another position."

"Surely Lady Harrowden will not blame you for decisions made by a young woman who has no character, one who has been left to an indifferent upbringing, and who has had no time to have a sense of decorum properly instilled by you? It is ridiculous. You are worrying for nothing, Selena."

There was truth in what he said, but he didn't understand that she would pay for it with her position if she made no push to retrieve Rebecca. When she was able to respond, it was in a voice subdued with emotion. "You are wrong. Lady Harrowden has already told me she holds me responsible. I will not be given a letter of character, and I will not be able to find another post."

Lucius waved it off impatiently. "What does it matter whether

Lady Harrrowden gives you a glowing reference? There is surely some other position for you to hold besides governess."

"And who will give me such a recommendation?" Selena challenged. "*You*? If the *ton* does not easily forgive a member who belongs to it, how much less will they forgive somebody whose rank is beneath them?"

A muscle twitched in Lucius's jaw, already tense with emotion. "I do not know to whom you are referring, Selena. You are not beneath them. You are a gentleman's daughter."

"It matters not," she cried. "My family is shrouded in scandal. They take one look at your dress, they know of your financial situation. They know who has cut you, and what connection still exists. Even if you are a hanger-on—and I refuse to be one—there is no future for an impoverished female with no references."

Lucius raised his own voice. "You are lumping everyone in Society together. Not everybody thinks that way. Not everyone has such a prejudice. Some people look beyond outward appearances and judge the inside worth."

Selena shook her head. "Impossible. You have not been in my shoes. It is the same everywhere."

Lucius took two steps forward and took Selena by the arm. "No, it is not." His voice came out in a growl of frustration. "I have been trying to find a way to tell you that I *love* you, but you have not let me get close enough."

Lucius let go of her arm and exhaled with impatience. "Have you not by now discerned that I don't care what other people think? If I asked you to marry me, it is because everything in me wants you for my wife. I don't want a position, or wealth, or somebody who is free of scandal—one that was not of your own making, I might add. I just want you, and I'm not going to change my mind."

Selena closed her eyes. She would not be persuaded by his tempting words. It would only hurt that much more afterwards. "You will soon enough change your mind...sir."

After a brief pause, she opened her eyes and raised them to his. She saw surprise and—she thought—a flash of hurt. He continued to stare at her, and the seconds ticked by in silence.

At last, he shook his head and said in a soft voice, "I had not thought you could be so obstinate. It seems you are unwilling to hear. I believe it is not the *ton* that is prejudiced, Selena. I believe it is *you* who are. And if you are bent on classing people by rank, so that you may determine where you fall, no one will be able to convince you otherwise. And *that* would be a tragedy."

Selena fell silent. The truth pierced her heart like a shaft. She looked at him. "Lucius, I—"

The door opened.

24

LADY HARROWDEN'S cane thumped on the floor with every step as she advanced into the room. To Lucius's relief, she did not seem to notice his proximity to Selena or the tension that radiated from them. "It appears that girl has fled with my dreadful nephew. Alice said the footman cannot find Richard, and his carriage is missing."

Lucius met Selena's glance briefly. There was too much left unfinished between them. Although she had refused him *again*, and he had scolded her, he did not waver in the hopes of convincing her. She had recognized the truth in his words and would come to see reason, he was sure of it.

Selena opened her mouth to respond to the countess but was not given the chance.

"It is a flight to the border, as sure as anything," Lady Harrowden glowered. "You must do something. This house is already steeped in scandal with tradesmen coming to the front door and refusing to deliver something as simple as meat. If Richard has indeed ruined this estate, as I suspect he has, we cannot add to it an elopement with a young woman who was supposed to be under my protection. Selena, I hold you personally responsible to find her. You must stop this marriage from taking place."

Lady Harrowden turned to Lucius. "I have known you since you were a boy. If you would like to make up for your lapse of not sticking to your promise, you may do so now. Take Miss Lockhart and find that girl. Stop this elopement."

Lucius met her gaze unflinchingly. Yes, he had lapsed in his promise, but he thought he had more than made up for it by finding out news of her nephew and engaging a solicitor to oversee her affairs. However, it only took a split-second for him to calculate that her command fit his objective with precision. If he were alone with Selena in a carriage for hours, as they chased after the errant couple—who would not be found in time, of that he was sure—he would have time to press his suit.

Selena's reasons for saying no were based on past hurts and fear but did not represent the desires of her heart. He had to convince her that he could protect her, and that anyone who would scorn her for her father's transgressions was not someone he would have any dealings with. The contentment Selena would bring to his life was worth any Society he needed to cut to keep her there. It wanted only time to win her over.

"Very well, my lady," he said. "But I will do this correctly. I will get my coachman and undergroom and a closed carriage. I will not subject Miss Lockhart to the discomfort of late January weather in an open carriage, as we are likely to be riding for hours in it."

"That's the first sensible word you've spoken," Lady Harrowden grumbled.

Lucius turned to go, and she added, "Stay a minute, Lucius. Those fools will have to marry now, and I suppose her fortune will save the estate from immediate ruin. But their marriage must not be done by elopement. I happen to know that the archbishop is in Hertfordshire on a visit—in Graveley. I will pen a note that you will take to him in order to request a special license."

Lucius opened his eyes in surprise. "Willingly," he said. "But I must warn you that there is small chance of them being found before they have gone too far. They seem to have had a head start of several hours."

"Nevertheless, you will try. If I know the pair of them, Rebecca will wish to stop at every stage, and Richard will have his pockets to let before they leave the county, or he will drive his carriage into a ditch or some such thing." Lady Harrowden made her way to the desk and sat. "I have hopes of their being found."

She wrote a brief note, sanded and sealed it, and handed it to Lucius, which he took. He turned to Selena.

"Miss Lockhart, if you will accompany me to the door, I have some instructions to give you for the journey." He saw her swallow in apprehension, but she followed him. When they arrived at the front door, which was blessedly empty due to the lack of servants, he leaned in.

"I have no expectation of reaching this couple. I will accompany you to satisfy Lady Harrowden's request. But I will not compromise your reputation in any way, even if that means abandoning the pursuit. And—" He caught her gaze and held it. "I look forward to continuing our conversation." He watched her eyes grow wide, before she hurried away.

WHEN HE CAME AN HOUR LATER, Selena was standing in the entrance, dressed in her warmest clothing, Miss Woodsley's maid at her side. Lucius, however, had no intention of allowing the awkward presence of a maid to interfere with his suit. He was determined to win Selena's hand, and this would have to be done without the encumbrance.

He addressed both ladies. "I am sorry to say we have no room for the maid. We will bring Miss Woodsley back in our carriage once we catch up to them, but it will be a tight fit with her luggage as well. Miss Lockhart, I assure you, your reputation will be perfectly safe, as I have my coachman and undergroom."

Selena's lips settled in a prim line that spoke volumes. He knew she didn't like being manipulated, but he was going to win this round, especially if it meant fighting to convince her that she would be happier married to him than in a life of service.

She turned to Miss Woodsley's maid. "Tell Lady Harrowden we have left. I will do my best to bring Miss Woodsley home to you."

Lucius helped her into the carriage then climbed in after her, before closing the door behind them and rapping on the roof. The horses surged forward.

He leaned against the corner of the seat and, with a look of mild amusement, said, "I did not expect assistance from such quarters as Lady Harrowden. But she has practically handed you over to me."

Selena drew back with a raised eyebrow. She looked wary, but unafraid, as she rubbed one gloved hand over the other. "I hope you have not invented some nefarious purpose in my being alone with you, Lucius. I had thought I might trust you."

"You know very well you may trust me, my dear," Lucius said. "I have honorable intentions. But here I may convince you to become my wife, without fear of interruption."

"You may talk," she said, facing forward, and he thought he saw a dimple appear on her cheek. "But I still own my own mind."

"Yes, but yours appears to be deranged in some way, for you seem to think that because of something your father did years ago, you must resign yourself to a life of spinsterhood. And here you have received a perfectly respectable offer of marriage and have so far turned it down. You cannot convince me that this speaks to your sanity."

"If you are so concerned for my sanity," she countered, her lips now trembling toward a smile, "I wonder that you should wish to marry me at all."

Lucius folded his arms, his own lips quirking upward. "I have no doubt in my mind that your sanity will fully be restored. Once you have agreed to become my wife."

"My," she exclaimed. "Once you are fixated on a subject, you do not leave it alone easily enough."

"No," he said. "But since I have promised to protect your reputation and cannot, in good conscience, kiss you—which experience tells me does the best job of convincing you—I must use my words alone."

A tiny gasp escaped from Selena's lips, and she looked heavenward. "Your restraint hints at your being a gentleman, but a gentleman would not allude to such a delicate matter as a wayward kiss," she said severely.

He laughed.

"Lucius." Selena turned to him in all seriousness. "I am sensible of the honor you do me in asking me to become your wife. My faith is not lacking in the sincerity of your offer. It is rather that I do not think you know what you are asking. The incident that happened at the ball was just one example of what I'm to expect if I reenter Society. And..."

She paused, and he waited, wondering what else was in her adorable mind. She bit her lip. "I know you expressed regret for not having come to my aid, but I assure you, I hold you no ill-will. I just believe that this is one small incident of many that will await us if I become your wife. What I am afraid of is seeing the affection you may now hold for me turn into regret, when you must share everywhere in the scorn that will greet me."

Lucius's burst of optimism took an abrupt dive, and he grabbed her hand. "Ah, now we've come to the heart of it. When Downing dared to humiliate you in front of everyone, you had no protectors. I should have been one, but I had not yet decided to take up that role. I was wrong, and I heartily regret it. At first, I thought it was only my conscience that troubled me for not having taken up your defense, but I quickly learned that my feelings had grown deeper than I suspected. It is not affection I feel for you, Selena—affection has such shallow roots, it can be ripped out. What I feel for you is love."

She turned to him, her serious gray eyes studying him.

"And I will not let this happen again," he said. "You will not face whispers when I am your protector. Society will know that they must answer to me for any ill-treatment they dare to heap upon you. I will not press you for an answer now, but I want you to know that once decided, I am not the fickle man you think me to be."

Lucius squeezed her hand, then pulled his away and turned to look through the window at the rolling countryside. He was smart enough to know that silence and time would do more to add strength to his argument than an influx of words could ever do. Nevertheless, his body seemed to urge the carriage forward—not to find Rebecca—but to bring Selena closer to the answer he knew they both desired.

25

SELENA WAS SWAYED by the jolting carriage as they went over the remaining distance to Graveley, which she had been told was not much farther, although they'd stopped briefly at several inns on the road to inquire after the runaways.

She didn't feel any alarm in getting farther and farther from Harrowden Estate. On the contrary, she felt free. What would it be like to be under the protection of such a man as Lucius? Under his sardonic exterior he had revealed himself to be kind. It had been some time since she found someone so easy to talk to—and he made her laugh.

And that kiss! Selena's heart skipped a beat when she thought about it. If she agreed to his proposal, this would be what she woke up to every day. Selena tugged at the tips of her gloves, toying with their seams. It was getting harder and harder to refuse him, or to remember why she should.

After a short time, they arrived at the village of Graveley, and the sounds of human activity outdoors broke into her thoughts. Lucius opened the carriage door and helped Selena down, before guiding her into the posting house.

"As you know, Lady Harrowden has charged me with business

here," he said. "I will see the archbishop as quickly as I may, and will leave my servants with you as protection." He went over to the innkeeper and conferred with him for several minutes, then returned.

"I've had a private parlor readied for you while I am away, and I have the directions now of where to go. The innkeeper's wife is preparing a luncheon for you, and I shall not be long."

SELENA, alone in the parlor, ate from the delicious fare that had been set before her, and although she was prone to feeling jumpy from having set out on such an unanticipated mission, she experienced a surprising amount of peace. The food tasted better than anything she remembered having tasted, the sun beamed gaily through the window of the parlor, she was under the protection of an honorable man, and...

She leaned her chin on her hand. *And I hope I might remain with him always.*

I am in love. The reality hit Selena like a bolt.

As if responding to the beckon of her heart, Lucius entered the room at that moment. "Selena, I do not think—"

He stopped short and studied her, as she stared up at him wistfully. Selena knew her feelings for him were written all over her face. In three strides, he was at the table, where he took his seat next to hers, clasping her two hands in his. "My dear, what is it?"

She smiled and shook her head. It was nothing she could voice. "You do not think *what*, Lucius?"

He kept his eyes trained on her for a few seconds longer, but when she did not enlighten him, he smiled and brought one of her hands to his lips.

"I do not think we should continue on this mad pursuit. Harrowden's carriage passed through here in the early hours of the morning. It did not even stop, but one of the hostlers recognized the crest as it rode by. We will never reach them, and I refuse to compromise your reputation for them."

Selena was still affected by his kiss on her hand, wishing for something she could not identify. She did not answer right away. At last, she looked up. "In some ways, I agree with you. We cannot go much farther and still reach Harrowden before the end of day. I do not wish to bring down scandal on my name, if they are determined not to be caught." She knit her brows. "However, I feel we ought to do everything we can to try to stop them. Who knows, but perhaps their carriage has overturned, and they are even now in need of assistance. And did you not get a special license for them to be married? Perhaps it is not too late to catch them." It was a bold move on her part, but she reached out to touch his gloved hand. "Why do we not continue for one more stage and see if we can find them. And if they are truly gone, we will return home."

There was a look in Lucius's eyes that Selena could not quite identify when he answered. "Very well. We shall do as you suggest. And to answer your question, I was indeed successful and managed to have an audience with the archbishop, where I acquired a special license." He smiled, and she could have sworn she saw mischief lurking in his eyes.

"You are surprisingly docile to agree to my plan without argument." Selena narrowed her eyes. "If I have learned anything of you, it is that you enjoy defending your case. Have you something up your sleeve?"

Lucius stood. "I always have something up my sleeve. One must be prepared." He held out his hand, and she allowed him to help her rise. Despite his air of mystery, Selena could not help but trust him completely.

They climbed into the carriage, and he tapped on the roof. Soon the carriage went from the cobblestones to the dirt road, and Selena was lulled by the rocking motion. She was so at ease, she nearly fell asleep. When she felt the touch of Lucius's hand on hers, she looked up at him, startled.

"My dear, apart from this liberty I have taken of holding your hand, I will not give you any unwelcome advances while you are under my protection," he said. "You have my word on it."

Selena's pulse beat erratically in her throat. His touch was not precisely *un*welcome, but she did not wish for more, as she knew her reputation would not recover. She was also not sure if she could trust herself to put a proper stop to things. She looked ahead but did not pull her hand from under his.

At her silence, Lucius carefully threaded his fingers through hers, and she was aware of the sensation of warmth that crept through her gloved hand and spread to her whole being. The daylight was beginning to dim, and his voice rumbled in the shadows of the carriage.

"I am most determined to make you my wife, Selena," Lucius said. "If I agreed to the harebrained scheme of chasing after two such simpletons as Harrowden and Miss Woodsley, it was only for the opportunity to spend time with you, unhindered by anyone else. And I see I was not mistaken to have done so, or I would not be sitting next to you, holding your hand now."

He gave a small squeeze, and his touch sent Selena's pulse racing. He leaned back against the seat and did not say anything further. Selena began to grow accustomed to the warmth and weight of his hand and became drowsy again.

Suddenly, the carriage lurched to a halt and careened to one side. Selena fell on top of Lucius as the carriage toppled over completely, and he snaked an arm around her waist and grinned, as her eyes widened in alarm.

"Hush, darling," he said. "There is nothing to fear. You are with me." Very carefully, he extricated himself from their embrace and stood to open the carriage door that was now the ceiling. He pulled himself up and out of the carriage, then sat on the side of the coach. His boots swung jauntily above Selena, and it looked to her as if he were enjoying himself. Despite herself—and her awkward position—Selena smiled.

"Aye," he called out. "Worley, this is a first for you. Now we're in a fix, aren't we?" She heard the mumbled apologies of the coachman, who seemed to be explaining that he'd tried to avoid some small animal and had tossed the carriage into a ditch. Lucius cut his protestations short.

"Never mind that. Jim, unhitch the horses, and I'll take the one with the saddle." He looked down at Selena, who had righted herself to a seated position, his boots dangling not far from her face. He swung his legs out of the carriage then bent over at the waist and leaned down into the body.

"Stand up, and I shall pull you out," he ordered, his face lit with amusement.

"Just like that?" Selena said with an answering smile. She had clearly injured her head in the crash if she could find anything to smile about.

"Just like that," he repeated.

She stood, and Lucius leaned down and grasped her by the waist. As he slid down the exterior of the coach, he lifted her up, taking care not to harm her against the edge of the carriage. He landed on the ground, and Selena was still leaning over its side in a most undignified way. It made her laugh helplessly.

"Lucius, this is most disgraceful. I insist that you see me to the ground straight away," she commanded.

Lucius, his lips still stretched in a broad smile, lifted her the rest of the way out of the carriage and set her on the ground. After a moment, he pulled his hands from her waist. She turned from him to look at the accident, and when she saw the state of the carriage, all humor fled. Both wheels were broken on one side, and the undergroom was unhitching one of the horses from the carriage.

"This is terrible," she said. "How will we get back to Harrowden tonight?"

"Do not fear," Lucius said. "I have a plan." He signaled for the lad to bring over one of the saddled horses, and he held it by the bridle. "We are going to ride. I will climb up, and I will pull you in front of me."

He called out to the coachman. "Worley, how far is the nearest town from here?"

The coachman looked up from examining the wheel. "I would say about two miles more, sir."

Lucius swung up into the saddle and leaned down and reached out his hands to Selena. "Face out, and I will pull you up."

Selena did so and felt his hands on her waist from behind. Then, before she knew it, she was sitting snug against Lucius's chest, with her legs on one side and cradled in his arms.

The undergroom was now checking the forelocks of one of the other horses, and Lucius called out to the coachman again. "I want you and Jim to stable the other horses in the next village. Send someone to come and fix the carriage, and have everything ready for us to go back in two days' time. This should be enough for your needs." He tossed a small sack of coins to his coachman.

"Yes, sir," Worley said.

Selena felt apprehension creep up her spine, as they began riding forward. She was so close to Lucius—more than she'd ever been to any other man. "Two days?" she said in a small voice.

He bent down to look at her. "Don't be afraid, Selena. I will not let any harm come to you."

Her eyes fixated on the hint of stubble on his chin. "How can that be? When we will not return to Harrowden for two days? Even if you do not take advantage of my situation, my reputation will not recover. Not only will I be shunned everywhere—even worse than I already am —but..." She tugged on his lapel. "Lucius—I will not get another position anywhere. I will be destitute. I do not think you have thought through the implications for my situation."

"Your situation has long chafed me," Lucius said, tightening his hold around her. "I cannot bear to see you treated with disdain by the likes of men like Downing, or to be under the insolent gaze of Lord Harrowden—or even to be ordered about by Lady Harrowden and silly chits like Miss Woodsley. As I have already told you, I will not rest until you are my wife, and you will learn that I am not a man to give up easily."

He leaned down and kissed her forehead. "Do not waver back and forth any longer. Selena. Say you will be my wife—and not because you must in order to save your reputation—but because you wish it."

Her defenses were worn down, and Selena sighed loudly. "I will be your wife then"—adding in a voice that was more timid— "and because I wish it." She darted a panicked glance at his face before dropping her gaze. She had worn her heart on her sleeve.

Please don't mock me.

He tightened his arm around her waist, and when she looked at him, his face held such a look of joy. It transformed his features entirely. He leaned down and planted a kiss on her lips.

"Watch the road, Lucius," she admonished, her lips curving upward.

She breathed in sharply as realization struck. "But, Lucius, we still have not solved the problem! Even if you marry me, I will be in your company without a chaperone overnight—never mind that we are not in the same room. That alone will ruin my reputation. Oh, why did we not bring Alice? We could easily have found room for her."

"Confound Alice," he said. "She would have been *de trop*. I have not underestimated the danger to your reputation, dearest, but as I said—I always come prepared." A smile played on his lips, as he looked straight ahead. "In my coat pocket, I have a special license—"

"For Rebecca and Lord Harrowden," Selena exclaimed. "What good can that do us?"

"Do you think I would lose an opportunity to get a special license for them and not request one for us?" he said. "That would have been bacon-brained."

Selena looked at him in shock. Such a thing had never occurred to her.

"It's hard enough to convince you stubborn girl that you are—to marry me," he continued. "I can see that it will never do, with my sister constantly sowing seeds of doubt—although you may be sure that she and I have had a talk and we now understand one another perfectly—and cow-hearted men like Downing making you doubt your worth. His Grace has given me the direction of the vicar at Campton, and I will marry you tonight." He flashed her a proud grin. "Now that you have finally said yes."

Nestled in his arms, Selena was flooded with joy. She could not believe that such joy belonged to her "Oh, Lucius," she breathed as she opened her eyes wide to him. He pulled his horse to a sudden stop and fixed his gaze on her.

"Why did you stop?" she asked.

With one hand around her waist, and with the reins wrapped around the other, he pulled her close. "For this." Lucius kissed her until she was faint with longing, pulled up tight against him and cradled in his arms. He pulled away at last, his breath coming quickly, and his eyes glowing in the near darkness. A smile grew on both their faces as their gazes held.

"So where do we find this vicar?" Selena asked shyly.

❧ 26 ❧

Two days later, Sir Lucius and Lady Clavering arrived at Harrowden Estate, and Selena shot Lucius a glance full of misgiving. They had spent the two days following their impromptu wedding ceremony selfish beyond permission, Selena had told her husband more than once, but he banished her objections easily.

"It is time someone thought about you, and that is my role now," Lucius had told her.

However, it was time to face the music. Lady Harrowden was likely to be incensed, and she had every right to be. It mattered little that Selena had the protection of her husband, she knew they were in the wrong.

Lucius saw her furrowed brow and cupped her cheek with his hand. "Do not worry about a thing." He laughed suddenly in recollection. "I should not think she could *eat* you." That made Selena smile.

As Lucius assisted her down from the carriage, the noise of another carriage crunching over the melting snow reached them. He looked up, then turned to Selena, his eyes twinkling.

"This should prove interesting. It's my brother, George, and from the looks of it, Philippa, as well. I suppose if I were to introduce my wife to my family, I would most like to start with those two."

"Lucius!" George reined in and greeted Lucius with a look of relief. "You are here. Briggs was surprisingly closed about your whereabouts, and as I know you did not leave for London, nor would you go visit Mother without absolutely needing to, I thought, perhaps, I might find you here."

George stopped suddenly, as his eyes lit on Selena, but it was Philippa who spoke. "You are both dressed for traveling," she exclaimed. "What has happened? This morning, Maria heard a rumor about Miss Woodsley running off with Lord Harrowden. I suppose you were persuaded to go after them? Good afternoon Miss Lockhart. Did you have success?"

Selena pressed her lips together and looked at Lucius for support. He reached for her hand and squeezed it, and both George and Philippa's eyes widened in surprise.

"Lucius, you have something to tell us," Philippa said, her smile broadening.

"I do. You are no longer addressing Miss Lockhart. You may call her Selena, for she is Lady Clavering now."

"Never say so, Lucius," George said in wonderment. "At last, you are leg-shackled."

Lucius held out his arm, and Selena slipped her hand through it for reassurance. "Leg-shackled is not exactly how I would term it," he said wryly. "This was a love match."

George clapped his hand over his mouth. "I beg your pardon Miss...Lady Clav...Selena," he managed at last.

"Your success with the ladies is assured, George," Lucius said in a droll voice.

Philippa clapped her hands together. "Oh, I just knew it. I could tell from the way you looked at each other that there was going to be a match."

Lucius frowned at her. "You knew nothing," he objected. "I assure you I was not so transparent."

"Perhaps not from the way you left her to fend for herself, Lucius," Philippa countered drily. "But I knew it would not be long before you came to your senses."

Selena took a deep breath. "I suppose there is no better time than the present to inform Lady Harrowden that our mission did not succeed." Lucius squeezed her hand in encouragement.

They began to walk toward the house, when George spoke up from behind. "And Maria," he added. "Unless she has already left, she is here visiting the countess now." Selena bit her lip and looked at Lucius but did not say anything.

The door opened before them, and they entered the house. To Selena's surprise, Mullings had returned, and she wondered if there had been a reversal in their financial situation at the estate. The butler's brief glance at Selena showed disapproval, and she longed to set him straight. She did not deserve such a censorious glance.

"Mullings," Lucius said. "Be so good as to inform Lady Harrowden that we are here."

Mullings walked forward in a stately manor and opened the door to the drawing room. "Sir Lucius Clavering, Mr. George Clavering, Miss Philippa Clavering, Miss Lockhart." He opened the door wider, and Lucius led Selena into the room.

Lady Harrowden did not let them get far. "This is outside of enough. You have returned, but after having left Miss Lockhart's chaperone at home, do you think she will be welcome here? Your reputation has been tarnished, Selena," the countess admonished. "And from what I can see, you did not find my nephew and Rebecca. On the whole, you have done nothing but botch the entire affair."

Maria stood when they entered. "Really, Lucius. I do not like the thought of you compromising any young lady, even if you went at the express request of Lady Harrowden." She turned to the countess. "My lady, you will admit this to be so. They will now have to marry."

"Unless it is possible to cobble together some excuse," Lady Harrowden said. "I did not think you to be so clumsy, Lucius. Who saw you? Where did you sleep these two nights?"

"*Hm*," Lucius ducked his head, and Selena knew it was to hide the smile that had appeared on his lips. He looked to be enjoying himself for all the world. *I'm glad someone is*, she thought in exasperation.

"The vicar at Campton saw us," he informed the countess, "right before he married us. And the innkeeper saw us at the Blue Bell Inn, when he showed us to our room."

Although, Philippa and George looked amused, Lady Harrowden turned an outraged face toward Selena, and she felt the familiar panic send a blush to her cheeks. She despised being under any sort of scrutiny, especially of the negative kind.

Looking vastly uncomfortable, Maria stood and advanced toward Selena. "Welcome to our family." Her lips stretched across her teeth in a grimaced smile and froze there. George coughed suddenly behind them.

"Lucius, how dare you disoblige me by marrying her?" Lady Harrowden said. "You did not ask my permission, and Miss Lockhart is under my employment. I would have said no."

Lucius widened his eyes but spoke in a measured tone. "My lady, you can hardly dictate her steps, as she is of age. But I did not need your approval and nor did Lady Clavering. It was to avoid such ridiculous objections as these that I married her by special license—and I have you to thank, by the way, for the introduction, which allowed me to obtain it."

Lady Harrowden gasped.

"I married only to oblige myself," Lucius added. Selena glanced up at her husband and warmed under the protection of his loving gaze.

He turned back to the countess. "It is true we did not meet with success where your nephew and protégé were concerned, but I believe they were most determined to be married in their way. However, as you said, Miss Woodsley's income will stave off the most pressing debts of the estate, and one can hope your nephew has learned his lesson. From what little I know of him, he is not keen to lose his exalted position in Society, and I believe he won't be eager to plunge himself into ruin now that he has this second chance."

Lucius glanced back at the door to the entryway, a questioning look in his eyes. "By the bye, I see Mullings has returned. How is that?"

Lady Harrowden puckered her wrinkled lips and paused before answering. "My nephew had dismissed Mullings, because he thought he was too loyal to me. Your solicitor discovered the misunderstanding and has brought him back to serve here until he can follow me to the dower house. Although," she continued waspishly, "I don't see how I can remove there now without a companion." She shot an accusing look at Selena.

"I believe I have someone who can take Lady Clavering's place," Maria said. "Perhaps we may discuss the idea now."

LUCIUS SHIFTED, revealing that the interview was at an end. "I suppose you will see Lord and Lady Harrowden in a matter of a couple of weeks. In the meantime, I will send a maid to collect Lady Clavering's effects. And now, it is time we returned home."

Philippa ducked her head as though she were trying not to smile. She peeked at them as they walked past her toward the door. George offered a single salute, and he and Philippa went to sit near the fire with Maria and Lady Harrowden.

Selena and Lucius left to the sounds of Lady Harrowden speculating in shocked accents on which was more scandalous of the two—Lord Harrowden and Miss Woodsley's elopement or Lucius and Selena's suspiciously sudden marriage without the banns even being read. Maria was applying herself to soothe the countess's agitation.

Mullings opened the front door to show them out, and Lucius leaned in to have a word. "The next time we come to visit the countess, you may introduce Miss Lockhart as Lady Clavering." He paused to level a glance at the old butler. "And I hope you will do so in a manner that is worthy of my wife."

The butler abandoned his stiff posture and studied the floor. "Yes, sir."

Selena and Lucius left the estate, stepping into the wintry landscape, bright with snow, but with a thawing wind that melted the drifts as it blew. They climbed into the waiting carriage, and Lucius gave a tap on the roof to start.

He stretched and sighed in deep appreciation before turning to Selena, who could not hide her look of adoration. He opened his arm, and she slid into his embrace. A comfortable silence stretched as they rode, and a ballooning sensation of happiness prodded his lips into a grin.

Lucius put his boots up on the seat across from them.

"Lady Clavering, I don't believe you are familiar with my hunting box, where we will reside until we may remove to my estate. I hope you will find it to your liking. True, there are occasionally damsels in distress, who knock on the door at odd hours, but otherwise, it is quite tolerable, I assure you."

Made in the USA
Middletown, DE
23 April 2020

91358603R00139